D1357237

DEATH AT THE TERMINUS

By Edward Marston

THE RAILWAY DETECTIVE SERIES
The Railway Detective • The Excursion Train
The Railway Viaduct • The Iron Horse
Murder on the Brighton Express • The Silver Locomotive Mystery
Railway to the Grave • Blood on the Line
The Stationmaster's Farewell • Peril on the Royal Train
A Ticket to Oblivion • Timetable of Death
Signal for Vengeance • The Circus Train Conspiracy
A Christmas Railway Mystery • Points of Danger
Fear on the Phantom Special • Slaughter in the Sapperton Tunnel
Tragedy on the Branch Line
The Railway Detective's Christmas Case • Death at the Terminus
Inspector Colbeck's Casebook

THE HOME FRONT DETECTIVE SERIES
A Bespoke Murder • Instrument of Slaughter
Five Dead Canaries • Deeds of Darkness
Dance of Death • The Enemy Within
Under Attack • The Unseen Hand • Orders to Kill
Danger of Defeat

THE OCEAN LINER MYSTERIES
Murder on the Lusitania • Murder on the Mauretania
Murder on the Minnesota • Murder on the Caronia
Murder on the Marmora • Murder on the Salsette
Murder on the Oceanic • Murder on the Celtic

DEATH AT THE TERMINUS

EDWARD MARSTON

Allison & Busby Limited
11 Wardour Mews
London W1F 8AN
allisonandbusby.com

First published in Great Britain by Allison & Busby in 2023.

A CIP catalogue record for this book is available from
the British Library.

First Edition

ISBN 978-0-7490-2824-4

Typeset in 11/16 pt Sabon LT Pro by
Allison & Busby Ltd.

Printed and bound by
CPI Group (UK) Ltd, Croydon, CR0 4YY

To Jane Conway-Gordon, my literary agent, who helped me to bring Robert Colbeck into existence

CHAPTER ONE

Spring, 1865

York railway station was a cauldron of noise and activity. Hundreds of passengers were bustling about, many of them accompanied by well-wishers eager to offer a few words of farewell. Porters darted everywhere, sizing up those in need of their services and deciding how much, if anything, they would receive by way of a tip. Children's voices were raised above the hubbub. The spacious booking office was filled with stragglers, buying tickets to take them to a variety of destinations. Slamming doors augmented the general din. Pigeons flew everywhere, swooping dangerously. A woman screeched in dismay as her dog pulled its lead from her hand, barking joyously as it chased the birds.

It was a scene so familiar to the stationmaster that he ignored it. His ears had long ago become immune to the general clamour of his working day. All that concerned him was doing his job properly. After taking out the watch from his waistcoat pocket, he noted the time, then glanced up at the large clock above his head. Watch and clock were in perfect agreement. He was content.

His peace of mind, however, was soon shattered. Emerging from nowhere, the guard ran quickly along the platform, dodging passengers as he did so. He jumped into the brake van and pulled the door shut behind him. Soon afterwards, there was a loud explosion. An eerie silence followed, broken only by the sound of a violin played by a bearded old man in search of an audience. Everyone stared in horror at the flames licking their way hungrily out of the brake van. Nobody moved. Almost a minute passed before the door finally opened, and the guard staggered out, his clothing alight and his cries piteous. People found their voices again, yelling in alarm as he lurched towards them and backing way in a panic.

The guard never reached the buckets of water lined up against the wall. Yards away from them, he had used up the last of his energy. All that he could do was to collapse in a heap on the platform, curling up to form a human inferno that continued to blaze away until the fire buckets were emptied over him.

CHAPTER TWO

Victor Leeming was so upset by the order that he raised his voice.

'I can't go to York, sir,' he protested.

'Why not?'

'It's my son's birthday next week. I can't possibly miss that.'

'You may have to,' warned Colbeck. 'Our duties as detectives always come first. We can't expect murders to fit themselves neatly into our respective diaries. They happen at random. Our task is to respond to them.'

'But it's so far away.'

'I'm sorry, Victor. As a father myself, I know how important a child's birthday is. Look,' he advised, 'try to take an optimistic view. If we solve this crime quickly, you could be back in London in plenty of time to join in the birthday party.'

'What chance is there of that happening?' groaned Leeming.

Their discussion was cut short as the cab in which they'd been speeding along began to slow down. When it came to a halt outside the railway station, Colbeck paid the driver then led the way to the ticket office. It was only when they were walking towards their platform that they were able to resume the conversation.

'Whose birthday is it?' asked Colbeck. 'David or Albert?'

'Albert.'

'Ah, I see the problem. He's your younger son.'

'It's no fun being in that position,' said Leeming. 'I was a younger son myself. You spend your entire life being overshadowed by a brother who is older, bigger and whose clothes are passed on to you. I can't ever remember getting something to wear that was new,' he wailed. 'The one day of the year when you feel important is on your birthday. It's a time when you get noticed at last. That's why I've always made such an effort to be there for Albert every year.'

'You must do so again, Victor.'

'A crime on this scale could take weeks to solve.'

'Don't be so defeatist.'

'I'm being realistic, sir. This is no minor infringement of the law. A brake van was blown up in a crowded railway station. That's serious.'

Colbeck smiled. 'So is Albert's birthday.'

Gregory Maynard walked up and down the platform to relieve his tension. He was a big, heavy, pale-faced man

12

in his sixties and the exercise was soon making him pant. The charred remains of the brake van had been towed into a siding. As he glanced across at it, his heart missed a beat. It was a calamity for the North Eastern Railway. Since he was the Chairman of the Board, he was suddenly thrust into the crisis, forced to make instant decisions, and having to confront a small army of newspaper reporters. York railway station was no longer a busy, noisy, overcrowded place that met the needs of thousands of passengers. Largely deserted, it now had the air of a cemetery.

'Ah, there you are, Gregory,' said a man, hurrying up to him. 'I came as quickly as I could. This is dreadful news.'

'It's my worst nightmare, Neville,' said Maynard, stopping abruptly. 'The sheer effrontery of it is staggering. The whole place is in chaos.'

'I know. I've seen the queue of trains outside the station.'

'It's a terrible shock for the NER.'

'I sympathise with you,' said the other, 'but I see it from a different angle. As lord mayor, I am bound to put the reputation of the city first. What happened here yesterday is a hideous advertisement for York. Think of the repercussions if people start to fear that this is a place of danger.'

Neville Timms was a middle-aged man of medium height whose loud voice, expansive paunch and gesticulations made him seem bigger than he really was. The arrival of the railway some twenty years or more earlier had transformed the city, giving it a greater importance, and increasing its commercial potential. Timms was proud of the way that it had burgeoned.

'What do the police say?' he asked.

'This case is beyond their abilities, Neville. If the railway policemen who work here had been doing their job,' said Maynard, rancorously, 'this crime might never have been committed. As for the city police, they're completely bemused. That's why I've gone above their heads.'

'What do you mean?'

'I sent a telegraph to Scotland Yard yesterday.'

Timms frowned. 'Would the Metropolitan Police Force show any interest in a crime committed so far away from London?'

'Oh, yes. They have a detective who is willing to travel the length and breadth of the whole country, if necessary. His forte is railway crime.'

'Who is this person?'

'Inspector Robert Colbeck.'

It was not until they were almost halfway to their destination that their compartment finally shed its other passengers and allowed them the privacy needed to discuss the case. As the train set off north once more, Leeming pressed for detail.

'What did the telegraph say?' he asked.

'It was a study in brevity, Victor. Little detail was given beyond damage to the brake van and the death of the guard. Reading between the lines, however, I sensed a real challenge for us.'

'How did the superintendent react?'

'He was reluctant to send us out of London.'

'For once, I agree with him.'

'He said we were needed there.'

'What changed his mind?'

'I did,' said Colbeck. 'York is one of the most beautiful cities in the country. It also has an important connection with the development of our railway system, thanks to a man named George Hudson.'

'The Railway King,' said Leeming. 'Even I have heard of him.'

'But for an inheritance, he might have remained relatively unknown. Instead, he used his sudden wealth to invest in the railways at a time when a mania developed. Hudson was one of its main beneficiaries. York was duly proud of him. He was its lord mayor at one point. When a railway station finally arrived in the city, they named the street beside it after him.'

'I thought he was accused of fraud and fled abroad.'

'That was when the bubble burst and fortunes were no longer so easy to make out of the railways. But he deserves credit for bringing York to life. Thanks to him, it's grown out of all recognition. The citizens are delighted.'

'One of them isn't,' said Leeming. 'He struck a blow against railways.'

'Let's get the full details before we form a judgement.'

'It's happened in other places. People who feel that the railways have ruined their lives – those who used to make stagecoaches, for instance – have caused untold damage. That's what happened in this case, I fancy. Someone took his revenge.'

'He didn't have to kill a guard to do that,' argued Colbeck.

'What do you mean?'

'He could have destroyed the brake van without spilling

a drop of blood. If it was simply a case of vandalism, we would have stayed in London. What's taking us to York, I suspect, is a murder victim.'

'Why, in God's name, couldn't the killer wait until my son had had his birthday?' demanded Leeming.

'It's a question you'll be able to put to him, Victor.'

'I'll wring his neck!'

'Leave that task to the hangman.'

'If I miss Albert's birthday, he'll never forgive me.'

'You'll be there somehow.'

'And why do people always turn to us in an emergency?'

'It's because we have a reputation, Victor. You're only thinking of your younger son, and so you should. But there's a very different question fluttering about in my brain.'

'What is it, sir?'

'Well,' said Colbeck, 'in his prime, George Hudson was seen as a hero by the people of York. He was then despised as a villain. His name will have been removed from that street near the station. I wonder what it's called now.'

CHAPTER THREE

Estelle Leeming was mending the torn sleeve of her husband's shirt when she heard the cab pulling up outside her front door. The sound brought her to her feet. Hansom cabs rarely came to any of the houses in that part of the city. Looking through the front window, Estelle saw that she had a visitor. Madeleine Colbeck was getting out of the vehicle to pay the driver. Putting the shirt aside, Estelle rushed to open the front door and welcome her friend, throwing her arms around her. After a warm embrace, she ushered Madeleine into the house.

'What a lovely surprise!' she said.

'I'm sorry that I couldn't come earlier, Estelle, but I was held up.'

'No excuses are needed. It's just such a pleasure to see you again.' She eyed her visitor's hat. 'That's new, isn't it?'

'Yes, I wanted to celebrate spring with a new bonnet.'

'It suits you, Madeleine,' said the other. 'Now sit down and make yourself at home while I brew some tea.'

'Let me tell you my news first. It concerns Victor.'

Estelle's face clouded. 'Nothing's happened to him, has it?'

'No,' said Madeleine. 'He's not hurt or anything. It's just that he's had to go away at short notice. Earlier on, Robert sent me a letter by hand. He and Victor have gone to York to investigate what might well be a murder.'

'Oh dear!'

'I don't have any details to pass on, but I thought you should know that you mustn't expect to see your husband for a while.'

Estelle was aghast. 'But it's Albert's birthday next week.'

'Victor knows that.'

'How long is he likely to be away?'

'I've no idea,' admitted Madeleine. 'Listen, why don't you make that pot of tea, then we can talk properly?'

Estelle nodded and went off into the kitchen. Madeleine sat down and looked around the little room. It was very cosy and quite spotless, reminding her of the home in which she'd been born and brought up. Though she enjoyed living in a large house in a more affluent part of the city, she still felt more at ease in a humbler dwelling. Madeleine was an attractive, intelligent, well-dressed woman in her thirties who had had the good fortune to meet and marry Robert Colbeck. Her friendship with the sergeant's wife was one of the benefits. A strong bond had been forged between them.

'I'm so sorry,' said Estelle, popping into the room. 'I

should have asked about Helena Rose.'

'She's a little darling most of the time,' replied Madeleine, 'but, every so often, she can be a little devil.' They shared a laugh. 'How are the boys?'

'I'll tell you when I've made the tea.'

Spotting her husband's shirt, Estelle gathered it up and tucked it away in a drawer. Now in her late thirties, she had kept her youthful prettiness along with her freckles. Her distinctive auburn hair was brushed neatly back into a bun.

'It never gets any easier, does it?' she said, pausing at the door.

'What doesn't?'

'Sharing your life with a detective. Once they disappear on a case, you never know when you're likely to see them again.'

'It can be vexing,' conceded Madeleine. 'Until you get used to it, that is.'

'I've never managed to do that somehow.'

'There's one thing to comfort us, Estelle.'

'What is it?'

'Well, we may miss our husbands when they go away,' said Madeleine, 'but it works both ways. Robert and Victor will certainly be missing us!'

Reaching York had been a relatively straightforward business. Getting to the station, however, was more of a problem. The train bearing the detectives ground to a halt some distance away from it. They soon learnt that they were at the back of a long queue of trains. Leeming fretted but Colbeck was more hopeful, believing that the man who had sent for them would have anticipated the delay and found a means of circumventing it. His instinct was sound. Minutes after their abrupt halt, Colbeck gazed out of the window and saw a man in the uniform of a porter, walking beside the track and holding up a placard.

'Look,' said Leeming in delight. 'It's got your name on it, sir.'

'Then it's time for us to get off the train.'

Colbeck was on his feet at once. The two of them were soon climbing out of the train with their valises and hailing the man with the placard. He welcomed them, then took them to a carriage, parked in the road parallel with the track. Fifteen minutes later, they were being shown into an office at the station. Two men awaited them. As the pair rose to their feet, Gregory Maynard and Neville Timms introduced themselves to the newcomers. In return, Colbeck introduced himself and Leeming.

'I don't know who rescued us from that queue,' he said, 'but I'm eternally grateful to him.'

'It was my doing,' said Maynard.

'But it was my carriage that brought you here,' said Timms, pompously.

As the two men took it in turns to explain who they were, Colbeck was able to weigh them up. Maynard seemed the more pleasant of the two, serious, civilised and genuinely grateful that the detectives had come to their rescue. Timms, by contrast, looked like a wily politician who had engineered himself into the position of lord mayor, and who was keen to remind them of his status.

'What we'd really like to hear,' said Colbeck, interrupting

Timms in full flow, 'is what happened.'

'I can tell you that,' said Maynard.

'Were you here at the time, sir?'

'No, Inspector, I was not.'

'Then I'd prefer to speak to someone who was – like the stationmaster.'

'Staines has told me everything,' insisted Maynard.

'I need to hear it from his own lips, sir.'

'Besides,' added Leeming, 'we would ask the stationmaster questions you would never think of putting to him. Why are you hiding him away?'

'Staines is busy,' said Maynard, unimpressed by the sergeant's appearance and manner. 'The station is open. He has a job to do.'

'There must be someone who can act as his deputy,' said Colbeck, reasonably. 'We won't take him away from his duties for long.'

Maynard headed for the door. 'I'll see what I can do, Inspector.'

'Listen,' said Timms, waiting until Maynard had left the room, 'you must make allowances for Gregory. This whole business has shaken him to the core. I apologise for his abrupt manner. As a rule, he is quite charming. While we're waiting,' he went on, 'I can give you the salient details.'

'Only the stationmaster can do that, sir,' said Leeming. 'What was the name of the guard, by the way?'

Timms squirmed. 'To be honest . . . I don't know.'

'Didn't you ask for it?' said Colbeck in surprise.

'Well . . . I didn't have the opportunity.'

'What happened to the body?'

'It was removed yesterday.'

'Was the guard married? Does he have a family?'

Timms shrugged. 'I haven't a clue.'

'You have a strange lack of curiosity, Lord Mayor,' said Colbeck. 'A railway employee is killed in broad daylight, throwing this station into a state of confusion, yet you have no idea of his identity. Don't you have any sympathy for the poor man?'

Timms took a deep breath before speaking. 'Whoever he is,' he promised, 'I'll make sure that the city will provide a plaque to honour him. We have high civic standards here.' Thumbs inside his lapels, he struck a pose befitting his status. 'When you think of York,' he asked, 'what is the first thing that comes into your mind?'

'The Minster,' replied Colbeck.

'What about you, Sergeant?'

Leeming grinned. 'Cocoa.'

Word of the explosion had spread throughout York. Ignorant of the facts, people were nevertheless quick to offer their theories as if speaking with authority. Sarah Scawin heard two of her employees doing just that in the reception area.

'Don't you have work to do?' she asked, sharply.

'Yes, Mrs Scawin,' said the hall porter, dutifully. 'I'm sorry.'

'So am I,' added the maid to whom he'd been talking. 'Excuse us.'

Sarah's eyes never left them until they had vanished. As the owner of the hotel close to the railway station, she always made her presence felt. She was a handsome, full-bodied woman in her late fifties, a watchful widow who had devoted herself to running the hotel that bore her name and reflected her character. It had a clientele that consisted largely of businessmen and commercial travellers, birds of passage who found its efficiency, its facilities, and its proximity to the station ideal for their purposes. Scawin's Hotel was dwarfed by the Royal Station Hotel not far away, yet it was still able to compete effectively with its rival. The personality of its owner had much to do with its success.

As two people came in through the front door, she spread her arms.

'Welcome back, Mr and Mrs Warburton!' she said, smiling broadly.

'That's amazing,' said the man, agog. 'We've only stayed here once – a year or so ago – yet you've remembered our names.'

'Guests deserve to be remembered – especially when they book in here a second time. I hope that you enjoy your stay.'

The Warburtons were an elderly couple with clear evidence of wealth. Sarah remembered something else about them.

'You live in Holtby, I believe,' she observed.

'That's right,' said the husband. 'We were driven here in our landau and intend to catch an early train tomorrow morning.' He sighed. 'If, that is, it's still running.'

'What's going on here, Mrs Scawin?' asked his wife, nervously. 'The station seems to have come to a standstill with trains queuing up outside it, and policemen on duty everywhere. We found it rather intimidating.'

Sarah took a deep breath before speaking. 'Why don't you book in first?' she suggested. 'Then I'll explain what happened at the station yesterday. It's . . . rather distressing . . .'

In the course of their work, the detectives had dealt with many stationmasters and found them, as a rule, efficient and personable. In Frederick Staines, they sensed that they had found someone rather different. Tall and skinny with grey hair poking out from beneath his hat, he had a resentful look in his eye and a defensive posture. When he came into the office with Maynard, he was introduced to the detectives. After giving Timms a nod of recognition, Staines sounded hurt at being dragged away.

'Should be out there,' he said, jerking a thumb over his shoulder. 'My job to sort this mess out.'

'We won't keep you long,' said Colbeck, 'but we do need your help.' He waited until Leeming had taken out his notebook and pencil. 'To begin with, Mr Staines, please tell us the name of the murder victim.'

'Jack Follis,' grunted the stationmaster.

'Was he good at his job?'

'Yes, he was.'

'We'll need his home address so that we can contact his family.'

'Jack had no family. Parents died years ago. No brothers or sisters.'

'Was he married?'

'Oh no,' said Staines. 'Jack was not the marrying kind.'

'Where did he live?'

'Here in York.'

24

He gave an address that Leeming wrote down in his notebook.

'Now,' said Colbeck, 'what exactly happened?'

Staines was terse. 'Wish I knew.'

'You were there at the time.'

'Doing my job.'

'What about Mr Follis?'

'Jack wasn't.'

'I don't follow, Mr Staines.'

'Should have been by the brake van.'

'Then where was he?' asked Colbeck.

'Don't know. Suddenly appeared and ran down the platform. Jumped into the brake van. It exploded with a loud bang. You can imagine the shock it caused.'

'Frankly, Mr Staines, we can't. It would help us if you'd be more specific. You're in possession of information that will help us to catch the person who was behind this outrage. Don't you care what happened on your watch?'

'Yes,' retorted Staines, clearly offended. 'Love my station. Always have. Want to get back out there to get it running properly again.'

'Well, you won't do that if you obstruct the inspector,' warned Maynard. 'He needs all the facts – and he needs them more politely. Inspector Colbeck and Sergeant Leeming have come all the way from London to lead this investigation. If you can't assist them in every way,' he warned, 'we will be looking for a new stationmaster.'

'Sorry, Mr Maynard,' said Staines, shaken by the threat. 'Truth is, I'm very upset. Jack was a friend. Didn't mean to be rude.' His gaze shifted to Colbeck. 'What else do you need to know, Inspector?'

'Mr Follis should have stayed beside the brake van,' said Colbeck. 'Is that correct?'

'It was his duty.'

'So where did he go?'

'Wish I knew.'

'Has he wandered off before?'

'No, not Jack.'

'Are you quite sure?'

'Yes, I am,' said Staines, raising his voice. 'If he had, I'd have reported him.'

Colbeck exchanged a glance with Leeming. They both knew that he was lying.

Sarah Scawin always let the duty manager run the hotel during his shift. It allowed her to float around the public areas, speaking to guests, encouraging her staff, sorting out any problems and – to use her own words – 'keeping an eye on things'. When she drifted into the lounge, she expected to see four people on duty, but one was missing. At the sight of their employer, the remaining three smiled at her and got on with their work. Sarah, meanwhile, went into the room at the rear of the bar. A shapely young woman was seated in the corner, dabbing at her tears with a handkerchief. When she realised that she was not alone, she leapt apologetically to her feet. Sarah was sympathetic.

'That's quite all right, Mary,' she said.

'I'll go back to work straight away, Mrs Scawin.'

'No, you won't. Our guests like to be served by a pretty young woman with a pleasant manner, not by someone who's been crying her eyes out.'

'I feel much better now,' said Mary.

'Well, you don't look better.'

'I'm sorry.'

Sarah put a consoling hand on her shoulder. 'Who told you?'

'One of the guests,' replied the other. 'He was on the station when it happened. Everyone seemed to know the name of the—'

'Try not to brood on it, Mary.'

'I can't help it, Mrs Scawin.'

'Then you're no use to me, I'm afraid. Take the rest of the day off.'

Mary was shocked. 'Are you giving me the sack?'

'No, I'm simply saving you a lot of embarrassment. Everyone who comes into that lounge is talking about what happened. It will be sheer torture for you.'

'Yes, Mrs Scawin, it will.'

'Dry your eyes and slip away quietly. The others will cope.'

'What about tomorrow?'

'That depends on how you feel. More to the point,' said Sarah, 'it depends on how you choose to look at what happened. I can understand why you're grieving now but things may look very different tomorrow. You may realise that, in fact, there may be a benefit for you in this tragedy. You've been spared any further pain . . .'

Mary was startled. 'How can you say that?'

'Wait and see.'

But the other woman didn't even hear her. A fresh supply of tears was already coursing down her cheeks. She was inconsolable.

CHAPTER FOUR

They were seated in the office, ignoring the sounds of trains and passengers moving around outside. After the stern reproach from Maynard, the stationmaster was on his best behaviour, answering all the questions put to him by Colbeck and hoping that the interrogation would soon finish. Leeming had filled several pages of his notebook.

'Let's come to the important question,' said Colbeck. 'Do you have any idea who might have been behind this incident?'

'Yes, I do,' replied Staines.

'Well?'

'I blame the Irish.'

'Do you have a large Irish community here?'

'Yes, we do,' explained Timms, 'and they have been

troublesome. In the wake of the potato famine twenty years or so ago, they started coming to this country in large numbers.' He wrinkled his nose. 'York had more than its fair share of them.'

'You can't blame people for trying to better themselves,' said Leeming. 'Many who stayed in Ireland died of hunger.'

'Why should they pick on the railway?' asked Colbeck.

'We're an easy target,' said Staines. 'They've tried to sneak on to trains without buying a ticket, or been caught trying to steal things, or simply turned up drunk and started a fight here. Some of them know how to behave themselves but there's a hard core that love to cause mischief.'

'Is there strong Fenian sentiment among them?'

'Yes, Inspector,' moaned Timms. 'We've had clear evidence of it.'

'Most of them live in the Bedern area,' added Staines. 'It's one of the poorest parts of the city. Large families are crammed into filthy slums. The place stinks.'

'We've tried to improve conditions,' said the lord mayor, defensively, 'though I'm not sure that they deserve it.'

'Everyone deserves basic amenities,' Colbeck put in.

'Our resources are limited, Inspector.'

'I've heard that excuse before.'

'In the last census, over forty-five thousand people were recorded living in York. That number places a huge responsibility on me and my council.'

'What about you, sir?' asked Colbeck, turning to Maynard. 'A serious crime has occurred on your railway. Who would you blame?'

'I'm wondering if we should point the finger elsewhere,

Inspector,' said the other, thoughtfully. 'Anarchists have been busy across the north. They cause damage for the sheer pleasure of it.'

'They tend to exist in small cells, don't they?'

'It only takes one of them to fashion a bomb.'

'And we are a sitting target,' complained Staines. 'This is not simply a terminus, it's a badly designed station. Trains come in one way then back slowly out. There's also a lot of coupling and uncoupling of engines, and that slows everything down even more.'

'You'd have been watched,' said Colbeck. 'Nobody was acting on the spur of the moment. The bomber – if that's what he was – knew when and where to strike.'

'How do we catch the devil?' asked Maynard.

'First, we need to gather more information, sir. Masses of people were milling about before the explosion. Some were close enough to the brake van to be injured by burning splinters of wood. One or more of them must have seen something suspicious.'

'They'll have to be contacted.'

'The best way to do that is to offer a reward for information leading to the arrest of the person or persons responsible,' said Colbeck. 'How soon could you have posters printed and put up?'

'It could be done in a matter of hours,' promised Maynard.

'And I'll make sure that a reward notice is in tomorrow's newspapers,' said Timms. 'First of all, however, we must arrange some accommodation for you.'

'That's my responsibility, Neville. I was the person who had the sense to summon help from Scotland Yard.'

Maynard turned to the detectives. 'I'll book rooms for you at the Royal Station Hotel.'

'If you don't mind,' said Colbeck, 'we'd prefer to stay at the smaller hotel next door to the station. That will suit us.'

'May I ask why?'

'Big hotels tend to be impersonal. We prefer somewhere with character.'

'As you wish, Inspector.'

'Before that, however, we'd like to see the exact spot where the brake van was when it exploded. Would you be so good as to conduct us there, Mr Staines?'

'Yes, of course,' said the stationmaster, partially mollified.

'Then let's go, shall we?'

Staines opened the door and led the detectives out on to the platform. Timms looked at his companion with a quizzical expression.

'What do you make of them?' he asked.

'The inspector is obviously a man of great experience and so is the sergeant.'

'I was less impressed.'

'Why?'

'The one is a dandy and the other looks as if he's never been taught how to dress properly. Frankly, they don't inspire confidence. We're dealing with a very strange couple, Gregory.'

'They get results,' said Maynard. 'that's all I care about. The local police have been dithering for hours. Colbeck talks as if he knows exactly what to do.'

* * *

Madeleine Colbeck had a full life, dividing her time between family and friends while pursuing a career as an artist. Having delivered her latest painting of a railway scene, she was enjoying a break from her studio and finding moments when she could rest. She was relaxing in an armchair when she had an unexpected visitor. Madeleine was thrilled to see Lydia Quayle being shown into the house by the maid. After hugging her friend, she took her into the drawing room.

'I hope that you don't mind my dropping in, Madeleine,' said Lydia.

'Of course, not – you couldn't be more welcome.'

'Thank you.'

'As it happens, you've caught me at the perfect time. I finished my latest commission and am having a rest from cleaning oil paints off my hands.'

'You deserve a break from time to time. How is Helena Rose?'

'She's as lively as ever,' said Madeleine, smiling fondly. 'Well, you can see for yourself in a while. She's in the nursery with my father. Helena will be overjoyed to see Aunt Lydia.'

'Watching her grow up has been a real joy for me.'

'Oh, I've got some news for you,' said Madeleine. 'Robert has gone to York to investigate a murder there. He sent someone here with a message for me.'

Lydia laughed. 'Am I supposed to guess who the messenger was?'

'You already know. It was Detective Constable Hinton.'

'How is Alan?'

'He looks much better than he did when he came back from that assignment in the Black Country. That beating he took there would have put a lot of men off returning to such a dangerous job, but not Alan Hinton.'

'Did he . . . mention me?'

'As if you need to ask!' teased Madeleine. 'He asked how you were and wanted to pass on his love and best wishes.'

Lydia smiled. 'That was kind of him.'

Tall, poised and beautifully dressed, she had striking good looks. At an early stage of her time in London, she had been troubled by a stalker. Alan Hinton had not only come to her assistance, he'd traced and arrested the man responsible. It had been the start of a friendship that had deepened over time.

'There's no need for me to ask what Alan wants, is there?'

'He wants to be up in York, working with Robert and Victor Leeming. It's a case that involves someone blown up in a brake van.'

Lydia pulled a face. 'How dreadful!'

'Yes,' said Madeleine. 'Estelle was horrified when she heard that. It's a case that could keep them away for a long time – and it's Albert's birthday next week.'

'Oh no!'

'The thought that Victor might miss the celebrations really upset her.'

'I don't blame her.'

'Albert will be really hurt if his father isn't there.'

'Is he the one who wants to be an engine driver?'

'He's changed his mind about that, Lydia.'

'What does he want to be now?'

'A policeman.'

'Like father, like son.'

'Estelle has warned him that it will be a hard life, but it hasn't put the lad off. Mind you, it didn't put Estelle herself off. When she fell in love with a policeman, she was happy to marry him.'

'The same is true of you, Madeleine. You learnt to live with the dangers.'

'In my position,' said the other, meaningfully, 'you would do the same.'

'Behave yourself,' warned Lydia, pushing her affectionately. 'I came here in the hope of a cup of tea, not for advice about my private life, however well intended it might be.'

Frederick Staines was a different man when he was back in the station he loved. His resentment disappeared to be replaced by a readiness to help in any way that he could. After showing the detectives where the brake van had been standing, he pointed to the place where he had been at the time of the explosion. Colbeck noted that he was some distance away from the guard. Leeming, meanwhile, made a rough sketch of the train's position. He was careful to include the fire buckets that the guard had failed to reach.

'What a terrible way to die!' he said.

'We'll miss him,' said Staines, sadly. 'Jack was a real character. I hope you catch the man who killed him, Inspector.'

'Oh, we'll catch him,' promised Colbeck, 'but I'm not entirely sure that the guard was meant to die. Simply blowing up the brake van would be enough to spread panic. Now that you've explained the sequence of events to us, you see, I'm having doubts.'

'I was there,' Staines reminded him. 'I saw the brake van explode.'

'But how would the man who placed that bomb in there know that it would go off at the precise time when the guard returned? He couldn't have had any control of the device, could he? It was bad luck on his part that Mr Follis stepped into the van shortly before it was due to explode.'

'What are you saying, sir?' asked Leeming.

'I'm not convinced that he was the target.'

'He must have been,' argued Staines.

'The person who placed that bomb aboard,' said Colbeck, 'knew exactly how big the blast would have been. He'd have stayed well out of reach of it. All he wanted was to cause trouble. It might even be that killing someone was a bonus to him.'

'He deserves to be blown to pieces himself!' said Staines with feeling.

'Don't worry. He'll get his just desserts.'

'I'd light the bleeding fuse myself.'

'Calm down, Mr Staines,' advised Leeming. 'I'm very sorry that your friend was killed but there's no point in making threats when your anger is raging. We must be as cold and brutal as the man who caused all this mayhem.'

'The sergeant is correct,' said Colbeck. 'You are an important figure in this investigation. When you described the explosion earlier, we could see the pain that it was causing you. Learn to cope with it, please,' he counselled. 'And when you're alone, try to remember if there's any detail that you missed – however minor it may seem – then pass it on to us.'

The stationmaster nodded. 'Have you finished with me now?'

'Yes, Mr Staines. You're back in charge now. The station is all yours.'

Giving them each a nod of farewell, Staines went off quickly.

'He lives for his job, doesn't he?' said Leeming.

'So do we,' Colbeck reminded him. 'Let's get on with it.'

The duty manager at Scawin's Hotel that day was Henry Kemp, a short, slim man in his thirties with a neat moustache decorating a pleasant face. Impeccably dressed, he was strolling towards the lounge when he met his employer.

'Ah, good,' said Sarah. 'I need to have a word with you, Henry.'

'As many as you wish, Mrs Scawin,' replied the other with a smile.

'I sent Mary Dowling home earlier on.'

'That was very wise of you. She was in no state to discharge her duties.'

'I sympathise with her, but we are here to serve the public. The last thing that guests want is to be served by someone on the verge of tears.'

'Mary's a conscientious girl. She'll be better by tomorrow, I guarantee. She'll have learnt to cope with the situation by then.'

'That's what I hope.' Sarah lowered her voice. 'Is there anyone else among the female staff that we need to keep an eye on?'

'I don't think so, Mrs Scawin. We did have worries about Annie Regan, but she's no longer employed here.

Annie had the sense to get well away from him.'

'Jack Follis really was a menace.'

'That's all in the past now.'

'You're right, Henry. Never speak ill of the dead – especially if they come to such a dreadful end. Now then,' she went on, 'you always have a keen ear for gossip. Do you know what the police are saying?'

'From what I hear, they're hopping mad.'

'Why?'

'Someone has been brought in over their heads,' said Kemp. 'He's a famous detective from London, I'm told, and the police are angry that he's taken over a case they believe belongs to them.'

'They can work together, surely?'

'Our police aren't like that. They want all the glory for themselves.'

'That doesn't bode well for the investigation, does it?'

'No, Mrs Scawin,' he said with a sigh. 'It doesn't. This man from London will get little help from the York constabulary. I feel sorry for the man. He doesn't know it yet, but he'll have to solve the murder on his own.'

CHAPTER FIVE

Superintendent Horace Nash had not even bothered to visit the station, preferring to send his officers there to make an initial report. It was only when he heard that Scotland Yard detectives had arrived to take control of a case on his patch that he was roused out of his chair. Nash was a big, solid, bull-necked man in his fifties with a natural authority. Before he left the police station, he stood in front of a full-length mirror and adjusted his clothing. After putting on his hat, he felt ready to do battle.

Driven to the station, he got out of the carriage and collected dutiful nods from the policemen he'd already despatched there. The first person he saw when he reached a platform was the lord mayor. Having braced himself for a confrontation with detectives he regarded as interlopers, he had to temper his mood and summon up a submissive smile.

'Good day to you, Lord Mayor,' he said.

'It's a very bad day, Superintendent,' replied the other. 'The NER has been attacked in the most frightening way. A guard was killed, and several people close to the brake van were injured when it exploded.'

'Yes, yes, I've seen the reports.'

'I'm surprised that they didn't make you come here at once.'

'I was . . . otherwise engaged,' said Nash, dismissively. 'But I'm here now to make a personal assessment. What's this about outside help being sought?'

'That was Mr Maynard's idea.'

'We should have been consulted beforehand.'

'He believes he acted correctly,' said Timms. 'According to him, there is nobody more experienced in dealing with crimes relating to the railway than Inspector Robert Colbeck. His reputation goes before him.'

'I've never heard of the man.'

'You will, Superintendent, you will.'

'Where is he now?'

'He's doing something that your officers should have done,' Timms told him with an edge in his voice. 'He and Sergeant Leeming are inspecting the remains of the brake van.' He pointed to the siding. 'There they are.'

When he spotted the two men, Nash's eyes widened in astonishment. While a tall, elegant figure was circling the wreckage, a sturdy, almost scruffy individual was writing in his notebook.

'What the devil are they doing?' asked Nash.

'They're searching for evidence, Superintendent. Inspector Colbeck wishes to see if there's any trace of the bomb that caused all the damage. He's also making an inventory – as far as is possible – of the items that were stowed in the brake van. The damage was extensive. Passengers who put luggage in there will be demanding compensation from the NER.'

'That's Mr Maynard's problem.'

'Ours is to catch the villain who caused this damage.'

'We'll do that, sir,' said Nash, jutting out his chin.

'You'll be working in a supporting role.'

'Oh, no, I won't. I intend to direct the operation.'

'Scotland Yard has the authority to take over the investigation.'

'They are not going to steal it from us, Lord Mayor,' said Nash. 'Speak up for us. Do you really want complete strangers pushing us roughly aside? Assert your authority as lord mayor. Insist that the York Constabulary handles this serious crime committed here.'

'Mr Maynard has a perfect right to send for outside help,' said Timms.

'And you have a perfect right to raise an objection,' urged Nash. 'Look at the pair of them,' he continued, pointing towards the brake van. 'Do they look like men who really know what they are doing?'

'Well . . . let's just say that I have reservations about them.'

'Left to me, they'd be on the next train back to London.'

'Come now, Superintendent. We must treat them with civility.'

40

'Oh, I'll do that, I promise you,' said Nash, darkly. 'When I wave that pair of intruders off, I'll have a smile on my face as big as the Minster.'

'The NER?' said Caleb Andrews in disgust. 'Robert has rushed off all the way to York to do the bidding of the North Eastern Railway?'

'He was summoned by name, Father.'

'That doesn't mean he has to dance to their tune, Maddy. If they're in another mess – and they've been in plenty – they should sort it out themselves. Robert's place is here with his family.'

'He has to obey orders, Mr Andrews,' ventured Lydia.

'In his position, he should be able to pick and choose.'

'I knew it was a mistake to tell you,' said Madeleine, clicking her tongue. 'Just because you worked all those years for the LNWR, you think that every other railway company is inferior.'

'Well, they are,' said Andrews. 'We're streets ahead of the others – especially the NER. Robert has my sympathy.'

The three of them were in the drawing room. When Madeleine and Lydia were alone, they could drink their tea and have a pleasant discussion. Now that Andrews had joined them, the mood had changed. He had reacted badly to the news of his son-in-law's latest assignment. When he launched himself on one of his combative rants, normal conversation was impossible.

'That's enough,' said Madeleine, sharply. 'Now that you've expressed your opinion, Father, we'll move on to a different subject. Did I tell you that I called on Estelle Leeming this morning?'

'No,' he replied. 'You didn't. How is she?'

'Very upset that Victor has gone away. It's Albert's birthday next week.'

'He'd love his father to be there,' said Lydia.

'It's his bounden duty,' insisted Andrews. 'These things matter to children. Look how upset Helena was when she thought her father wouldn't be back home before Christmas.'

'Victor's sons were in the same position,' Madeleine reminded him. 'They thought he'd be trapped in the Malverns. Luckily, he and Robert got back with days to spare.'

'I remember Albert well,' said Andrews. 'I once took him and David around the engine sheds to show them what life on the railway was like. Albert was a chirpy lad, full of questions. Both brothers wanted to be an engine driver like me.'

'That was then. Estelle says that Albert wants to be a policeman now.'

'That means she'll have a husband and a son away a lot of the time,' said Lydia. 'I don't envy her.'

'I think she'll be very proud of them.'

Andrews grinned. 'She'd be even prouder if Albert became an engine driver like me – as long as he didn't work for the NER, that is.'

'Father!' scolded Madeleine.

'I'm entitled to my opinion,' he said.

'You don't deserve that cup of tea.'

'I was just going to ask you for another one.'

'Only if you promise to behave yourself in front of Lydia.'

'Oh, don't mind me,' said Lydia with a laugh. 'I love to watch the way that your family works. Despite occasional disagreements, there's an underlying love and togetherness. My family wasn't like that,' she confessed. 'I hated my childhood. I always felt excluded. That's why I drifted away from my home.'

'Well, don't you dare to drift away from this one,' said Madeleine, wagging a finger at her. 'Helena Rose would be devastated, and so would Robert and me. You're one of us now, Lydia.'

'Yes,' affirmed Andrews, 'you certainly are. So don't you dare desert us. If you do, Maddy will set me on to you.'

They laughed happily.

It was ironic. Colbeck had examined the brake van with great care while Leeming stood yards away and took notes. Yet when the pair of them climbed back on to the platform, it was the sergeant who was covered in debris and the inspector who was spotless. Leeming caught sight of himself in the window of the restaurant.

'Look at the state of me,' he said, vainly trying to brush the dirt off.

'It was all in a good cause, Victor.'

'I hope so.'

Before the conversation could continue, they saw the lord mayor swooping towards them with a man in the uniform of a senior police officer.

'Allow me to introduce Superintendent Nash,' said Timms, indicating his companion.

'We're pleased to meet you, Superintendent,' said Colbeck. 'I'm sure that the lord mayor has told you who we are. Sergeant Leeming and I value this opportunity to lend York our expertise.'

'It's not expertise we need,' said Nash, gruffly. 'It's local knowledge. We know this city inside out, so it's vital that you act under our direction.'

'Mr Maynard has put us in charge of the investigation.'

'He's not empowered to do so.'

'We haven't come all this way just to be dogsbodies,' said Leeming.

'You'll do as you're told, Sergeant,' snapped Nash.

'I take my orders from Scotland Yard.'

'Not while you're in my city.'

'With respect, Superintendent,' said Timms, drawing himself to his full height, 'I am the lord mayor here. That means any major decisions affecting this city must be taken by me.'

'You promised to give me a free hand,' recalled Nash. 'Where law and order were concerned, you said, I was allowed to act as I wished. And my wish at this moment is that these . . . unwanted visitors from Scotland Yard need to be confined to a minor position in this investigation.'

'Why don't we move this discussion to a more private place?' said Colbeck, politely. 'If we stay out here, haggling like fishwives, we'll soon draw a crowd.'

'An admirable idea,' agreed Timms.

He led them to the office they had used earlier and, once they were all inside it, closed the door behind him. Colbeck, Leeming and Timms each took a seat, but Nash remained on his feet in the belief that it gave him an advantage. He tapped his chest.

'I speak for the police here,' he emphasised, raising his

voice, 'and I refuse to let my officers be at the beck and call of two complete strangers.'

'We were sent for,' insisted Leeming.

'Not by me, you weren't. The position is this. If you don't agree to do exactly what I tell you, I will take you off this case altogether.'

'And how do you propose to do that?' asked Colbeck, quietly.

'I'll bring our senior legal advisor here to educate you in the law of the land.' Leeming burst out laughing. 'Did I say something funny, Sergeant?'

'Yes, you did, Superintendent. And many others have said the same before you. When we dealt with a case in Great Malvern last year, an inspector from the Worcestershire Constabulary told us that we had no jurisdiction there.'

'I'm saying the same thing about York.'

'Then I'll have to tell you what I said to the person mentioned by the sergeant,' said Colbeck. 'As members of the Detective Department in the Metropolitan Police Force – the oldest force in the country – we have the right to assume control of any investigation that is deemed beyond the capacities of a provincial force.'

Nash's face reddened with anger. 'It is not beyond our capacities.'

'Bring whom you choose to debate the issue and I will be happy to acquaint them with the finer points of the law.'

'Inspector Colbeck used to be a successful barrister,' Leeming told them.

'Is that so?' said Timms, impressed.

'I have a degree in Jurisprudence from the University of

45

Oxford,' said Colbeck, modestly, 'and I was later called to the Bar.'

'Where did you study the law, Superintendent?' asked Leeming, wickedly. 'By the way, the inspector from the Worcestershire Constabulary had the sense to cooperate with us in the end. He stopped throwing his weight about.'

'I'm simply using the authority invested in me,' growled Nash.

'Perhaps you're being a little hasty,' suggested Timms.

'You back me, Lord Mayor, surely?'

'Well, in principle, yes. But these gentlemen come with excellent credentials, I'm told, and they are here at the behest of Mr Maynard.'

'Then he is the person I need to speak to.'

'Save your breath to cool your porridge,' murmured Leeming.

Colbeck rose to his feet. 'Is there anything else we can do for you, Superintendent?' he asked. 'The sergeant and I are not here to steal this case from under your noses. We would appreciate your assistance.'

'Pah!' exclaimed Nash in disgust.

'Somewhere in your city, it's conceivable, is the person who killed a guard and destroyed a brake van. If you could help us, please, we'll find him sooner rather than later.'

'You pursue your investigation, Inspector,' said Nash, issuing a challenge, 'and we'll pursue ours. I guarantee that we will solve this case before you.'

Without another word, he stormed out of the office and slammed the door.

'Is he always so tetchy?' Colbeck asked.

'The superintendent polices this city well,' said Timms,

loyally. 'And having been born and brought up here, he has a distinctive advantage over you.'

'We acknowledge that, sir.'

'Don't antagonise him, Inspector.'

'I had the feeling that he set out to antagonise us.'

'He certainly didn't come to offer us a warm welcome,' noted Leeming.

'I'll . . . speak to him,' said Timms, uncomfortably. 'There must be a way that you can work alongside each other.'

Colbeck was impassive. 'We'll see, sir.'

Sarah Scawin was in her office, going through her financial records. Her hotel had been doing well of late, but she feared that her run of success would not last. The blast in the adjacent railway station would deter passengers from coming there. She herself might think twice about travelling by train until the killer had been caught, and that was by no means a certainty. Meanwhile, there was bound to be a cloud over York railway station. Her hotel would suffer as a result.

There was a tap on the door. In response to her summons, Henry Kemp stepped into the office and delivered his message.

'They're here, Mrs Scawin.'

'Who are?'

'The detectives from London. I left them booking in for an indefinite period.'

'But they'd stay at the Royal, surely?'

'I heard Inspector Colbert say that they preferred to be here.'

'Then he deserves a welcome,' she said, rising from behind her desk and heading for the door. 'Thank you, Henry. I'd very much like to meet these gentlemen . . .'

Bustling along to the reception area, she was just in time to stop the new guests from being shown to their rooms. She spread her arms wide.

'Welcome to my hotel, Inspector Colbeck,' she said. 'I am Sarah Scawin. It's a pleasure to have you both staying with us. We'll be happy to provide everything you need.'

'Thank you, Mrs Scawin,' said Colbeck, impressed by her manner. 'Allow me to introduce Sergeant Leeming.' He pointed to his companion. 'You may be seeing a lot of us in the next week or so.'

'We're all delighted to have you in York.'

'Superintendent Nash isn't,' said Leeming. 'He made no bones about that.'

'We'll win him over in due course,' promised Colbeck.

'I doubt it, sir.'

'I can see why it was important for you to come here,' said Sarah, 'but the killer is unlikely to be in York, surely. He'll have fled the city and gone to ground a long way from here.'

'That may well be true,' agreed Colbert, 'but the trail starts here. We will pursue it until we find him, no matter how far away he might be.'

'We never give up, Mrs Scawin,' boasted Leeming. 'We once chased a killer all the way across the Atlantic Ocean.'

'Goodness!' she exclaimed.

'We caught him in the end. New York isn't a patch on York itself, I can tell you that. It's so dangerous over there.'

'Let's concentrate on the case in hand,' said Colbeck.

'Jack Follis requires all our attention. He was an outstanding guard, we're told.'

'I'm sure that he was,' said Sarah with a note of disapproval. 'I only wish that he was just as well behaved when he was off duty.'

'I don't follow, Mrs Scawin.'

'He was a pest, Inspector.'

'Did you know the man?'

'I knew him only too well,' she said, curling a lip. 'And so did the female members of my staff. It got to the point where I had to ban him from this hotel. I'm sorry for anyone who dies in such an appalling way,' she added, 'but I won't be mourning Jack Follis. He caused me far too much trouble.'

Horace Nash was still seething when he got back to his office. His attempt at taking control of the investigation had been thwarted. In Colbeck, he had learnt, he had a far more experienced and intelligent detective than he had imagined. Unable to bring him to heel, Nash had instead been rebuffed and humiliated. Even the support of the lord mayor could not be relied on entirely. The only way to assert his authority – and get rid of the Scotland Yard detectives – was to solve the crime before they did.

He had all the advantages. Nash knew every inch of the city in which he'd been born, and he had patrolled some of the most dangerous areas during his time as a young constable. His success had been unrivalled in the force. He had made countless arrests and shown a gift for detection that caught the attention of his superiors. Nash was eventually promoted above the heads of the people from whom he once took orders. They had to obey him now.

Sitting at his desk, he took out a ledger from a desk and opened it. In front of him was the name of everyone in the York Constabulary. He ran a finger down the list until he came to one that made him stop and smile. Nash had found the ideal man to keep watch on Colbeck and Leeming. They would be under constant surveillance. Everything that they did would be reported back to the superintendent, giving him a clear advantage. A smile spread slowly across his face. He felt certain that he would win the contest.

CHAPTER SIX

When they had left their luggage in their respective rooms, Colbeck and Leeming descended the staircase together.

'What do we do now, sir?' asked the sergeant.

'We part company,' replied Colbeck. 'The telegraph station is still open so I will send for help from Scotland Yard.'

'Do we need help?'

'I think so, Victor. You heard Superintendent Nash's threat. He hopes to show us up by solving the murder before we do. That means he'll have us watched like a hawk. We need someone to guard our backs.'

'Alan Hinton, perhaps?'

'I'll ask for him by name.'

'Another pair of eyes is always useful.'

'Yes – and Hinton knows how to be discreet.'

'What am I to do while you're at the telegraph office?'

'You need to talk to members of the staff here. Learn as much as you can about the guard. Follis has obviously stirred up bad blood in this hotel.'

'It sounds as if he was a ladies' man.'

'There's one lady on whom his charm failed to work,' said Colbeck, 'and that's Mrs Scawin.'

'What did you think of her?'

'Well,' said Colbeck, 'she's obviously a redoubtable woman. Running a hotel like this needs a strong hand, and that's what Mrs Scawin clearly has. Follis was a threat to some members of her female staff, so she leapt to their defence.'

'I'll see what I can find out, sir.'

'When I've despatched the telegraph, I'm going to pay a visit to the guard's lodging. It will be interesting to hear what his landlord thinks of him. We'll meet up here later and compare notes over dinner.'

'Good,' said Leeming. 'I'm starting to feel hungry. Oh, by the way,' he added, 'would you like me to find out what Hudson Street is called now?'

'I already know – it's Railway Street.'

Constable Roger Pendle was a tall, lean man in his thirties with the kind of face that could best be described as unmemorable. Pale and impassive, it lacked any features that would imprint themselves on anyone's memory. As he stood dutifully in the superintendent's office, he listened with care to his orders. Nash issued a warning.

'Be careful,' he said. 'You must remain invisible. Get

close enough to find out what they're up to and keep a record of it in your notebook.'

'I understand, Superintendent.'

'You'll need to change out of that uniform and book a room at Scawin's Hotel. That's where they're staying.'

'How would you describe them, sir?'

'In a word, they're Londoners,' said Nash with contempt. 'They've got a sense of importance that folk who live in the nation's capital always have. I despise it. They behave as if they're doing us a favour when they're simply getting in our way. That's why you must shadow them.'

'What if they split up, sir?'

'Stay with Inspector Colbeck. He makes all their decisions.'

'Is he easy to pick out?'

'Oh, yes,' said Nash, derisively. 'He'll be strutting around York like a turkey-cock. You'll have no difficulty picking him out. Colbeck dresses like a member of the aristocracy.'

Alan Hinton was about to go off duty at Scotland Yard when he was summoned. He hurried along to the superintendent's office. Ordinarily, he would creep there with trepidation because he knew that a reprimand was probably waiting for him on the other side of the door. This time, however, he sensed that there would be good news for a change. After knocking, he entered the room with a smile. Edward Tallis glowered.

'What are you smirking at?' he demanded.

'I'm sorry, sir,' said Hinton, face becoming blank.

'Detective work is a serious business. You can't do it

properly if you're grinning like a chimpanzee.'

'I realise that.'

Tallis reached for the telegraph on his desk. 'Inspector Colbeck has sent a request,' he said. 'He needs assistance.'

'I'll be happy to provide it, sir.'

'You don't know what it entails yet. Tomorrow morning, you are to catch the earliest train to York. Book a room at Scawin's Hotel. Don't disclose that you are a detective.'

'Why not?'

'Just do as you're told, man.'

'Very well, sir.'

'The inspector's orders are sometimes baffling, but they usually make sense.'

He paused to select a cigar from the box on his desk and sniffed it. Tallis was showing signs of age, but his eyes retained their distinctive glint, and he still had the straight-backed look of a former soldier.

'Is there anything else I should know, sir?' he asked.

'Try to keep out of danger,' said Tallis, showing a rare glimpse of sympathy. 'The last time you worked alongside Colbeck, as I recall, you took a fearful battering. I don't want to see you in that state again.' He bit the end from his cigar then looked up. 'Well, what are you waiting for, Constable? You've had your orders.'

Gabbling a farewell, Hinton was out of the room in a flash.

When he got to the house where Jack Follis had been living, Colbeck encountered an unforeseen problem. Olive Cusworth, the guard's landlady, was unaware that her lodger had been killed. Breaking the news of his death to her would require tact. She was a short, fair-haired, dainty woman in her late fifties with a high voice and nervous laugh. When she learnt that he was a detective, her face crumpled.

'Is Mr Follis in trouble?' she asked.

'He's done nothing wrong, as far as I know, Mrs Cusworth.'

'I can't believe that he would ever break the law. He's too . . . honest.'

'I'll take your word for it,' he said. 'Perhaps we could sit down.'

'Yes, of course, Inspector.' She lowered herself into an armchair.

Colbeck sat opposite her, trying to work out how she would react to the news about the guard's death. They were in a spacious drawing room with a window overlooking the River Ouse. He could smell the polish on the furniture. Evidently, the guard had found excellent accommodation.

'How long has Mr Follis been here?' he asked.

'Two years this August,' she replied. 'We couldn't have had a better lodger. We regard him as the son we never had.'

'I see.'

'Why are you so interested in him, Inspector?'

'Well,' he began after taking a deep breath, 'there's been an unfortunate incident at the railway station. It involved Mr Follis.'

'He's not hurt, is he?' she asked, clasping her hands together. 'Please don't tell me that he's in hospital. I couldn't bear that.'

'There's no escaping the truth, Mrs Cusworth. He's not in hospital. I'm afraid that it's worse than that.'

'Worse!' she cried. 'What do you mean?'

'Mr Follis passed away yesterday at the railway station.'

'Are you saying that he's dead?'

Colbeck nodded. 'It's the reason we were summoned from London,' he explained, softly. 'It was not a natural death, I fear.'

'Then how did he die . . . ?' The words hung in the air as she took in the full horror of what she had just heard. 'Will we never see him alive again?'

'No, Mrs Cusworth.'

Without warning, she let out such a howl of pain and loss that it echoed throughout the house. It awakened her husband, who had dozed off in his chair in the adjoining room. Struggling to his feet, he hobbled into the drawing room on his walking stick. Colbeck could see that he was much older and frailer than his wife. Simon Cusworth was shrunken, grey-haired and hollow-eyed. When he spoke, his voice was like the croak of a frog.

'What's going on, Olive?' he asked.

'Mr Follis is dead,' she gasped.

'Never! He was always so full of life.'

'This gentleman is a detective inspector from London.'

'I'm sorry we meet under such unfortunate circumstances,' said Colbeck. 'It's been my sad duty to inform your wife that Jack Follis was killed at the railway station yesterday by a person or persons unknown.'

The old man's jaw dropped. 'He was murdered?'

'That's one possibility.'

'Why? He was the nicest man in the world.'

'You don't need to hear the full details until you've adjusted to the idea that he's gone for good. I can see that he was rather more than a lodger to you both.'

'He was,' said Olive. 'Jack was . . . one of the family.'

'Before I can arrest whoever contrived his death,' said Colbeck, 'I need as much information about Mr Follis as I can possibly get.'

'What would you like to know, Inspector?'

'First of all, Mrs Cusworth, I'd appreciate a look at his room.'

'Yes, of course.'

'You take him up, Olive,' said her husband. 'Climbing those stairs is a real ordeal for me. Besides, I'd like some time alone to come to terms with what we've just heard. Jack Follis dead? No,' he went on, shaking his head in disbelief. 'I can't accept that we'll never see him again and hear that wonderful laugh of his.'

'You stay here, dear,' said his wife, quietly. 'I'll take the inspector up.'

She led the way out of the room and into the hall, pausing at the bottom of the staircase. Gathering her strength, she went slowly up the steps in front of Colbeck as if forcing herself to go on. After leading the way along the landing, she came to a halt and pointed to the room at the far end.

'That's where Jack – Mr Follis, I mean – lived.'

'Aren't you coming in with me?'

'Oh, no, I'm too upset to do that, Inspector. If I see his belongings, I may disgrace myself by bursting into tears. I'll be downstairs with my husband. We need to console each other.' She bit her lip. 'You go into his room on your own. It's not locked. He kept it very tidy. That was typical of him.'

* * *

Victor Leeming began his search for information by talking to Henry Kemp. The duty manager weighed his words carefully before speaking. He agreed that Jack Follis had caused problems at the hotel and supported the ban placed on him. Kemp could not be drawn, however, into making any comments about his employer beyond the fact that Sarah Scawin maintained high standards at the hotel and took a justifiable pride in its success. Since he had learnt so little from the man, Leeming went in search of someone less discreet and more forthcoming. He found Eric Featherstone.

'Did you know a man called Jack Follis?' he asked.

The porter chuckled. 'Who didn't?'

'I'm told that he was very popular with some of the female staff.'

'It's true, Sergeant – though I don't really know why. I mean, Jack was not what you'd call good-looking. He just had this sort of energy about him. There was always a grin on his face and a spring in his step.'

Leeming had deliberately chosen the oldest of the porters, a man who had worked at the hotel for many years and who knew everything there was to know about it. Eric Featherstone was a tubby individual in a uniform that was slightly too small for him. He had a well-trimmed beard, flecked with grey hairs, and a strong local accent. He was clearly delighted to be part of a police investigation.

'What happened when he was banned from the hotel?' asked Leeming.

'Oh, Jack soon got round that.'

'How?'

'Well, he came here in disguise a few times. It was Mr

58

Kemp who recognised him eventually. He not only threw Jack out, he threatened to have him arrested if he so much as stepped in here again.'

'Did that work?'

'It seemed to, Sergeant.'

'Seemed?'

'Aye, there was no sign of him. He'd found a new way to get in here, see. Jack bribed the night porter to let him in after midnight. It worked well for a week or so, then the porter, Billy Daunt, was caught in the act.'

'What happened to him?'

'Billy was sacked on the spot, and it was the last time Jack sneaked in here.'

'When did this happen?'

'A couple of weeks ago.'

'So Follis stopped trying, did he?'

Featherstone chuckled again. 'I reckon he was just biding his time,' he said. 'Besides, he had other women that took a fancy to him, ones that didn't work here. Most of them was single because Jack liked them young, but, now and then, there were rumours about him and married women. Jack enjoyed playing with fire.'

It was an unfortunate choice of words. Leeming had heard more than one description of how Follis had died an agonising death.

Madeleine Colbeck was in the drawing room when she heard the doorbell ring. The maid went to open the front door and Madeleine caught the faintest sound of a voice. It was enough to make her leap up and go into the hall. Alan Hinton was standing in the open doorway. After dismissing the maid with a nod, she beckoned her visitor into the hall and closed the door behind him.

'How lovely to see you again, Alan!' she said.

'I just called in to pass on some good news.'

'Have you been sent for?'

'Yes,' he said, glowing with pleasure. 'I'm catching an early train to York tomorrow morning.'

'That's wonderful news. Congratulations!'

'Thank you. Since I'll be seeing Inspector Colbeck tomorrow, I thought I might act as a postman for you.'

'Yes, please! If you'll excuse me, I'll write a letter at once. But you don't need to stand out here while I go off. Why don't you wait in the drawing room?'

'Thank you,' he said. 'I will.'

While Madeleine disappeared, Hinton went across to the drawing room and opened the door. Expecting it to be unoccupied, he was both surprised and delighted to see Lydia Quayle seated on the sofa. At the sight of him, she jumped to her feet.

'What are you doing here, Alan?'

He grinned. 'I'm just enjoying my good luck.'

'That makes two of us,' she said.

They stood there in silence, gazing fondly at each other.

Jack Follis's room was a revelation. It was much larger and better furnished than Colbeck had expected. Railway guards had an important job to do but they were not well paid. Colbeck had lost count of the number of times that his father-in-law had complained about the inadequate rewards of being a railwayman. It seemed as if Follis had fared better than most. The room contained a double bed, a three-piece suite, and a selection of rather insipid water colours. Above the fireplace was a large, gilt-framed mirror. Tucked away in a corner was a mahogany wardrobe. When he opened the doors, Colbeck found a suit, hat and overcoat hanging there. Three ties and a pair of shoes were the only other items.

Getting on his knees beside the bed, Colbeck lifted the trailing coverlet to reveal a small chest. When he pulled it out, he saw that it was unlocked. In a household like that, Follis had obviously felt that his possessions were safe. Opening the trunk, Colbeck found an assortment of shirts, socks and underwear. He also discovered something that he didn't expect to find. When he lifted out a bunch of keys, he dropped them back into the chest again and heard a hollow sound. He guessed at once what had caused it. The chest had a false bottom. After emptying everything out, Colbeck lifted the carefully fitted wooden panel out to expose items that Follis had thought precious enough to conceal.

Chief among them was a bundle of letters with a ribbon around them. He felt at once elated and embarrassed, glad that he had stumbled on something that would give him a real insight into the life and character of Jack Follis while feeling that he was somehow trespassing on someone's privacy. Colbeck had to remind himself that the guard had been murdered and that it was his duty to gather every shred of evidence that might lead to the arrest and conviction of the killer.

Removing the ribbon, he picked up the first letter.

CHAPTER SEVEN

Leeming had been busy. After speaking to five different employees at Scawin's Hotel, he drifted out to the station and chatted to one of the railway policemen on duty there, a tall, wiry, middle-aged man with a fringe beard. When he heard that Leeming was a detective from Scotland Yard, the policeman was immediately wary of him, stepping slightly away.

'There's no need to be frightened of me,' said Leeming. 'Over the years, we've had good cause to be grateful to railway policemen. They've helped us to solve many crimes.'

'I'm glad that someone appreciates us.'

'What do you mean?'

'When he was here earlier,' said the man, 'Superintendent Nash gave each one of us a mouthful of abuse. It was as if he blamed us for setting that brake van alight.'

'Let's forget the superintendent, shall we? In my opinion,' said Leeming, thinking of Edward Tallis, 'something very nasty happens to people when they're promoted to that rank. What's your name, by the way?'

'Walters, sir. Ben Walters.'

'Do you enjoy working at this station?'

'I do and I don't.'

'You're confusing me.'

'I like it here because there's always something going on.'

'And why don't you like it?'

'Look around you, Sergeant,' said Waters, taking in the whole station with a sweep of his arm. 'York railway station is a mess. To begin with, it's too small for a city like this. Traffic will increase and we simply don't have room to expand.'

'It does look cluttered,' observed Leeming.

'It was built over twenty years ago at the junction of Toft Green and Tanner Row. Unlike the makeshift station we used to have, this one is built inside the city walls. That was a big mistake.'

'Yet it looks very impressive from the outside.'

'It's the inside that matters.'

'What's the problem?'

'We're a bottleneck, Sergeant. You've seen the trouble that trains have getting in and out of here. There's a ridiculous waste of time.'

Leeming let him sound off for a few minutes then became serious.

'Who do you think blew up that brake van yesterday?' he asked.

'Whoever it was, he probably had an Irish accent.'

'Someone else mentioned the Irish.'

'They're a menace,' said Walters. 'They hang around the station with no intention of catching a train. We clear them away time and again. Their children are almost as bad. Some of them are trained pickpockets.'

'What would the Irish hope to gain by destroying a brake van?'

Walters lowered his voice. 'Satisfaction.'

Superintendent Nash was in his office, sifting his way through the information that his officers had gathered about the apparent murder of the guard. He felt that he had all the relevant information to hand. It was time to show his rivals from Scotland Yard that he and his force could compete with them. Accordingly, he called for his carriage and was driven to a house that nestled on the banks of the Ouse. When he knocked on the front door, a maid came to open it, quailing at the sight of a police uniform.

'Is Mr Cusworth here?' he asked.

'Yes, he is,' she replied, 'but he's had to go and lie down. He tires easily.'

'Is there a Mrs Cusworth I can speak to?'

'Who is it, Minny?' asked Olive as she came into the hall. 'Oh dear!' she said when she saw their visitor. 'It's another policeman.'

'Are you Mrs Cusworth?' asked Nash.

'Yes, I am.'

'I'm Superintendent Nash of the York Constabulary and I'm leading an investigation into the untimely death of a man named Jack Follis.' She brought both hands up to her face. 'You've obviously heard what happened to your lodger.'

'My husband and I were shocked.'

'Who was behind the murder, we can't be certain. But there may well be evidence in Mr Follis's possessions that could lead us to the killer. Because of that,' he went on, 'I must ask your permission to search his room.'

'But the other policeman has already done that, Superintendent.'

Nash gulped. 'Other policeman?'

'Inspector Colbeck from Scotland Yard.'

'He's been here?'

'Yes, he left half an hour ago.'

'What exactly did he do?'

'He searched Mr Follis's room then went away.'

'Did he take anything with him?'

'I don't think so,' she said. 'He was so considerate and broke the dreadful news to me very gently. I was grateful to him for that.' She stood back from the door. 'You're welcome to come in and see the room for yourself, Superintendent. I'll get someone to make you a cup of tea. Do you take milk and sugar?'

Too angry to speak, Nash turned on his heel and climbed into the waiting cab. As he was driven away, he realised that Colbeck might have secured valuable evidence ahead of him. He had underestimated the inspector badly. Nash vowed that it would never happen again.

'What else did this man, Walters, tell you?' asked Colbeck.

'He thinks the killer will turn out to be Irish,' said Leeming.

'Why?'

'They cause a lot of problems at the station, apparently.'

'That doesn't mean one of them would stoop to murder.'

'No, it doesn't, sir, but you have to remember that the lord mayor thought that the Irish could be involved as well.'

'True,' agreed Colbeck. 'It's not impossible that the guard's death had a political element to it, I suppose.'

'It's a pity we don't have Brendan to call on. If you or I go into the Irish community, we'll stick out like sore thumbs. Brendan Mulryne would mix with them easily. He's helped us out before.'

'There are two problems, Victor. First, we have no idea where he is. Second, if we dared to bring him into the investigation, Superintendent Tallis might find out and he was the person who had Mulryne kicked out of the Metropolitan Police Force. No,' decided Colbeck, 'we'll have to settle for Alan Hinton.'

They were in Colbeck's room, exchanging information before they went down to dinner. Leeming was feeling pangs of hunger.

'Why don't we discuss everything in the dining room?' he asked.

'It's because we might be overheard and some of the things that I discovered must be kept private. Otherwise, they could cause a lot of embarrassment.'

'Who for, sir?'

'I'm not naming names.'

'What did Follis's landlord say about him?'

'It was his wife who did most of the talking. Mrs Cusworth was responsible for inviting Follis to stay at their house in the first place. It happened by complete chance.'

Colbeck went on to explain how Olive Cusworth had arrived at the station one morning when Follis was the guard on the train she was catching. Someone loitering near the exit had decided she was defenceless and seized his chance, grabbing her handbag and trying to run away. Alerted by her cry of alarm, Follis had chased after the thief and caught him, overpowering the man and dragging him back to the station to hand him over to one of the railway policemen. Mrs Cusworth was so grateful to get her handbag back that she offered the guard money. When Follis refused to accept it, she insisted that there must be something she could do for him. The guard said that he was searching for a room to rent in York. If she knew anyone ready to take in a lodger, could he please have their address?

'And she immediately offered him a room at her house,' guessed Leeming.

'Oh, no,' said Colbeck, 'it took months before that happened. She had to persuade her husband first and he had grave doubts. In the end, she won him over. He agreed to take in Follis for a trial period.'

'And?'

'That was almost two years ago. Mr Cusworth took to him immediately. He told me that Follis was one of the family. There can't be many railway guards enjoying accommodation of that quality.'

'What did you mean when you talked about embarrassment?'

'I found a cache of letters hidden away in a chest – love letters.'

'There's nothing wrong in that, sir,' said Leeming. 'A lot

of people keep souvenirs like that. I know that Estelle does. She's kept every letter I ever sent her. They meant a lot to her – even though my spelling was poor.'

'It's the thought that counts.'

'Jack Follis is entitled to keep letters from his sweetheart.'

'You don't understand, Victor. These were not billets-doux from a woman he loved. Each one was written by someone different, pledging love and devotion.'

'Are you saying that . . . ?'

'Yes, I am. The women involved had each fallen for his charms. What I was looking at was a record of his conquests.'

Leeming was taken aback. 'How many were there?'

'Well over a dozen,' said Colbeck. 'One of those letters was written by someone who works in this very hotel. It was barely literate but the emotions it conveyed were sincere. Like all the others, she had surrendered to Follis.'

'What did you do with the letters?'

'I removed them. I didn't want Mr and Mrs Cusworth learning the truth about their lodger. It would distress them beyond measure.'

Leeming was appalled. 'What sort of man was he?'

'We'll talk about it after we've had dinner. Now remember to say nothing about the case while we're in public. We may be overheard.'

'Would the superintendent really have us watched?'

'Yes,' said Colbeck. 'He'll use every weapon in his armoury.'

Having booked a room at the hotel, Roger Pendle wandered around to inspect the facilities. He was outside the dining

68

room when he saw two figures approaching him. Colbeck fitted the description given to him by Superintendent Nash. Since they were deep in conversation, the two detectives hardly noticed Pendle as they went past. He walked away for ten minutes or so then returned to the dining room. After noting where Colbeck and Leeming were seated, he made sure that he had a table within earshot of them. His work had begun.

Horace Nash was brooding in his office when he had a visitor. Gregory Maynard came into the room, carrying a reward poster. He placed it on the desk.

'I thought that you should have a copy of this, Superintendent,' he said.

'Thank you, sir.'

'I've had copies put up in the railway station and at various points throughout the city. Inspector Colbeck is confident of a good response.'

'Ha!' sneered Nash, glancing at the reward on offer. 'You'll have a very large response if you're offering a hundred pounds to anyone who can give you information that will lead to an arrest. People will flock in to tell you cock and bull stories in the hope of getting their hands on that kind of money.'

'Colbeck will filter them out very quickly. The worst offenders will be handed over to you. Barefaced lying will only hinder the investigation.'

'It's already been hindered, Mr Maynard.'

'I don't follow.'

'You shouldn't have been so high-handed,' said Nash, rising to his feet. 'Before you summoned outside help, I should have been consulted.'

'This crime took place on railway property.'

'Railway property that is part of the city I'm employed to police.'

'Colbeck will naturally turn to you for assistance.'

'I've told him not to bother, sir. I resent being pushed aside to make way for someone who doesn't know anything about York. While he and the sergeant are floundering, we'll devote our resources to the capture of the villain responsible for the death of the guard, and the incidental wounding of those close to the brake van when it exploded.'

'This is ludicrous!' shouted Maynard.

'The fault lies with you.'

'The York Constabulary should work in harness with Inspector Colbeck, not in competition with him.'

'I'm nobody's lackey.'

'Is the lord mayor aware of this extraordinary decision?'

'He was present when I made it, sir.'

'And did he support you?'

'He shares my pride in this city. Why bring foreigners into this investigation when you already have a fully functioning police force here?'

'Colbeck specialises in crimes on the railway system.'

'Well, he didn't impress me.'

'I expected better of you, Superintendent.'

'And I expected better of you,' retorted Nash, bluntly. 'I regret what happened to the guard, but not as much as I regret the way that you acted in this matter. You can take this away with you,' he went on, picking up the reward poster and thrusting it at Maynard. 'We don't need to offer money to catch the killer. We'll use good, old-fashioned policing and a detailed knowledge of this city. It puts Colbeck at a severe disadvantage.' He grinned. 'You'll end up as a laughing stock, sir, and so will this precious Railway Detective of yours.'

Snatching the poster from him, Maynard stalked out.

They had almost finished their meal when Sarah Scawin came across to their table. She looked as purposeful as ever.

'Is everything to your satisfaction?' she asked.

'Yes, thank you, Mrs Scawin,' replied Colbeck.

'I must compliment you on the beer you serve,' added Leeming.

'And on the quality of your menu.'

'Thank you,' she said, beaming. 'May I ask why you chose this hotel and not the Royal? It has facilities that we can't offer you.'

'Size is not everything, Mrs Scawin,' said Colbeck. 'During a case that took us to the Malverns, our superintendent stayed in an imposing hotel near the railway station. It was far too big and too busy.'

'We had the sense to stay in a very small hotel,' explained Leeming. 'Like this one, it was run by the person who owned it.'

'Everything had the benefit of a woman's supervision,' said Colbeck, 'in the same way that Scawin's Hotel does.'

'I treasure that compliment, Inspector.'

'It's well deserved.' He lowered his voice. 'May I ask if you still have an employee by the name of Mary Dowling here?'

She blinked in surprise. 'We do, as a matter of fact.'

'I believe that she was . . . a friend of Jack Follis.'

'How on earth do you know that?'

'Her name came up in the course of our enquiries,' said Colbeck. 'I'd like to know a bit more about her.'

'Call in at my office when you've finished your meal,' she suggested.

'We will.'

'It's not something I care to discuss in public.'

'Of course.'

'Please excuse me,' she said, before moving on to speak to other guests.

Frederick Staines had come to the end of his shift and was preparing to hand over to another stationmaster. When he noticed Ben Walters patrolling the platform, he intercepted him.

'Did I see you talking to Sergeant Leeming earlier on?' he asked.

'Yes,' answered the railway policeman. 'He wasn't as bossy as the bobbies in our local constabulary. They look down on us. Sergeant Leeming didn't do that.'

'Why did he speak to you?'

'He wanted to know if I had any ideas who caused that explosion.'

'What did you tell him?' asked Staines.

'I gave him my honest opinion,' said Walters. 'I blame the Irish.'

'Good man. I told the detectives the same thing. I feel it in my bones, Ben. This is their revenge. Because we've clamped down on them recently, they decided to hit back at us.'

'I agree. I mean, who else could it possibly be?'

'Mr Maynard wondered if it might be some anarchists.'

'Do we have any of those in York?'

'They exist in every city,' said Staines, grimacing. 'They're not just people with an axe to grind. They're enemies of order. Mr Maynard told me about a leaflet of theirs he saw at Leeds station after some vandalism there. It was as if they were boasting about what they'd just done.'

'Why weren't they rounded up and arrested?'

'You need to find them first, Ben. Anarchists are not easy to pick out. On the surface, some of them look like ordinary, law-abiding people. It's only when they get together for secret meetings that they show their true colours.'

'The Irish are easier to identify. Their voices give them away.'

'Be fair,' warned Staines. 'We mustn't blame all of them. We've got Irish lawyers, doctors and businessmen here. They're as trustworthy as you or me. It's just the ones in Bedern. I reckon the man who planted that bomb came from there.'

'That's what I told the sergeant, Fred.'

'If it was left to me, I'd get the police to raid Bedern in large numbers and arrest the known troublemakers. It's the only way to find the man who was behind the murder of Jack Follis.'

Horace Nash led from the front. Having placed his men in strategic positions, he gave the signal and the police moved in. They did not stand on ceremony. Banging on doors or forcing them open in some cases, they charged into houses in search of known criminals. It happened so quickly that they met with little resistance, just howls of rage and streams of abuse. Patrick McBride was their main target. For that reason, Nash made sure that he performed the arrest, taking three constables with him in case of resistance.

'What the hell are you doing?' roared McBride as he was handcuffed.

'We're taking you in for questioning, Pat,' said Nash.

'You have no right to barge in here.'

'We've every right. You're our main suspect.'

'For what, for Christ's sake?' yelled McBride.

A big, hulking man in his forties, he tried to shake off the two policemen holding him. McBride was one of the leaders of the Irish community. Having just served a sentence for stealing meat from a butcher's shop, he was delighted to be free once more. His freedom, however, was clearly threatened.

'What the devil am I supposed to have done, Superintendent?' he demanded.

'You know only too well, Pat.'

'I've been as clean as a whistle since I was let out.'

'Oh,' mocked Nash, 'so you've repented of your evil ways, have you?'

'I'm innocent, I tell you!'

'You were born guilty, man!'

'I'm being arrested without a charge. That's illegal.'

'Then let's do this by the book, shall we? You're being charged with planning the murder of Jack Follis, a railway guard, yesterday.' He nodded to the policeman. 'Take him away.'

Amid a hail of protests from the rest of his family, McBride was dragged out.

Nash was happy. Going out into the street, he gave full details of the raid to the reporter from the local newspaper whom he had invited along. Everyone in the city would hear about the way that he took decisive action and bravely arrested a well-known criminal.

CHAPTER EIGHT

The lord mayor liked to be on good terms with everyone of importance in the city. Until now, he had always regarded Gregory Maynard as a close friend, but there was nothing friendly about the latter's demeanour when he called at the lord mayor's house that evening. Having finished eating dinner with his family, Timms had hoped to relax in the drawing room. Instead, he was now in his study, being confronted by an angry visitor.

'Calm down, calm down,' he urged.

'Why did you do it?' demanded Maynard.

'Do what?'

'Give your support to Superintendent Nash's actions. The man has a duty to assist Inspector Colbeck. Instead of that, he's actively obstructing him.'

'That's not true.'

'It sounds like it to me.'

'Horace Nash feels that you went over his head.'

'Yes, I did – because I want the best man possible to lead the investigation.'

'That's not a ringing endorsement for the York Constabulary.'

'Be honest, Neville,' said Maynard. 'They have their limitations. It's not entirely their fault, perhaps, because they've never been given adequate resources to police a city of this size. But there are also inherent faults – Nash is one of them.'

'He has his strengths.'

'I've yet to spot any of them. What I have noted in the past is how many serious crimes go unpunished in York. As lord mayor, you must be worried.'

'I am,' admitted Timms.

'Then why did you side with Nash?'

'Strictly speaking, I didn't do that.'

'He seems to think that you did. More importantly, so does Inspector Colbeck. He's entitled to guaranteed support from the local police. It wouldn't surprise me if he refers the matter to Scotland Yard.'

'Oh, I hope it doesn't come to that. There could be repercussions.'

'You endorsed Nash's decision.'

'I . . . did have doubts about it.'

'Then why didn't you call the superintendent to heel? If you'd had the sense to do that, we wouldn't be in the position of waiting to see which of two opposing teams will solve the murder.'

'Oh dear!' said Timms, running a hand through his

thinning hair. 'I do wish that we weren't in this situation.'

'You are partly to blame.'

'Let me speak to Horace Nash.'

'It's too late for that,' said Maynard. 'He'll browbeat you as usual.'

Timms felt insulted. 'I resent that accusation,' he bleated.

'Then prove to me that you can stand up to him.'

'I'm not sure I should try to do so. The simple truth is that I have some sympathy for his position. He doesn't feel that Colbeck should control this investigation, and I'm bound to say that I have qualms about the inspector myself. I have many more qualms about Sergeant Leeming,' he continued. 'In my opinion, he lacks the intelligence for the rank he holds.'

'I'm told he's proved his worth on countless occasions.'

'You'd never think it if you look at him.'

'That's a matter of opinion,' said Maynard. 'If Colbeck has faith in him, that's good enough for me. However, I came here to ask why you took Nash's side against a detective with a remarkable history of success behind him?'

'I did so,' affirmed Timms, 'because I trust Nash far more than I trust Colbeck. You keep trumpeting the inspector's virtues. I've yet to see any of them.'

'That's because you don't want to see them. From the moment he got here, Colbeck has been working quietly and effectively behind the scenes, gathering the intelligence that will lead to an arrest. Horace Nash, by contrast, didn't even bother to come to the railway station until the day after the explosion.'

'He was dealing with matters of importance.'

'What's more important than the murder of a guard, the destruction of his brake van, the disruption of train services and the spreading of panic throughout the entire station? Nash's behaviour is indefensible,' yelled Maynard. 'And so, by extension, is yours.'

'I resent that remark,' said Timms, wounded.

But his response went unheard. Turning on his heel, Maynard had already left the room and headed for the front the door. The conversation was over.

Roger Pendle came down to the dining room in Scawin's Hotel in the hope of finding a vantage point from which he could watch Colbeck and Leeming. After twenty minutes or so, however, there was no sign of them. He began to wonder if they would be having breakfast that morning. Sarah Scawin came into the room to see if everything was operating smoothly. Pendle sidled over to her.

'Can you tell me if Inspector Colbeck is still staying at the hotel?' he asked.

'Yes, sir,' she replied. 'He and the sergeant are here until further notice.'

'I see.'

'If you wish to speak to them, you'll need to get up earlier. They were the first guests in here today because they were eager to start work at the station.'

Pendle cursed himself for not keeping watch more carefully on the detectives. Abandoning the remains of his breakfast, he thanked Sarah for her information then scurried out of the dining room.

* * *

Word of the reward money had spread quickly throughout the city. By the time they reached the stationmaster' office, Colbeck and Leeming found a queue waiting for them. Frederick Staines greeted the detectives and wondered when he could have his office back.

'As soon as we have information we can act upon,' said Colbeck, 'we will be gone. We're grateful for your cooperation, Mr Staines. We won't inconvenience you any longer than we need to do so.'

'Then I wish you good luck, Inspector.'

When the stationmaster moved away, the detectives began their work. While Colbeck questioned the witnesses, Leeming took note of their names, addresses and evidence. Ben Walters, the railway policeman, stayed outside to control the queue. Obvious fraudsters were given short shrift, threatened with arrest, and sent packing. Most of those who had come were genuine, recalling what they had seen two days earlier as they walked past the brake van. None of them, however, provided evidence that was decisive enough to be acted upon.

While the majority were eager to help, one man of middle years entered the office in a state of belligerence. Short, fat, oily and oozing self-importance, he issued a demand.

'I want my money,' he insisted.

'Then you must give us information that justifies it,' said Colbeck.

'I'm not talking about the reward. I had goods to the value of a hundred and forty pounds in that brake van. They were burnt to cinders. I expect compensation.'

'Then you must take your complaint to the railway company, sir.'

'I want my money NOW!'

'Our priority,' said Colbeck, levelly, 'is to catch the man who caused the explosion in that brake van. You only lost your goods, sir. The guard lost his life.'

'That's immaterial.'

'I disagree.'

Rising out of his seat, Colbeck took him by the scruff of his neck and pushed him out on to the platform. He handed his spluttering captive over to Ben Walters.

'Escort this man out of the station,' he said. 'He needs to go home and write a letter to the North Eastern Railway company, giving full details of the property he lost when it was destroyed in the explosion in the brake van.'

Glad to have something to do, Walters marched the man away.

The detectives, meanwhile, continued to work their way through the queue. People came from all walks of life. Some had been passengers on the train involved in the explosion. Others had been well-wishers, standing on the platform to wave friends or loved ones off on their journey. All were anxious to help the investigation but none of them, it transpired, had evidence that caused the slightest flutter of excitement in Colbeck and Leeming. When they were alone for a moment, the sergeant groaned.

'We could be here forever, sir,' he said.

'Be patient, Victor.'

'This is the kind of job that Alan Hinton could do, leaving us to get on with the more important task of searching for the killer. He's still in the city, I'm sure.'

'We'll see.'

They looked up as another person stepped into the

office. Now in his late forties, he had the remains of what had once been a handsome face. Colbeck noticed the studious air, the rounded shoulders, and the bristling eyebrows. Although he wore a frock coat and top hat, the man looked somehow shabby with baggy trousers and shoes covered in dust.

Colbeck introduced himself and Leeming, then handed him over.

'Name, please, sir?' said the sergeant.

'Nicholas Ewart,' replied the other in a firm voice. 'And before I go any further, let me say that I am not here in search of the reward money for myself. If, by chance, what I tell you leads to an arrest, I wish the hundred pounds to go to the Minster. It's in dire need of it.'

'That's very kind of you, sir,' said Colbeck.

'I'm an archaeologist,' explained the other, 'and I've devoted my life to the study of York's history. The Minster has a special place in my heart,' he went on with a broad smile. 'As a boy, I used to sing in the choir there.'

He might have lost his chorister's voice, but his youthful enthusiasm was quite intact. When he talked, his eyes lit up. Leeming asked for his address. Ewart named a street that was in the shadow of the Minster.

'Right,' said Colbeck, 'so you believe that you may have seen something yesterday that might be of value to us. Is that correct?'

'Yes, Inspector,' said Ewart.

'What were you doing at the station?'

'I was there to wave my sister off. After staying with me for a few days, Ellen was returning to Leeds. I helped her into her seat then stood back.'

'How far away were you from the brake van?'

'Thirty yards or so at most,' said Ewart. 'I have excellent eyesight and a good memory. At first, of course, I assumed that the man was waiting to get on the train himself, but he just stood there. No,' he corrected, 'he wasn't standing, he was lurking. He kept glancing up and down the platform.'

'Can you describe this individual?' asked Colbeck.

'Oh, yes, Inspector. He was short, slight and had a dark complexion. I'd put him in his thirties. He was dressed like a tradesman – a carpenter, perhaps or a builder of some sort. He was carrying a small bag in one hand. I guessed – wrongly, perhaps – that it might contain his midday meal.'

'How long did he stay beside the brake van?'

'I suppose it must have been – what? – nine or ten minutes. Most of the time, porters were putting luggage aboard and he always stepped out of their way. For obvious reasons, I was far more interested in my sister than in a stranger. Then,' said Ewart, 'he did something that struck me as odd.'

'What was it?' asked Leeming.

'He disappeared.'

'Into the brake van?'

'Yes, Sergeant. And when he came out, he no longer had the bag.'

'What happened then?'

'He left the station, and I thought no more of it. Then, five minutes or so later, the guard came running down the platform and jumped into the brake van. I daresay you know what happened soon after.'

'What did you do, Mr Ewart?' asked Colbeck. 'Did you report what you'd seen to one of the railway policemen?'

'Regrettably, I didn't.'

'Why not?'

'There were people injured in the blast, Inspector, so I helped some of them to get clear of the brake van. It was blazing merrily. My main concern, of course,' he stressed, 'was to calm my sister down. Ellen was in a terrible state. She lost her husband some months ago and is still very fragile. I climbed into her compartment and tried to soothe her.'

'In the circumstances, sir,' said Colbeck, 'you behaved as you should.'

'The man I've described to you went clear out of my mind.'

'If you saw him again,' asked Leeming, 'would you recognise him?'

'I'm not sure,' admitted Ewart, 'but I hope so.'

Roger Pendle saw the queue on the platform and realised that he had tracked down the detectives. When he ambled past the stationmaster's office, he caught a glimpse of them, seated behind a table. Colbeck was talking to an elderly woman while Leeming was writing something in his notebook. Judging by the length of the queue, Pendle decided that they would be fully occupied for some time. However, he took no chances. Having missed seeing them in the hotel dining room, he was not going to make the same mistake twice. He therefore melted into the crowd, moving up and down but always keeping one eye on the stationmaster's office.

There had been a good response to the reward notice. While Pendle knew that some claims would, inevitably, be bogus, others might yield valuable information about the man who caused the explosion in the brake van. Pendle worried that the detectives would secure an advantage over the York Constabulary. If Colbeck and Leeming went on to solve the crime, Superintendent Nash and his officers would be left with red faces. The thought irked Pendle.

When they had finally worked their way through the queue, Colbeck and Leeming were able to have a rest and review their findings. One testimony stood out from the rest.

'Mr Ewart gave the most reliable account,' said Colbeck. 'He's highly intelligent and has a passion for his work.'

'Other people described a man loitering near the brake van,' recalled Leeming, 'but they didn't provide the same detail as Mr Ewart.' He grinned. 'I don't see him as a choirboy, somehow.'

'I was interested in his work as an archaeologist.'

'Why is that?'

'It's a testing profession. When you're involved in a dig, you spend a lot of your time on your knees, sifting through soil. You'd have to be dedicated to spend a whole lifetime doing that.'

'That's what I told my younger son.'

Colbeck was surprised. 'Albert doesn't want to be an archaeologist, does he?'

'No, of course not,' said Leeming. 'He's set his

heart on being a policeman. I've warned him about the dangers involved, not to mention the hard work. We spend ages sifting through tons of rubbish before we find something of value. Look at this morning, for instance,' he continued, tapping his notebook. 'We've spoken to dozens of people yet only one of them was worth listening to.'

As soon as he left the railway station, Nicholas Ewart went straight back to work. He joined his team at the trenches they had dug and peeled off his hat and coat. After examining a few items discovered that morning, he picked up a trowel and knelt beside the others. Ewart's scholarly zeal inspired them. When he unearthed the remains of a leather shoe, he held it aloft as if he had just found buried treasure.

The dig was in Coppergate and it had taken a long time to secure permission for the archaeological work. A few passers-by took an interest in what was happening but, to most citizens, it was a nuisance because they were forced to walk around the site. Ewart made sure that all the finds were taken away at the end of the day and locked up. He also arranged for the two trenches to be guarded at night in case someone tried to damage them. Even though he was in charge, he took his turn on the night shift, protecting the site from interference of any kind.

He was still on his knees when he heard a familiar voice.

'Good morning, Nicholas,' she said, looking down into the trench. 'I knew that I would find you here as usual.'

'It's my calling, Mrs Brightwell,' he said, rising to his feet.

'Have you found anything?'

'My assistants have found all sorts of things – coins, ceramics, antler work, metal work and so on. My claim to fame is that I dug up the remains of a Viking shoe.'

'Congratulations!'

'I'll need to examine it properly before I can place a date on it, but it's the kind of discovery that spurs us on to keep digging.'

'That's what I like to hear.'

Miriam Brightwell was a handsome, immaculately dressed middle-aged woman with a cultured voice. Unlike most people, she was fascinated by the way that Ewart was bringing the past to life again. He had cause to be grateful to her because she had made a generous donation towards the excavation. For that reason, she was allowed to see the display of finds whenever she wished.

'You all seem to be working with such caution,' she observed.

'It's what I've taught them to do. I've been to sites where they use spades and shovels too robustly. They destroy some of the artefacts they're searching for. That doesn't happen here. The trowel is our preferred tool. We exercise great care.'

'Well,' she said, 'I won't hold you up any longer.'

'You are always welcome, Mrs Brightwell.'

'I look forward to seeing the Viking shoe that you dug up earlier.'

'I daresay that we'll have a number of other new finds for you to enjoy.'

'Goodbye, Nicholas.'

'Goodbye,' he called, waving her off.

Moments later, he was down on his knees again, lost in his work.

Another queue had formed outside the stationmaster's office, but it was a relatively small one. Colbeck and Leeming were able to deal with the new witnesses quite briskly. The last of them had been a young man who had been standing on the platform two days earlier, minutes before the explosion.

'He noticed someone lurking near the brake van,' said Leeming, 'and he was able to give us a rough description of him.'

'It wasn't as detailed as the one Ewart supplied.'

'I still think they were both looking at the same man, sir.'

'We must allow for the fact that people were milling about on the platform at the time. Like Ewart, the latest witness would only have caught glimpses of the suspect. They were both there to see someone off, not to monitor the brake van. Right,' said Colbeck, 'let's see if there's anybody else outside.'

Before he could even leave his seat, however, the inspector saw the door open to admit Alan Hinton. He beamed at them.

'I'd forgotten you were coming, Alan,' said Leeming.

'I hadn't,' said Colbeck. 'Have you checked into the hotel yet?'

Hinton nodded. 'Yes, sir. I did as you advised – though I'm not quite sure why there's a need for secrecy.'

'Put simply, the situation is this. The local constabulary feel that they can do a better job than we can, so an alternative investigation has been set up.'

'That's ridiculous!'

'I agree, Alan. What it means, unfortunately, is that we will be watched to see what advances we make. I want you to find whoever is assigned to keep an eye on us. He'll be staying incognito at Scawin's Hotel.'

'Just like you,' Leeming pointed out.

'How do I keep in touch with you?' asked Hinton.

'We'll slip notes for you under your door.'

'Yes,' said Colbeck. 'Any instructions will be given to you face to face in the privacy of our rooms. We're on the top floor, by the way. I'll give you the numbers.'

'Thank you, sir.'

'Did the superintendent send a message?' asked Leeming.

'No, but Mrs Colbeck did.' Hinton took the letter from his pocket and handed it over to the inspector. 'I knew that your wife would welcome the opportunity to send you her news, sir.'

'That's very considerate of you,' said Colbeck.

'What do I do now?'

'Pretend that you are another so-called witness in search of the reward. It's highly likely that this office is being watched by someone deployed by Superintendent Nash, the head of the constabulary.' Colbeck winked at him. 'Let's put on a display for him, shall we?'

Roger Pendle kept shifting his position on the platform, but his gaze never left the stationmaster's office. His patience was at last rewarded. Colbeck came out of the office with the young man who had recently entered it. The latter pointed towards the end of the platform as if indicating a point where the brake van had been on the previous day. The two men seemed to be having an earnest conversation. They walked along the platform to a point near the collection of fire buckets. Colbeck kept nodding at his companion, as if grateful for the account he was being given. The witness then left the station altogether.

Pendle was worried. It looked as if the man had brought valuable information regarding the explosion. The advantage might well swing in favour of the detectives from Scotland Yard. That was disturbing news. Pendle didn't relish the idea of passing it on to Superintendent Nash.

CHAPTER NINE

When he arrived at his desk, Neville Timms found a letter awaiting him. Recognising the superintendent's hand, he tore the missive open and learnt that a significant arrest had been made during the night. The lord mayor was elated. His decision to support the York Constabulary had been vindicated. Nash had succeeded where the Scotland Yard detectives had failed. Timms might even get an abject apology from Gregory Maynard. It would be something to savour.

Minutes later, he was being driven to the police station. As soon as he arrived, he was admitted to Nash's office. The superintendent was glowing with pride.

'You read my letter, I see,' he said.

'It's wonderful news!'

'When I act, I do so decisively.'

'What you didn't tell me was the name of the man you arrested,' said Timms. 'How did you pick up his scent so quickly?'

Nash guffawed. 'I wouldn't call it scent,' he said. 'The man stinks to high heaven. I had to hold my nose before I put the handcuffs on him.'

'What is his name?'

'Patrick McBride.'

Timms was shocked. 'I thought he was in prison.'

'They let him out weeks ago.'

'Did he really plant a bomb in the brake van?'

'I don't know,' said Nash, hunching his shoulders, 'but he's certainly capable of ordering it. The way I see it is this. McBride rules Bedern. While he was behind bars, there was a sharp drop in the number of crimes committed by the Irish. McBride may not have put that bomb in place himself, but I'll wager that he gave the order for someone else to do it.'

'What has he been charged with?'

'The murder of Jack Follis.'

'But you've just told me that it wasn't him.'

'It was someone acting under his command, and that makes him equally culpable in my view. Let's be brutally frank, Lord Mayor. Only someone from the Irish community would have the gall to plan something like this. By arresting their leader, I've set the cat among the pigeons.'

Timms was sceptical. 'I'm not sure about this.'

'Am I supposed to let that villain roam free?' bellowed Nash.

'There's no need to shout, Horace.'

'Then don't make me do so. I expect you to back me to the hilt.'

'To some extent,' said Timms, 'I do. But I think you may have been rather hasty.' Nash snorted. 'I'm only being honest.'

'Wait until you read a copy of the evening paper. A reporter was present at the arrest. He appreciated the speed and commitment that we showed. When we dragged McBride out of his hutch, the reporter clapped his hands.'

'I wish that I could do that.'

'The case is solved, man. Doesn't that please you?'

'It's only partially solved,' argued Timms. 'You may have the man who gave the orders, but where is the person who placed that bomb in the brake van?'

'I'll get the name very soon.'

'How?'

'McBride will give it to me.'

'He'd rather die than do that, Horace!'

'I disagree,' said Nash with a complacent smile. 'When you realise that you're in the shadow of the hangman, you start to behave like a sensible human being. I'll get that name. In the hope of making one of his underlings take all the blame, McBride will hand him over without a flicker of regret.'

'The Irish are always fiercely loyal to their own kind.'

'Not in this case – just you watch.'

When she welcomed her father to the house, Madeleine Colbeck knew what to expect. As soon as Caleb Andrews had kissed his daughter, his eyes sparkled with curiosity.

'Has Robert solved the crime yet?' he asked.

'Give him a chance, Father,' she said. 'He's only been there five minutes. If the case was as simple as you seem to think, Robert wouldn't have needed to send for Alan Hinton yet again.'

'Is that what happened?'

'Yes – Alan called in here yesterday evening to tell me. He very kindly agreed to take a letter for Robert. I told him how much his wife and daughter missed him.'

'Did you mention me?'

'No – why should I?'

'Because I'm part of the family, that's why,' he said, aggrieved. 'You might have asked him if he wanted my advice about brake vans or the duties of a guard.'

'Someone in York can tell him that.'

'But I can speak with more authority, Maddy.'

'You've got a more important job to do here. Helena has been asking about you ever since we had breakfast. She's dying to play that game you taught her yesterday.'

He was nonplussed. 'What game?'

'Don't worry,' said Madeleine, laughing. 'If you can't remember it, your granddaughter certainly can.'

'It's coming back to me now, Maddy,' he said with a grin. 'You know, when Robert was sent off to York, I was quite jealous at first. Then I remembered that George Hudson lived there for a while. He did more damage to the railway system than any man in Britain.'

'You used to say the same thing about Mr Brunel.'

'Hudson was worse.'

'There was a time when you admired him,' she remembered.

'That was before I knew he was a crook. What sort of man flees the country when he gets into hot water? He should have stayed and defended himself.'

'As far as railways go, Mr Hudson belongs in the past.'

'Oh, no, he doesn't, Maddy. I bet that his footprints are all over York. He was a lord mayor at one time. Next thing you know, he launches the York and North Midland Railway.'

'I've heard you rant about it many a time, Father,' she said, trying to escape another lecture. 'Why keep on about it?'

'Because the truth needs to be remembered,' he said with conviction. 'The past is important, Maddy. It shaped the world that we live in.'

'I suppose that's true,' she conceded.

'Don't ever forget it.'

She sighed. 'I won't, Father.'

'When you were little, you loved hearing stories about the past.'

'That was different. The stories were not real. They were made up.'

'You believed them at the time. They brought you a lot of pleasure in the same way that looking back over the years pleases me. Show respect to history, Maddy. It's the best teacher you can have.'

When one of his assistants unearthed a cowrie shell, Nicholas Ewart was called over, He identified it at once, suggesting that it might have been used in trade, as had the various coins they had found. But it was a copper brooch that proved to be the find of the day. After cleaning it off with great care, Ewart let his team handle it in turn. He was thrilled by its quality. It would be something to show to Miriam Brightwell when she came to inspect the items they had reclaimed from the distant past.

Now that the queue outside the stationmaster's office had virtually disappeared, Colbeck went back to the hotel. Leeming was left to handle any stray visitors who might turn up with their differing claims to the reward money. On his way out, Colbeck was unaware whether he was being followed but he'd taken steps to find out. Hinton's room overlooked the entrance to the hotel. The detective constable had been asked to keep watch through his window when Colbeck returned. Minutes after he went into his room, the inspector was, as arranged, joined by Hinton.

'You obviously saw me arrive,' said Colbeck.

'Yes, sir,' replied Hinton. 'Ever since I got back here, I've been sitting beside the window with my eyes peeled.'

'Did you notice anyone following me?'

'No, Inspector.'

'Are you quite sure of that?'

'I'm absolutely certain of it, sir,' said Hinton, emphatically.

'That's reassuring,' said Colbeck. 'Now, please take a seat, and I'll bring you up to date with what's been happening here. If nothing else, yesterday was eventful. The sergeant and I had a mixed welcome . . .'

Left alone in the stationmaster's office, Leeming had seen the procession of witnesses dwindle then cease. He was about to abandon his post when a woman suddenly appeared in the doorway. Miriam Brightwell apologised profusely for not bringing her testimony earlier and hoped that it might still be of use. Leeming offered her a seat and made a note of her name and address.

'What is it that you saw, Mrs Brightwell?' he asked.

'Well, not a great deal, really. It's just that I remember a man – a rather ugly, uncouth individual – standing near the brake van as I walked past. I usually give such people a wide berth but not in this case.'

'What time would this be?'

'Five or ten minutes before the train was due to depart.'

'And did you see this man enter the brake van?' said Leeming.

'No,' she replied. 'I just noticed that he'd somehow vanished. When I looked again shortly afterwards, he was back again. I watched him slink towards the exit.'

'Please give me as full a description as you can of this man.'

'That may be difficult,' she admitted. 'My mind is not as retentive as it used to be. But I do remember his face and the way that he kept looking around furtively.'

'What age was he?' asked Leeming, pencil hovering above his notebook, 'and what was he wearing?'

'Well, now, let me see . . .'

On hearing the news of an arrest, Gregory Maynard was in a quandary, unsure whether he ought to congratulate Horace Nash or suspect him of making a serious mistake. Anxious to confront the superintendent, he went to the police station. As soon as he heard the name of the man now locked in one of the cells, Maynard came to a decision.

What had happened was an act of madness.

'Patrick McBride?' he said. 'Are you serious about this?'

'Deadly serious,' Nash retaliated. 'Because I acted on instinct, I caught the villain who plotted the destruction of that brake van.'

'What evidence do you have?'

'It's the evidence of my own eyes. I've watched McBride for years.'

'Then you ought to have remembered that there's a definite pattern to McBride's misbehaviour,' said Maynard. 'Whenever he's committed a crime in the past, he's always disappeared from the city straight afterwards. I know that from personal experience. He caused wanton destruction of property at the railway station, then shot off to Whitby.'

'I know. We tracked him there.'

'And what happened?'

'McBride produced half a dozen "witnesses" who swore that he'd been there for the previous few days. The case against him collapsed.'

'Exactly!'

'I caught him this time before he managed to take to his heels.'

'McBride didn't need to run. That proves he's innocent.'

'He's the leader of the criminal community in Bedern. You know that as well as I do. Whenever a serious crime occurs in this city, you can be certain that McBride is involved somehow.'

'That argument won't stand up in court. In a trial for murder, the judge and jury need cast-iron evidence.'

Nash smiled confidently. 'It will be forthcoming.'

'Does the lord mayor know about the arrest?'

'Yes, of course.'

'What was his reaction?'

'Mr Timms had the grace to applaud my actions,' said Nash, airily, concealing the fact that the lord mayor had had misgivings. 'I was rather hoping that you might do the same. After all, I've saved you and your railway a fair amount of money.'

'I don't follow.'

'Well, you won't have to pay any more hotel bills for Inspector Colbeck and the sergeant. Now that I've arrested McBride, they can go back to London on the next train – and good riddance to them!'

'You'll regret your decision to act independently.'

'And you'll regret your decision to invite outsiders to this city,' snarled the other. 'Tell them that they are no longer needed.'

'I'll tell them the complete opposite,' said Maynard, hotly.

'And what's that?'

'They are needed more than ever.'

After working in the trench for over an hour, Nicholas Ewart allowed himself a breather. He hauled himself to his feet and used a handkerchief to mop his brow. Though he had always been fit and active, the exercise was starting to tire him. Looking around, he was rewarded by the sight of the people who had volunteered to help him search for the remains of the Viking occupation. They were young, for the most part, and, in some cases, had had to be schooled in the way to search for and handle artefacts. When one of them found something important, the whole team celebrated. Ewart loved their youthful exuberance.

He became conscious that someone was watching him. He looked up to see an old man, leaning on the fence and gazing down at the trench. The bystander wore a tattered coat and a cap that had seen better days. A clay pipe was in his mouth but there was no sign of smoke.

'You the boss?' he said to Ewart.

'Yes, I am.'

'What'll 'appen to them things you digs up?'

'They'll be dated as accurately as we can manage,' said Ewart, 'then they'll be put in chronological order. When that's done, I'll catalogue them before putting them on display in the museum.'

'Will I be able to see 'em?'

'Members of the public will be welcome.'

'Good. Never knew we 'ad Vikings 'ere.'

'Most people who live in York didn't realise it,' said Ewart. 'We're trying to educate them.'

'Thank ye, sir!'

Removing the pipe, he spat on the ground then sauntered happily on his way.

When he had explained to Alan Hinton what had happened so far, Colbeck gave him his instructions and sent him on his way. The inspector's intention was to return to the station to see if any other witnesses had come forward. As he came downstairs, however, he was intercepted by Henry Kemp, the duty manager.

'I didn't realise that you were still in the hotel, Inspector,' he said. 'In fact, I was about to send a message to you at the station.'

'You can give it to me now, Mr Kemp.'

'Mrs Scawin is very anxious to see you, sir.'

'Did she say why?'

'A young woman has turned up,' said Kemp. 'She is asking for the person in charge of the investigation into the death of Jack Follis. I'd better warn you that she is . . . in a state of distress.'

'I'll go to her immediately,' said Colbeck, moving off.

When he got to Sarah Scawin's office, he knocked on the door and was invited in. The scene that greeted him told its own story. An attractive woman in her late twenties was weeping into a handkerchief. Standing beside her, trying to soothe her, was the hotel owner. Sarah was relieved to see Colbeck.

'Thank you for coming, Inspector,' she said. 'I have assured this young woman that you were a man of discretion and would understand why she was unable to give her name.'

'You are under no compulsion to do so,' he told the visitor.

'There you are,' said Sarah. 'You can speak freely.'

The woman dabbed at her tears with a handkerchief. Colbeck gave her time to recover. He had already made two deductions. The first one was that the visitor was unlike the female members of staff who had been pursued by Follis. They were young, innocent girls from the working class. This woman, by contrast, wore a coat and hat of real quality. When she had finished crying, she looked up and gave Colbeck a nervous smile, allowing him to see just how beautiful she was.

The smile vanished almost immediately to be replaced by

101

a look of shame. Colbeck's second deduction was accurate. She was married.

When she felt able to speak at last, her voice was soft.

'I met Mr Follis by accident some weeks ago,' she admitted. 'He was kind and attentive. I felt that I could trust him. Every time I caught a train, he seemed to be there. We always exchanged a word or two.'

'You don't need to go into detail,' said Sarah. 'The fact is that a friendship of sorts grew up between you. That's what you told me earlier.'

'Yes, Mrs Scawin. It's true.'

'Do you live in York?' asked Colbeck. The woman nodded. 'Are you in the habit of travelling by train?'

'Not really,' confessed the other.

'When you did go to the station, you met Mr Follis?'

'Yes, Inspector – as a rule. Nothing happened between us, I swear. It's just that my husband is . . . away for long periods.' She lowered her head. 'I was lonely. I was flattered by Mr Follis's interest.'

'What happened two days ago?' prompted Sarah.

'I'd rather not say, Mrs Scawin.'

'The inspector will understand.'

'He'd disapprove of me, and I'd hate that.'

'You are quite wrong,' said Colbeck. 'My sole concern is to find the man responsible for the untimely death of Mr Follis. From what you've already told me, I can see that you're as eager as I am to see the killer arrested and punished.'

'Yes!' she said with sudden anger. 'I am, I am.'

It was slow, patient work but the story was eventually dragged out of her. The friendship with Follis reached a point where he suggested they meet somewhere in private. Embarrassed at first, she eventually agreed to think it over. Follis had extracted a promise from her. On the previous day, she would come to the station to tell him if she would meet him in private.

'I told him the truth, Inspector. I'm a married woman, and I'd never break the vows I made at the altar. I was shocked I'd even let Jack – Mr Follis – make such a proposal. Our friendship had to end.'

'What did he say to that?' asked Colbeck.

'Nothing at all. He just glared at me and ran off along the platform. You know what happened next. He was killed in the brake van.' She burst into tears. 'It seemed like God's judgement on the two of us. Jack lost his life, and I must bear some of the blame for turning him down and making him run away like that.'

'You mustn't think like that,' said Sarah with a consoling hand around her shoulders. 'It was simply a case of rotten luck.'

'I can't thank you enough for being brave enough to come forward,' said Colbeck with sincere gratitude. 'You've provided important details. I don't need to hear any more.'

'If only I'd talked to Jack for a few minutes,' said the woman through her tears 'he'd still be alive. But I . . . rejected him and sent him to his death.'

Roger Pendle had been told to report to the superintendent if he had discovered anything important. When he got to the police station, however, he had a long wait while Horace Nash had a meeting with his colleagues. By the time he finally went into the superintendent's office, Pendle had to disguise his irritation.

'Well,' asked Nash, 'what did you find out?'

'Colbeck and his sergeant have adjoining rooms on the top floor.'

'Did you hear anything through the doors?'

'No, sir,' replied Pendle. 'That would have involved an unnecessary risk. Hotel guests and porters were everywhere.'

'Then what did you find out?'

Opening his notebook, Pendle used it to give a succinct account of what he had been doing. Nash was disappointed that the constable had not been able to find out what the detectives had learnt from Sarah Scawin when they joined the hotel owner in her office. Omitting that he had got up too late to watch them eating their breakfast, Pendle moved on to the activities at the railway station.

'Those reward notices attracted dozens and dozens of people,' he said. 'At one point, there must have been forty or fifty people in the queue.'

'Did any of them have evidence enough to win the money?'

'No, sir. In fact, some were fraudulent. Sergeant Leeming threw a couple of them out of the stationmaster's office. It was only at the very end that someone seemed to arouse their interest.'

'Why do you say that?'

'A young man went in to tell them what he saw. The inspector was so interested in what he heard that he came out on to the platform and walked to the point where the brake van blew up. The man was pointing as if he had something important to pass on,' said Pendle.

'I was worried that the newcomer might have valuable information – the kind that might lead to an arrest.'

'They're too late, Pendle.'

'I don't understand, sir.'

'An arrest has already been made,' said Nash, inflating his chest, 'and I was the person who made it. I don't think you need shadow Colbeck any longer. We already have the culprit in custody.'

'That's good news, Superintendent.'

'Yes, it is. In effect, the case is closed.'

CHAPTER TEN

The woman had now left the hotel, grateful for Colbeck's discretion and for Sarah Scawin's sympathy. She had told them enough to reveal the strength of her feelings for the guard. Colbeck was curious.

'Jack Follis seems to have had considerable charm,' he observed.

'Oh, there's no question about that, Inspector. I could see the effect that he had on my employees. He beguiled them.'

'The lady who left here moments ago was an unexpected victim of his charm. Ordinarily, I wouldn't have expected someone like her to look twice at a railway guard. She moves in a different world.'

'Quite so,' said Sarah. 'She must be tortured with guilt.'

'Yes,' he agreed. 'She's a married woman guilty of befriending another man, and she's persuaded herself that she was somehow responsible for the guard's death. I think she views that as God's punishment for the feelings she entertained for Follis. She was clearly in agony.'

'Thank you for being so understanding, Inspector.'

'I was glad you summoned me. Without realising it, she told me something of great importance to this investigation. However,' he went on, 'let's turn to someone else. Earlier today we questioned lots of people who claimed to have valuable information about the explosion. Most were of no value at all, but one man's testimony stood out. His name was Nicholas Ewart. I wondered if you had heard of the gentlemen.'

'Oh yes,' she said with evident approval. 'Mr Ewart is well known in York. He is fascinated by the city's history. I once heard him give a talk about the Viking occupation. It was fascinating. He's a real scholar.'

'There was no doubting that.'

'Yet he was able to explain things so clearly to ordinary people like me.'

'I'd never make the mistake of calling you ordinary, Mrs Scawin,' he said with a smile, 'because you are a remarkable woman. But I take your point. Mr Ewart is a born teacher.'

'He's a close friend of Archbishop William.'

'That doesn't surprise me in the least.'

'What might surprise you is the way that he behaved when his wife died.'

'Oh?'

'She had been ill for some time,' explained Sarah, 'so he

knew that her days were numbered. Most people who lose a partner they adored are stricken with grief. It happened to me, so I speak from experience. Mr Ewart was different. Instead of a period of mourning, he threw himself into his work as if it was the most important thing in the world. It was almost as if he wanted to block out painful memories by keeping himself fully occupied. That struck me as odd.'

While he drove himself on remorselessly, Nicholas Ewart did not expect his team to work as intensely. Even he decided to finish when the light began to fade. With the aid of his team, he moved trays of the day's finds to his house. Once he had washed his hands and brushed off his trousers, he adjourned to the Minster. Ignoring the pain in his knees, he prayed in a side chapel. When he eventually rose to his feet, he realised that he had company. It was the archbishop.

'How is the excavation going, Nicholas?' he asked.

'We've had a good day, Your Grace. I came here to give thanks.'

'That's as it should be.'

'The more we find, the more intriguing it becomes. Most people seem to think that the Vikings were no more than barbarians who came here solely to kill and loot. It's simply not true.'

'They had to fight when they first arrived here.'

'Oh yes, they were sturdy warriors. We've found ample evidence of that. But we've also found countless examples of a more peaceful way of life. They were, after all, here for the best part of a hundred years.'

'Yes, that's true. I'll be interested to see what you've found.'

'You're welcome to come to the house at any time, Your Grace.'

'I'll hold you to that, Nicholas.'

William Thomson spoke with obvious affection for the archaeologist. It was almost three years since he had been elevated to his position as Primate for England. During that time, he had established himself as a devout man with strong opinions on the future of the Anglican church. Tall, imposing and now in his mid-forties, the archbishop had large side whiskers and a prominent forehead. Some thought him vain, even aloof, but Ewart found him kind and approachable.

'I have to admire your industry, Nicholas,' said the other.

'It's a labour of love.'

'You've met with a lot of opposition, I know, but you soldier on regardless.'

'We did get a lot of abuse at the start,' admitted Ewart. 'Some people used to yell obscenities at us as they passed. Others thought the trenches were a place where they could dump their rubbish during the night. We found a dead dog in one trench.'

'Heavens!'

'We doubled the number of guards on night duty after that.'

'What about the cost of it all?'

'I managed to talk the city council into giving us some funding, but we also have generous donations from certain individuals. Chief among them is Mrs Brightwell.'

'The Minster has also benefitted from her kindness,' said Thomson, thankfully. 'When her husband died, he left her with a large fortune. Mrs Brightwell is determined to spend some of it on the Minster – and on what she considers to be good causes.'

'Luckily, we are one of them.'

'She is a true Christian.'

'Yet she is willing to invest in an archaeological project about a people who had a very different form of religion,' observed Ewart. 'I've managed to persuade her that Vikings were not simply bloodthirsty pirates. Here in Jorvik, as they called it, they worshipped their own gods. But they also had an established system of law and social organisation, not to mention a rich poetic culture. Mrs Brightwell understands that.'

'Don't forget that her husband had a sizeable library,' said Thomson. 'I was shown it when I visited the house. It was exceptional and Mrs Brightwell has made good use of it. She is a highly educated woman.'

Miriam Brightwell closed the book she had just finished reading and set it down on the little table beside her. Sitting back in her armchair, she reflected on what she had learnt from the volume. She was eternally grateful to her husband for urging her to read widely and educate herself. Their library had become a source of pleasure and instruction for them. It had opened her eyes in every way. Whenever she finished reading a book, memories of her husband flooded back. Chief among them was a recollection of the number of occasions when they had sat side by side in the library, reading a book apiece and being transported by someone's imagination.

Rising to her feet, she replaced her volume in its original position and ran her eyes along the shelves in search of something else. It took several minutes. When she had finally made her choice, she settled down in her armchair and opened the book.

Mrs Brightwell was soon lost to the world yet again.

'When was this?' asked Leeming.

'Earlier this afternoon,' replied Colbeck.

'Who was this woman?'

'She would only speak if her identity was concealed.'

'Why did she go to Scawin's Hotel?'

'I suspect that she knew the owner by reputation. Mrs Scawin inspires trust. A terrified young lady would only have turned to a woman in the first instance.'

It was early evening and Colbeck had gone to the station in search of Leeming. Since the trickle of witnesses had at last come to a dead halt, the sergeant was able to hand the office back to Frederick Staines, the helpful stationmaster. The detectives were now side by side on a bench on the platform.

'Did this woman say anything of importance?' asked Leeming.

'She did, Victor. My earlier theory may be vindicated.'

'What theory, sir?'

'I'll come to that. First, let me describe her . . .'

Colbeck gave a succinct account of the woman's confession, stressing how unlike she was from Follis's other known victims. He emphasised that it took a huge effort for her to come forward with her evidence.

'She would never have dared approach the local police.'

'I'm not surprised,' said Leeming. 'But I don't see what theory of yours she supported. All that happened was that she came close to being led astray by Follis.'

'She rejected him. That must have stung a man who regarded women as there to be taken. He was so upset that he fled. The stationmaster remembers the angry expression on his face as he shot past.'

'I'm sorry, sir. But I'm still confused.'

'Think it through,' advised Colbeck. 'If she had agreed to a rendezvous with him, he would have strutted along the platform with his chest out, proud of his latest conquest. The brake van would still have exploded – but Jack Follis would not have been inside it.'

Leeming slowly realised what he was being told. He was unconvinced.

'My theory,' said Colbeck, 'is that Follis might not have been the bomber's target, after all.'

'Of course he was!' declared Leeming.

'I believe that he died by accident.'

Alan Hinton had been given the task of finding out as much as he could about the investigation led by the local constabulary. He therefore spoke to some of the policemen who pounded the beat. What they saw was a well-dressed man with a pleasant manner, who treated them with respect. The two constables he approached were different in height, build and age. The older one was bigger and clearly more experienced than his companion, who looked rather callow. Hinton therefore directed his questions at the older man.

'Is it true that someone was blown up at the railway station recently?'

'It was, sir,' said the other. 'Me and Sidney heard the bang.'

'What did you do?'

'We rushed to the station to see what'd happened. It was too late to save the poor devil. He was burnt to a frazzle.'

'Who is leading the investigation?' asked Hinton.

'Superintendent Nash.'

'Do you have a Detective Department here?'

'No,' said the other. 'We manage very well without one. When the murder was committed, detectives from Scotland Yard were sent for, but our superintendent didn't think much of either of them.'

'Why was that?'

'They're strangers. They've no idea where to start.'

'Superintendent Nash showed them up,' said the other policeman with a grin.

'That's right, Sidney,' agreed the older man. 'While them detectives is still trying to find their way around, the superintendent arrested the killer.'

Hinton was astonished. 'Who was he?'

'Patrick McBride.'

'Is he a known criminal?'

'Oh, yes,' said the older policeman 'He's the worst in York.'

Patrick McBride yelled at the top of his voice until a duty officer came to see why the prisoner was making such an ear-splitting noise.

'Shut up!' he warned. 'Close that gob of yours or we'll close it for you.'

'I want to see a lawyer,' demanded McBride. 'It's my right.'

'All in good time.'

'I want him now.'

'Oh, do you?' teased the other. 'What else can we get for you – a tankard of beer, perhaps, or a nice fat tart to share your cell and help you pass the time?' His voice hardened. 'You've been arrested on a charge of murder. That means you've got no rights.'

McBride glowered at him. The policeman was a big, brawny man but he was dwarfed by the Irishman. As a result, he took care not to get too close to the bars in case the prisoner reached through them and grabbed him. McBride jabbed a finger at him.

'Let me talk to Nash.'

'You'll see the superintendent in court.'

'He's made a big mistake.'

The policeman cackled. 'They all say that.'

'Doesn't he have the decency to give me two minutes?'

'No, he doesn't,' said the other, vehemently. 'You showed no mercy towards Jack Follis. Why should anyone show mercy towards you?'

'I've never even heard of – what did you call him?'

'Jack Follis.'

'Don't know him from Adam.'

'Then why did you blow him up, you maniac? As for that howling and wailing of yours, remember this. If I get so much as a peep out of you, I'll come back with a few friends. Understand?'

Going through the outer door, he locked it behind him. Fuming with anger, all that McBride could do was to pace his cell and growl.

Colbeck and Leeming met at the hotel to discuss the case in comfort. Before long they were interrupted by Gregory Maynard. He came into the lounge and asked if he might join them.

'Of course, sir,' said Colbeck, indicating a chair. 'We're at your service, sir.'

'I'm glad that somebody is.' Maynard sat down. 'Have you heard from Nash?'

'No, sir – why?'

'He claims that he's solved the case.'

'Oh,' said Colbeck in surprise. 'Has he made an arrest?'

'A man named Patrick McBride is in custody. The superintendent raided the house at night and performed the arrest himself. He even took a reporter from the local newspaper along with him to make sure that he got publicity.'

'Who is this McBride?' asked Leeming.

'He's a deep-dyed villain,' said Maynard, 'and he's been guilty of many crimes over the years. But he draws the line at murder. It's one of the reasons I know he was not involved.'

He went on to tell them that McBride had caused so much trouble at the station that he was forbidden to come anywhere near it. By way of retaliation, Maynard claimed, the Irishman had vandalised the station one night before fleeing to Whitby on horseback. Though certain that he was the culprit, the police had no evidence to prove it.

'On what grounds was he arrested this time?' said Colbeck.

'It was purely on McBride's reputation.'

'The superintendent will need more than that in a court of law.'

'Nash believes he can get it,' said Maynard. 'If it was left to him, he'd have McBride hanged, drawn and quartered. It would certainly reduce the level of crime in the city. When McBride is at liberty, it goes up. That's a proven fact.'

'Yet you think he's innocent of this latest charge,' said Leeming.

'I do, Sergeant. He did not commit murder.'

'I don't think that anyone did, Mr Maynard,' said Colbeck, seriously. 'I've had reservations about this case from the start. In my opinion, Jack Follis was not intended to be a murder victim.'

Maynard was astounded. 'That's a preposterous claim, Inspector.'

'Wait until you hear me out. Evidence has come into my hands that explains why the guard was seen sprinting along the platform in a state of anger. I can't give you precise details,' explained Colbeck. 'Let me just say that he had been rejected by a certain woman. It was a savage blow to his pride. You know his reputation.'

'I do, indeed.'

'If he hadn't dashed back to the brake van, he wouldn't have been there when it exploded. The man who placed a bomb there wanted to cause damage and spread alarm – but he didn't come with murder in mind.'

'I find that hard to believe, Inspector.'

'It's only a theory, I grant you, but it has a lot of merit in my view.'

'I see none, I'm afraid.'

'Neither did I at first,' confessed Leeming, 'but I came to understand what the inspector was saying. It's changed the way we should approach the case.'

'Does it?' asked Maynard.

'Yes, sir. We've been looking for someone who hated Jack Follis.'

'Instead of that,' added Colbeck, 'we should search for someone with a grudge against the North Eastern Railway. That's what motivated the crime, in my view. The bomber set out to create panic at the railway station. In doing so, he mistakenly committed a murder. Do you follow my reasoning?'

'I'm beginning to,' said Maynard after some thought, 'but I can't say that it brings me any consolation. If the NER inspires someone to launch an attack of that scale on us, then we have a dangerous enemy still at liberty.'

'Unless that enemy is Patrick McBride,' Leeming pointed out. 'Maybe the superintendent has arrested the right man, after all.'

'No, I don't think so. McBride was let out of prison recently. He's keen to enjoy home comforts again. Even he is not stupid enough to take a risk like that. His wife and family mean a great deal to him.'

'In that case,' said Colbeck, 'we must look elsewhere for the man who planted that bomb in the brake van. At the start of the investigation, you thought that anarchists might be involved.'

'I wouldn't rule it out.'

'Have they been active elsewhere?'

'There was an incident in Leeds last year,' recalled Maynard. 'A bomb exploded at the entrance to the railway station. It caused massive delays. The police never caught those responsible, but they suspect that it was the work of an anarchist group. They hate the notion of an organised society. I've seen some of the leaflets they've put out,' he went on. 'They're full of threats of disruption.'

'Why should they pick on the NER?'

'I wish I knew, Inspector,' said Maynard. 'It's frightening to be in the dark like this. You must wish that I'd never brought you here.'

'Not at all,' said Colbeck. 'We love a challenge. My only regret is that we've been so embroiled in the case that we've had no time to explore the Minster.'

'Or to visit a cocoa factory,' added Leeming.

Caleb Andrews had been invited to dine with his daughter that evening, but he had already agreed to meet a group of retired railway employees. He was honest.

'Much as I'd love to join you, Maddy,' he said. 'I can't let my friends down. When I'm with them, I feel completely at ease.'

'I hope you feel completely at ease here as well,' said Madeleine.

'Most of the time, I do.'

'What do you mean?'

'Well, it's lovely being in this big house,' he explained, 'but I do get twinges from time to time. They remind me I don't really belong here.'

'Of course, you do!' she insisted.

'My little house can't compare with this one, but I'm happier there.'

'You just need to adjust, Father,' she said. 'It's what I had to do. I was born and brought up in that house and I loved it there. When I first came here, I was almost overwhelmed. Now, I'm completely at home.'

'That's as it should be, Maddy.' He opened the front door. 'Anyway, I'll be off . . .'

'Wait a moment. There's something I haven't told you.'

'Have I done something wrong again?'

'No, of course not. I thought you should know that I have company tomorrow morning. Estelle Leeming is coming.'

'Good,' he said. 'I'll be glad to see her. I'll tell her that young Albert ought to give up this stupid idea of joining the police and set his sights on being an engine driver. It's a much safer job.'

'Albert wants to follow in his father's footsteps.'

'Then his mother will hardly ever see him. Warn her, Maddy. The lad will be just like Victor – never at home.'

Nicholas Ewart was in a thoughtful mood as he returned home, reflecting on his visit to the Minster and his conversation with the archbishop. The fact that William Thomson took such an interest in his work was flattering. Ewart was happy at the way a friendship had developed between the two of them.

When he let himself into the house, he saw a letter on the hall table and recognised the handwriting of Miriam Brightwell. He opened the missive to find that she was asking if she could visit the house on the following evening to see the collection of Viking artefacts so far unearthed. Going straight to his study, Ewart dashed off a warm invitation, then called to a servant. When the man appeared, his employer thrust the letter into his hand.

'Deliver this to Mrs Brightwell's home,' he said.

Hinton followed his orders. He waited until Colbeck and Leeming had gone into the dining room, then watched to see if anyone was keeping them under observation. When he was convinced that they were not being watched, he had his own dinner, taking care to sit well away from his colleagues. After the meal, he went up to the top floor and joined them in Colbeck's room.

'What did you discover, Alan?' asked Leeming.

'I discovered that we're not very popular among the local police,' said Hinton. 'I spoke to half a dozen of them and got the same answer. They hate the idea of detectives from London daring to come here. Yorkshire people are independent. They resent being told what to do by someone from two hundred miles away.'

'It's a common reaction,' said Colbeck, tolerantly. 'We've had it wherever we go. Consequently, we need to prove our worth before we can garner any respect.'

'It's a case of us versus them, is it?'

'Not exactly, Alan. The police are trying to solve a murder that was not supposed to happen. We, on the other hand, are looking for someone bent solely on causing damage and spreading alarm.'

Hinton was puzzled. 'I don't understand, sir.'

'I didn't at first,' said Leeming.

Colbeck explained his theory but all that it did at first

was to corrugate Hinton's brow. It took the combined efforts of inspector and sergeant to convince him the notion had some value.

'What do we do next, Inspector?' asked Hinton.

'Your job is simple,' replied Colbeck. 'At the crack of dawn, I want you to explore Bedern and talk to some of the inhabitants.'

'I can do that right now.'

'That wouldn't be very wise,' said Leeming with a grin. 'From what we've heard, Bedern is the home of the Irish community. It will be lively enough in daylight. When it gets dark, I daresay it will be downright dangerous.'

'Oh, I see.'

'Don't take unnecessary risks, Alan,' said Colbeck. 'Remember what happened in Oldbury. You went out alone at night and ended up in hospital.'

'I remember it well,' said the other, ruefully.

'Did you bring a change of clothing?'

'Yes, Inspector.'

'Then wear it tomorrow. If you turn up in Bedern, looking well dressed, the chances are that nobody will speak to you. It's an area with extreme poverty. Keep your wits about you – or the pickpockets will start circling.'

CHAPTER ELEVEN

Shortly after first light, Nicholas Ewart arrived at the site and thanked those on guard for protecting it during the night. He was soon joined by other members of the team. Their sense of enthusiasm was undimmed. Ewart and the others were soon down on their knees, scraping away with their trowels. It was not long before the first significant find was discovered and handed to the archaeologist.

'It's pottery of the highest quality,' said Ewart, studying it through a magnifying glass. 'Let's hope we can dig up the rest of it.'

'What will happen to it, Nick?' asked one of his assistants.

'In the short term, I'll take it home so that I can gloat over it. Tomorrow – or maybe the day after – I'll take it to the museum for safekeeping.'

'Isn't it safe in your house?'

'I don't like to take unnecessary chances. On the other hand,' said Ewart, 'who is likely to want a fragment of a Viking pot? To me, it's a magical specimen. To the bulk of people, it's worthless.'

'Yesterday,' remembered the other, 'Mrs Brightwell said that she would love to see what we had dug up.'

'That's true. She's coming to view our recent finds this evening. Mrs Brightwell is not the only person who has shown an interest in our work. The archbishop himself is keen to view our collection.'

The assistant was impressed. 'How do you know?'

'I spoke to him at the Minster only yesterday. He's intrigued by what we're doing here.' His eyes twinkled. 'I'm rather hoping that we may get a mention in one of his sermons.'

After putting the shard of pottery on a tray, he went happily back to work.

Bedern ran south-east from Goodramgate to St Andrew-gate. As he walked through it, Alan Hinton found it hard to believe that Bedern meant 'house of prayer'. The area seemed so ungodly. It was an ugly, stinking, crowded street of slums in which whole families sometimes shared a single room. Laws had been passed to improve the accommodation, but the council had neither the money nor the urge to tackle the problem. Hinton had seen disgusting slums in various parts of London. Bedern could match any of them.

Wearing rough clothing, he attracted little attention, and, in any case, few people were about. It was only when he came around a bend that he realised why. A crowd was gathering quickly. The voices he heard were uniformly Irish. At the edge of the mass was a tall, striking figure whose top hat and frock coat made him stand out against the ragged mass around him. Hinton went over to speak to him.

'What's going on?' he asked.

'I'm leading a deputation to the police station,' replied the man.

'Why?'

'We intend to challenge a gross injustice. Pat McBride, a senior member of this community, has been wrongly arrested on a charge of murder. My name is Tom Quinn and I'm a lawyer. I represent these good people here,' he went on, 'and I mean to fight with every weapon at my disposal to get McBride released.'

'Are you sure of his innocence?'

'I know the fellow. He's no saint, I grant you that, and he's seen the inside of prison more than once. But he would never take the life of a fellow human being. Like any true Catholic, he knows that murder is expressly forbidden in the Bible.' He put an arm on Hinton's shoulder. 'Come and join us.'

'But I'm not Irish, Mr Quinn.'

'I don't care if you're Welsh, Scots or English. We need everyone we can get. The bigger the crowd, the more impact we can make. I've had dozens of people coming over from Walmgate to support us. They're Irish through and through. What do you say, my friend? Will you march beside us?'

'I think I will,' said Hinton, convinced that he might learn something of use. 'It sounds like a good cause.'

'Saving a life is the best cause there is.' Quinn offered his hand and Hinton shook it. 'Thank you, young man. You're one of us now.'

When he came down for breakfast, Colbeck discovered a letter waiting for him. Handing it over, the receptionist explained that it had been delivered during the night. Colbeck opened the letter and read its brief message. He then went into the dining room and was shown to a table. Minutes later, Leeming joined him.

'Good morning, sir,' he said. 'How are you?'

'To be honest, Victor, I'm rather mystified.'

'Why?'

'A letter was waiting for me this morning.'

'Who sent it?'

'I wish I knew. It was unsigned.'

'What did it say?'

'See for yourself,' said Colbeck, handing it over.

Leeming read it aloud. 'Owen Gale is the killer.' He scratched his head. 'Who the devil is Owen Gale?'

'We need to find out very quickly.'

'Why?'

'I think that a whole new dimension to this case has just opened up.'

Leeming was worried. 'Can we at least have breakfast first?'

During a rest from the punishing work of kneeling for long periods, Nicholas Ewart glanced up at the people walking past. He turned to one of his assistants.

'Look at them,' he said with a sad smile. 'They live in one

of the most beautiful cities in the country and they can't even spare it a glance. The Minster is invisible to them and so is the castle, the tower, the churches, chapels, ancient houses, civic buildings, and the amazing city walls that surround them all. Wherever you look, there's something quite remarkable.'

'Familiarity breeds contempt,' suggested his companion.

'It breeds something far worse – a deliberate blindness to the past. We have a splendid museum here, but how many of those streaming past us will venture inside it? As far as they're concerned, our Viking artefacts are better off below the earth.'

'Some people appreciate our work,' said the other.

'Too few of them, alas.'

'How do we change that?'

'We start in the schools,' said Ewart with conviction. 'We introduce children to the wonders of the past at an early age. When they're old enough to understand, we bring them to watch excavations such as this one. We try to implant in them the enthusiasm that we all share. Forgive me,' he said, holding up a palm. 'I'm asking for the impossible.'

'You never know. It might happen one day.'

'Pigs might fly one day.'

His colleague was concerned. 'I've never heard you being so defeatist.'

'You're right,' said Ewart, straightening his shoulders. 'This is no time to be downhearted. We're privileged to be able to do what we love most.' He slapped his assistant on the back. 'Let's get on with it, shall we?'

* * *

Colbeck and Leeming had spent almost the whole meal speculating on who Owen Gale might be. The sergeant began to wonder if the man existed.

'Someone is trying to have fun at our expense,' he said. 'It's happened before. We've had lots of anonymous letters trying to lead us astray.'

'I think this one is genuine, Victor.'

'Then why didn't the man who scrawled it sign his name?'

'How do you know it's a man?' asked Colbeck. 'It could equally well be a woman who sent it.'

'I never thought of that.'

'Let's finish our breakfast and make some enquiries.'

'We don't even know if Owen Gale lives in York.'

'Oh, I think he does, Victor. All we need to do is to find him.'

When the meal was over, they began their search by asking Sarah Scawin and Henry Kemp if either of them had heard the name. Both shook their head. Colbeck then decided that they might have more luck with Frederick Staines, a man whose job brought him into contact with large numbers of York residents. After listening to their request, the stationmaster pondered.

'Gale?' he said. 'Sorry – never heard of him.'

'It's someone with a connection to Jack Follis,' Colbeck told him.

'Try someone else.'

'I know just the person,' said Leeming as he spotted Ben Walters.

They went over to the railway policeman and mentioned the name to him.

'Owen Gale?' repeated Walters. 'Yes, I've heard that name before. I don't know where he lives but I can tell you where he works.'

'That's good enough,' said Colbeck.

'Gale has got a stall in the market. He's a fishmonger.'

'Thank you,' said Leeming.

'Why are you so keen to speak to him, anyway?'

'It's a private matter.'

Grateful that he had arrived in Bedern when he did, Hinton was feeling elated. He had been recruited by Tom Quinn and was part of an ever-increasing crowd that surged towards the police station. The irony of the situation was not lost on Hinton. He was a member of the Metropolitan Police Force, marching in support of a man with a long criminal record who had been arrested in connection with a murder. He could imagine all too well what Edward Tallis would say. The whole of the city's Irish community seemed to have turned out. Men and women walked shoulder to shoulder. Some of the women carried babies. Quinn led the way, but Hinton was no longer beside him. He chose to lose himself in the crowd. When the chant of 'Free McBride' went up, he found himself mouthing the name.

Horace Nash was ready for them. Warned about their approach, he was standing outside the police station with a grim expression on his face. Either side of him were three bulky policemen. When the crowd came into view, he held up both hands to quell the chanting, a gesture that only made the noise increase in volume. As Quinn brought them all to a halt, however, he only had to raise his hat in the air and the sound gradually died away, to be followed by a tense silence.

The superintendent ran his eye over the sea of faces before turning to Quinn.

'As a lawyer,' said Nash, 'you know the penalty for inciting mob violence.'

'There's been no violence,' retorted Quinn. 'This is a peaceful protest against a manifest injustice.'

'Patrick McBride has been brought in for questioning.'

'That's not what his family told me. He's being held against his will.'

'We're still gathering evidence against him.'

'I'd be interested to see it.'

'Then why didn't you approach me in the proper manner, Mr Quinn? There was no need to bring this rabble here. I don't buckle in the face of threats.'

'They are not rabble,' argued Quinn. 'They are concerned citizens who fear that a friend has been arrested on false evidence.'

'Get rid of them.'

'They'll stay as long as they wish, Superintendent.'

'Then that is tantamount to intimidation,' said Nash, taking a step towards him. 'Do you want me to summon the army to disperse this mob? I've already told them to be on the alert. If you expect me to bandy words with you in front of this crowd, you're badly mistaken.'

'I am a qualified lawyer. I demand access to my client.'

'As long as these people stay, you won't get a step closer to McBride. Disperse the crowd. Only then can we talk properly.'

Quinn needed only a second to reach his decision.

Turning around, he raised his voice so that everyone could hear it. He repeated Nash's demand. There was hostility at first, but the lawyer insisted that they had to remain within the law. With great reluctance, people began to drift away. Hinton wished that he could join Quinn and go into the police station, but there was no chance of that. He was merely one of the protesters. All that he could do was to follow the others.

Market day had brought in people from the surrounding villages to swell the already large numbers. There was ceaseless activity among the stalls. The detectives had to push their way through the throng before they located Owen Gale. Standing behind the counter, he was a short, stocky man in his fifties with his sleeves rolled up to expose his forearms. As soon as they got close to him, they were hit by the powerful aroma of dead fish. Gale served one customer, took some money from her, and put it away in a pouch in his apron. When he turned to what he expected was the next customer, he found himself looking at Colbeck.

'What can I get you, sir?' he asked.

'We've come in search of a few minutes of your time, Mr Gale.'

'How'd you know my name?'

'Someone mentioned you.'

When Colbeck introduced himself, and explained why they had come to the city, Gale became defensive.

'I'm too busy, Inspector,' he said, gruffly. 'I can't help you.'

'You've got two people serving with you,' said Colbeck, pointing to them. 'They can spare you for a while.'

'Why are you bothering me?'

'You may have information that may be of use to us.'

'Well, I don't.'

Gale folded his arms and gave a defiant stare. Leeming moved in closer.

'If you don't come with us, sir,' he warned, 'I'll have to arrest you.'

'But I've done nothing!' cried Gale.

'You are holding up a police investigation.'

'We may only need you for a matter of minutes,' added Colbeck. 'Then you can come back to your stall.'

After sizing them up, and realising that they were in earnest, Gale spoke to the two men who worked for him, then peeled off his apron. Colbeck led the way through the mass of bodies until they found a quiet spot near the edge of the market.

Gale was surly. 'What's going on?'

'If you'll permit me, sir,' said Colbeck, 'I'll ask the questions. Where were you two days ago?'

'I was helping to unload fish. Why do you want to know?'

'Are you aware that Jack Follis was killed that day?'

Gale grinned slyly. 'I had a drink to celebrate.'

'Did you know the man?'

'I knew of him and that was enough.'

'What was your connection with him?' asked Leeming.

'I got none.'

'We don't believe you.'

Gale shrugged. 'Suit yourself.'

'Let me show you what brought us here,' said Colbeck, taking the letter from his pocket and holding it up so that the fishmonger could read it. 'Well?'

'Who wrote that?' demanded Gale, shaking with anger. 'Who was it?'

'I was hoping you might tell us, sir.'

'Never even met Follis.'

'What about the person who wrote this?' asked Colbeck.

'There's no name there.'

'Do you recognise the handwriting?'

'No, I don't,' snapped Gale.

'You told us you knew about Follis,' recalled Leeming, 'but never met him.'

'That's right.'

'What were you told about him?'

'He deserved to be skinned alive.'

'Or set alight in a brake van?' suggested Leeming.

'I don't care how Follis died,' said Gale, venomously. 'I just hope he suffered. That's all I'm saying.' He looked from one to the other. 'Can I go back to selling fish now?'

Madeleine Colbeck was delighted to see her friend again. After ordering tea, she took Estelle Leeming into the drawing room.

'I don't suppose you've heard from Robert today,' said the visitor as she sat down. 'I'm hoping he'll say that their stay in York won't be too long.'

'I'm hoping the same thing, Estelle, but the mail hasn't arrived yet.' She joined her friend on the sofa. 'What I can tell you is that Alan Hinton has joined them. They obviously feel they need extra help.'

'Oh, I see. That's . . . rather worrying.'

'Don't give up hope. Albert's birthday is next week.'

'He's counting off the days, Madeleine.'

'I'm sure he is. By the way, how is his brother getting on? Does David like working on the railway?'

'I think he will do . . . in time.'

'Oh, I'm sorry to hear that he's not enjoying it. David was so keen.'

'He hadn't realised how much hard work a cleaner had to do. He comes home tired and filthy every day. David hoped he'd be a fireman before too long.'

'Oh, he's got years of waiting before he gets anywhere near the footplate,' said Madeleine. 'By that time, he'll be an expert on the way that steam engines work. And being a cleaner is not as dangerous as it used to be in the old days. My father told me about terrible injuries they used to get. When he was a cleaner, one of the engines in the shed exploded.'

'Good gracious! Was anyone hurt?'

'You'll be able to ask him, Estelle, because he'll be joining us soon.'

'I'm hoping that Helena Rose will be doing the same.'

'She certainly will. When I told her you were coming, she clapped her hands.'

Estelle laughed. 'I can't wait to see her again.'

Though he had not intended to join a demonstration, Hinton had been glad to do so. Rubbing shoulders with the denizens of Bedern had taught him something of their poverty and sense of being oppressed. In the face of what they perceived as a rank injustice to one of their own, they had bonded immediately. Glad to get away from the stench of Bedern, he began to explore the area, marvelling at how

133

ancient yet well preserved the city was. At every turn, there was something to catch his eye. His footsteps eventually led him to Coppergate, and he was intrigued by the sight of people kneeling in the trenches below. He paused to study them.

'Good day to you, sir,' said Nicholas Ewart, looking up.

'And the same to you,' replied Hinton.

'Are you interested in archaeology?'

'If that's what this is, then – yes – I suppose I am. What's all that stuff on the tray? Some of it looks like gold.'

'It's copper alloy – not quite as precious.'

'Is it very old?'

'I'd say it probably comes from the late ninth century when the Vikings were occupying the city.'

Hinton was impressed. 'How do you know that?'

'I've studied that period for many years. Friends tell me that I spend far more time in the past than in the present.' He looked at Hinton. 'I have a feeling that you don't live in York.'

'I'm . . . here for a short time.'

'Well, I hope that you enjoy your stay.'

'How long will it take to find my way around without getting lost?'

Ewart laughed. 'A minimum of five years,' he said. 'Where are you from?'

'London.'

'I thought I recognised that accent.'

'What do you do with the things you find?'

'Some of these items will be on display at the museum before too long. You'll be able to have a closer look at them.'

'If I'm still here,' said Hinton. 'How long will you go on digging?'

'Until we find a Viking horde,' said Ewart, hopefully.

After leaving the market, the detectives began the walk back to the station. They had not gone far before Colbeck became aware of something.

'We're being followed,' he warned.

'Are you sure, sir?'

'I'm certain.'

'Then why don't I get the same feeling?' asked the sergeant. 'Just when we need Hinton to watch our backs, there's no sign of him.'

'Keep walking until we reach the next corner. Then we split up. I'll go on towards the station while you pretend to go in the opposite direction.'

'If there is someone on your tail, I'll nab him.'

'The likelihood is that it will be a policeman sent to spy on us. He won't be in uniform, of course.'

'I'll pick him out, don't worry.'

When they reached the corner, they parted company. Maintaining the same pace, Colbeck carried on his way. He was still conscious of being followed. As he had expected, the person behind him was more interested in him than in Leeming. After a hundred yards or so, he stopped to look in the window of a shop. When he suddenly turned his gaze towards the street behind him, he was in time to see a figure dart out of sight into an alley. Moments later, Leeming went into the same alley and dragged out the person who had been following the inspector.

Colbeck was startled. It was a woman.

CHAPTER TWELVE

Superintendent Nash had had many battles over the years with Tom Quinn. While he could never bring himself to like the lawyer, he had been forced to respect him. Quinn was well versed in the laws of the land and able to produce a compelling defence for his clients. Nash began with a sneer.

'Why choose to represent scum like McBride?' he asked.

'Someone has to,' replied the other. 'And I don't regard him as scum.'

'Then you should examine his criminal record.'

'I'm aware of Patrick's occasional brushes with the law.'

'He's a menace, Mr Quinn.'

'He's still entitled to a defence.'

'Somehow,' asserted Nash, 'he is linked to the murder of Jack Follis.'

'When you produce evidence of it,' said Quinn, 'I'll be

happy to consider it. All I see is the flagrant use of police powers out of sheer spite. Pat McBride has a family to feed, Superintendent. He can't do that if he's locked up on false charges.'

'He's connected to this crime somehow.'

'That's wishful thinking on your part. Whenever a serious crime occurs in this city, McBride's name is at the top of your list of suspects.'

'And so it should be, Mr Quinn.'

'Has the lord mayor approved of your action?'

'Of course, he has,' lied Nash.

'Are you certain?'

'Yes, damn you!'

They were seated opposite each other in the superintendent's office, a place that Quinn had visited many times. The lawyer had not always been successful in defending a client, but he felt that he would gain the advantage this time. He had the entire Irish population of the city at his back. It was a show of strength that had not gone unnoticed. Apart from preventing free movement in the area, the baying crowd had alarmed other pedestrians.

'There are two ways of settling this, Superintendent,' said Quinn.

Nash was pugnacious. 'Don't you dare tell me how to do my job!'

'You can accept that McBride was wrongfully arrested . . .'

'Never!'

'Then this matter must be debated in court.'

'There are no grounds for that.'

'Oh, yes, there are,' argued Quinn, 'and you know it only too well. I'll just remind you of the occasions when we've tussled in front of a judge. You've been rapped over the knuckles more than once.'

'Be quiet!' yelled Nash.

'Loud voices don't always win arguments.'

'You're a low, cunning, Irish snake!'

'When you descend to slurs like that, I know you've lost the argument.'

'Get out of here, Mr Quinn!'

'Will Pat McBride be released without charge?'

'No, he won't.'

'Then we'll meet again in court,' said the lawyer, rising to his feet.

'And don't you dare bring that unruly mob here again.'

'I thought that they were very well behaved. One gesture from me and they dispersed peacefully. We low, cunning, Irish snakes are like that. Strange as it may seem, we're a law-abiding race at heart.' He waved a hand. 'Good day to you.'

'Out!' bellowed the other, jumping up and pointing to the door.

When the lawyer had left the room, Nash flopped into his chair and tried to calm down. Quinn had caught him on the raw and it stung.

Colbeck had assumed that the person following them had been given orders to do so by Superintendent Nash. Instead of catching a policeman, however, Leeming had grabbed a plump, middle-aged woman with staring eyes. Her name was Alice Kendrick and she was a stallholder in the market. She was now sitting between the detectives in a tea shop. Colbeck waited until she had had her first sip of tea before he questioned her. He was considerate.

'You wrote that letter, didn't you?' he said, softly.

'Yes,' she confessed.

'What did you hope it would achieve?'

'I thought that you'd question Owen Gale – and you did. I was in the market when you arrived. You took him off but only for a short while. When he was allowed to go back to his stall, I was angry.'

'Why?' asked Leeming.

'I hoped you'd arrest him.'

'We can't do that on the strength of an anonymous letter.'

'It's a serious charge,' added Colbeck, 'but you provided no evidence.'

'I hoped you'd squeeze it out of Mr Gale,' she said with rancour. 'It simply must be him. He needs to pay for it.'

'Why do you say that, Mrs Kendrick?'

'Because he's a nasty, brutal, evil man, that's why.'

'That's a serious accusation,' Colbeck warned her. 'If he heard you speak those words, Mr Gale could claim that it was slander and take you to court.'

'Why?'

'It's a means of protecting someone from false accusations.'

'Then I'm the one who should be protected from him. Mr Gale uses words about me I wouldn't dare tell you. He's got a foul mouth.'

'Is that all this amounts to?' asked Leeming with suspicion. 'You and the fishmonger have fallen out, so you want to get him into trouble.'

'It's the truth, I tell you,' she said. 'He's a killer.'

'Then how do you explain the fact that Mr Gale was unloading fish at the time when the brake van exploded?'

'He lied to you, Sergeant.'

'No, he didn't, Mrs Kendrick. I'd have known.'

'So would I,' said Colbeck. 'The sergeant and I have had a long experience of questioning suspects. We can usually pick out the ones trying to deceive us. Mr Gale was not at the railway station two days ago.'

Alice Kendrick was stunned. She sat there with a mingled pain and disbelief. They could see the glint of certainty vanishing from her eyes.

'In that case,' she said, lamely, 'Mr Gale paid someone to do it. He wanted the guard dead . . . and he got his way.'

'What's this all about, Mrs Kendrick?' asked Colbeck with sympathy. 'How did this idea that Mr Gale is a killer get into your head?'

'I know him of old, Inspector.'

'You obviously detest the man.'

'Wouldn't you?' she demanded. 'If he'd done it to you, wouldn't you want to show him up for the monster he is?'

'All we saw,' said Leeming, 'was an angry fishmonger. Mr Gale didn't look like a monster to me. What has he done to upset you so much?'

'He poisoned my cat.'

'Can you prove it?'

'No,' she said, grimly, 'but I know it was him.'

Estelle Leeming had always liked Caleb Andrews. Even though she knew that he could be cantankerous, she got on well with the old man. They came from similar backgrounds and talked the same language. Despite his many virtues, Colbeck could not relate to her in the same way. Fond as she was of him, she was always aware of the social and intellectual gap between them. There was no such problem with his father-in-law. While Madeleine was out of the room, Estelle enjoyed the opportunity of a private word with Andrews.

'We've been talking about my son,' she explained.

'Yes, I heard that Albert has a birthday very soon.'

'It was David, my elder boy, we were discussing.'

'Oh, I see. He's working for the LNWR now, isn't he?' She nodded. 'Then he must be having a rare old time. I know I did at his age.'

'David hasn't taken to it yet, Mr Andrews.'

'Why not? He's young, fit, and able. Doesn't he like the fact that he's now employed by the finest railway company in the country? More to the point, he's earning a wage for a job he loves.'

'The problem is that he doesn't love it.'

'Oh?'

'There are the hours, for a start. He hates getting up so early.'

'The lad will soon get used to that, Estelle.'

'I hope so,' she said. 'Then there's the language . . .'

Andrews was surprised. 'What's wrong with it?'

'Well, it's so crude. David gets called the most terrible names.'

'Then he must learn to defend himself. If people are getting at you, the only way to scare them off is to yell abuse in return. Those coarse words are not very nice, I know, but he must use them sometimes.'

'I can't believe that you ever used such language, Mr Andrews.'

'I did my best not to,' he claimed. 'Instead of swearing at someone, I used to clench my fist in warning. That usually frightened them off.'

'But David is so much smaller than everyone else.'

'He's a bright boy, Estelle. I'm certain that he'll find a way to cope. If he wants to be an engine driver, he must put up with the bullying and mockery. It happens to all cleaners. They're the lowest of the low.'

'Would you say that to him, please?'

'Can't you tell him yourself?'

'Yes, but I've never worked on the railway. David looks up to you. Ever since you took him and Albert around the engine sheds some years ago, you've become a sort of hero to the pair of them.'

'Have I?' said Andrews, delighted. 'Wait a moment,' he added on reflection. 'David may work for the LNWR but Albert's talking about the police force.'

'He wants to join as soon as he's old enough.'

'I thought you said I was a hero to both lads.'

'You are, Mr Andrews,' she replied, 'but Albert thinks his father is even more of a hero.'

'That's as it should be, Estelle. Mind you,' he warned with a grin, 'if Victor doesn't get home in time for Albert's birthday, he won't look quite so heroic.'

Before they resumed questioning her, they gave Alice Kendrick time to drink her tea and take a first bite out of her cake. Leeming was all for sending her on her way with a warning that she had wasted their time, but

Colbeck was sympathetic. He felt that there was more to her hostility to Owen Gale than a claim about a dead cat.

'You and Mr Gale are neighbours,' he recalled. 'How did you get along with him when you first met?'

'Not very well,' she said. 'He never showed any interest in us. In all the years we've known him, he never once invited us inside his house.'

'Did you ever invite Mr Gale into your house?'

'Of course, not! I disliked him on sight. So did my husband.'

'Does Mr Kendrick also think that he killed your cat?'

'He would do if he was able to think straight,' she replied with a sigh, 'but Sam doesn't know where he is most of the time. When I go to the market, I leave him at home. We've got a neighbour who looks in on him.'

'What happened to the cat?' asked Leeming.

'His name was Patch because he had this white patch on his back. He was quite harmless, though he did keep sneaking over to Mr Gale's house. You can't blame Patch. It was that smell of fish.'

'How do you know he was poisoned?'

'That's how Mr Gale threatened to kill him.'

'Did you find the animal dead?'

'No, I didn't,' she said, vengefully. 'But it had to be him. He hates us, and he hated Patch.'

'Did you report the cat's disappearance to the police?' asked Colbeck.

'Of course, I did. They said they searched for him, but I never believed them.'

'Why?'

'Cats come and go all the time. That's what they told me. They didn't really care if Patch was dead. In other words,' she said with disgust, 'Mr Gale got away with it. He killed the best friend I'd ever had.'

'That should be your husband,' said Leeming.

'Patch always came first, even before Sam.' She took a deep breath and tried to control her grief. They waited patiently 'Months after that,' she continued, 'Binny got a job at the railway station.'

'Binny?' repeated Leeming.

'Binny Gale, their daughter.'

'I see.'

'She was such a pretty lass – not ugly, like her father.'

'I'll take your word for it,' he said, stifling a yawn.

'That's how she met him, see.'

'Who?'

'That man, of course.'

'Which one?'

'The guard who was killed two days ago – Jack Follis.'

Leeming was suddenly interested. He took out his notebook.

Because the lord mayor was busy, Tom Quinn had to wait for some time before he was able to see him. When his visitor was eventually admitted, Neville Timms rose from his chair to give him a guarded welcome. The two of them sat down and eyed each other for a few moments. Quinn then fired his first question.

'Why did you offer Superintendent Nash your unconditional support?'

'I'm not aware that I did,' said the other, huffily.

'That, in effect, is what he claimed. We've crossed swords before, Lord Mayor,' he reminded Timms, 'and it was usually over the same thing. You allow the police chief to do whatever he wishes even if he is flouting the law.'

'I deny it, Mr Quinn.'

'He arrested Patrick McBride without just cause.'

'The superintendent is certain of the man's guilt.'

'Are you?'

'That's neither here nor there.'

'Nash claimed that he had your full support.'

'Well,' said Timms, prevaricating, 'that's not something I'm prepared to discuss. I've learnt to trust the superintendent. He does a difficult job well.'

'Then why did he rouse the whole Irish community to a peak of rage by his heavy-handed behaviour? If I hadn't been there to control them, there'd have been a riot. You ask Nash.'

Timms was alarmed. 'When was this?'

'Less than an hour ago.'

'Did you whip up the crowd?'

'They chose to follow me and scattered when I gave the order. Your police chief was all for summoning the army as if we were invading the city. Instead of that, we were simply protesting at a wrongful arrest.'

'Have you spoken to the superintendent?'

'I tried to, Lord Mayor. But those big ears of his don't seem to hear very well.'

'Leave the matter with me,' said Timms, uneasily, 'and I'll have a word with him. I can't promise that I'll do it today but . . . I'll be able to see him tomorrow.'

'That means another night in a police cell for McBride.'

'So be it.'

'I came here to secure his release.'

'Then you're going to be disappointed,' said the other, trying to inject some authority into his voice. 'Trying to hassle me will get you nowhere.'

'I was hoping to reason with you. McBride is no killer.'

'That's your view. Superintendent Nash disagrees with it.'

'I've got a feeling that you don't exactly back him to the hilt,' said Quinn, watching him shrewdly, 'but you lack the courage to admit it.'

Timms blenched. 'I think it's time that you left.'

'Why? I have a perfect right to come here.'

'And I have a perfect right to decide when the interview is over.'

'Very well,' said Quinn, 'but the matter won't end there, I warn you.' He got to his feet. 'You know, when you put that chain of office around your neck, you really look the part, indeed you do.' Crossing to the door, he opened it. 'But I've yet to see you doing anything that justifies the city's faith in you.'

Quinn marched out swiftly and left the door ajar.

Alice Kendrick lowered her voice to tell her tale. She spoke fondly of Binny, the one member of the Gale family who spoke kindly to her. Apparently, the girl had had a good word for everyone and always wore a friendly smile. When she secured a job as a waitress at the railway station, she had been delighted. It allowed her to meet people, learn new skills and start to blossom. Alice had seen the way that the job had transformed her.

'She grew into a lovely young woman,' she said.

'What happened then?' asked Leeming.

'He spotted her,' she said with a grimace.

'Jack Follis?'

'Yes. That guard. The local lads took a lot of interest in her, of course. Binny knew how to cope with them. But Follis was a grown man. He flattered her. At least, that's what I've been told. She started to come home later and later.'

'Didn't her parents object?'

'Oh, yes. They gave Binny warnings, and she obeyed them at first. Then it started again, so Mr Gale went in search of her one evening and found her talking to the guard outside the station. Her father went mad. Binny told me she'd never seen him like that before.'

'What did he do?' asked Colbeck.

'He threatened to kill Follis if he went near Binny again.'

'How did the guard react?'

'Binny didn't say. She was dragged home. The worst of it was that her father made her give up her job at the station. Instead, she was forced to help Mr Gale at the stall in the market. Binny hated it,' said Alice. 'The stink got into her hair and clothes.'

Leeming was impatient. 'Is there an end to this story?'

'That's what I was coming to,' she told him.

'Why do you think that Mr Gale was a killer?'

'Binny disappeared.'

'When was that, Mrs Kendrick?' asked Colbeck.

'It must be months ago now.'

'Wasn't there a search for her?'

'Yes,' she said with asperity, 'and it was a proper one – not like the search they pretended to have for Patch. The police had a team out looking for her. But it was no use. They never found Binny.'

'She may still be alive,' said Leeming, hopefully.

'Mr Gale doesn't think so.' She looked at them in turn. 'Neither do I.'

Returned to his hotel room, Hinton wrote details in his notebook of what he'd seen and done that morning. His experience in joining the march had a direct bearing on the case he was helping to investigate. Though he had never met Horace Nash, he knew his type very well. He had met superintendents like that before, tough, single-minded, peremptory men who used their powers to the full. The resemblance to Edward Tallis was strong but there were differences between the two of them. Nash had the appearance of a man prepared to bend the law to his advantage. That was the essence of Quinn's complaint against him. Tallis stayed strictly within the bounds of legality and expected his officers to do so.

Since his window commanded a view of the front of the hotel, Hinton kept glancing out of the window in case Colbeck and Leeming returned. When he'd finished writing his report, his mind drifted to his encounter with the archaeologist. The man's keen intelligence was clear, but he carried his knowledge lightly. Hinton was struck by his pleasant manner. He remembered an earlier case that took him to the University of Cambridge where he had dealings with undergraduates who made him cruelly aware of his educational shortcomings. The archaeologist had been different. During their brief chat, the man's readiness to talk openly to a total stranger was refreshing. Hinton resolved to find time to meet the man again.

For his part, Ewart had fond memories of the young man from London. Because so few people stopped to show an interest in his work, he remembered each one of them. Miriam Brightwell stood out from the others because she had educated herself to a high level. She had read books about archaeology, including the one that Ewart had written about the Viking Age. But she was a rarity, a woman who appreciated his eminence in his field and, in a sense, was like a student of his. The person Ewart had met had stumbled on the excavation and, out of sheer curiosity, wanted to know more. As a stranger in the city, he had seen it as a place of wonder. When he returned home, he would tell his friends about it.

A cry of joy brought Ewart out of his reverie. One of his assistants had just found a barrel padlock and was dusting it off with meticulous care. When it came fully into view, they could see that it was highly decorated. Ewart moved across to examine it.

'That's magnificent,' he declared. 'Well done!'

After sending Alice Kendrick on her way, the detectives came out of the tea shop and walked in the direction of Scawin's Hotel. Leeming was happy.

'We ought to do that more often, sir,' he said.

'Do what?' asked Colbeck.

'Talk to people who have evidence to offer in somewhere

149

like that little tea shop. It was so cosy. If we'd questioned Mrs Kendrick in the street, we'd never have got so much out of her. She'd have been tongue-tied. Buy her a cup of tea and cake, however, and she was able to relax.'

'I'll pass on your suggestion to the superintendent, Victor.'

'Don't do that,' said Leeming, hastily. 'He'd never accept it.'

'I'm not sure that I do. Mrs Kendrick was a special case. She was so upset when you pounced on her that she needed to be treated gently. But we can't do that for everyone who comes forward. Think of the cost if we treated all our witnesses to refreshments. That's what the superintendent would tell you.'

'Forget I even suggested it, sir.'

'You made a fair point,' said Colbeck. 'Now, let's turn to Mrs Kendrick.'

'I couldn't understand why she followed us like that.'

'Remember the first contact she made with us.'

'It was that letter.'

'She was hoping that it would send us off to arrest Owen Gale. She was obviously lurking near his stall in the market to see if we did just that. When we released Gale, she was horrified to see we believed he was innocent.'

'Is that why she followed us?'

'Yes, Victor.'

'Why didn't she speak to us?'

'Put yourself in her position,' said Colbeck. 'She's a decent, hard-working woman who is poorly educated. You could see from her letter that she could hardly write. As detectives from London, we would have looked intimidating to her. Mrs Kendrick trailed after us and tried to pluck up the courage to speak.'

'We're not that frightening, are we?'

'She might think so.'

'Maybe . . .'

'We were strangers to her, Victor. She didn't know if she could trust us. You could see that she had little faith in the local police. She must have wondered if we'd be any better than they were.'

'I suppose that's true.'

'But what really held her back was fear.'

'Fear of what?'

'Owen Gale.'

'Ah, I see now,' said Leeming. 'Mrs Kendrick was ready to give his name to us but not her own. If she'd come to us in person, she worried that we'd have told Gale where the information came from. So, when he turns out to be innocent . . .'

'He'd make her life a misery. We only had a chat with the fishmonger, but I saw enough of him to see that he could be an awkward neighbour.'

'Do you think he poisoned her cat?'

'I've no idea.'

'I hope she feels ashamed if Patch turns up again,' said Leeming. 'We lost a cat for almost six months. One day, in he strolls and settles down in his basket as if he was never missing. You never know with cats. They're funny creatures.'

They walked on in silence for a couple of minutes, then Colbeck spoke up.

'What was your assessment of Mrs Kendrick?'

'I felt sorry for her, living so close to that fishmonger.'

'But do you think she gave us reliable evidence?'

'Frankly,' said Leeming, 'I don't.'

'Why not?'

'She kept rambling off in all directions. That girl, Binny, was a friend of hers but she seemed to think more of Patch, her blooming cat.'

'I disagree. I think that she was genuinely fond of Binny Gale.'

'How can a terrible father like Gale have such a lovely daughter?'

'I don't know. We need to find out a lot more about that family. That's another job for Alan Hinton, I fancy. Gale knows us. He won't realise that Alan is a detective.'

'What do you think happened to the girl?'

'There's one obvious answer to that,' said Colbeck, sadly. 'Her father's intervention came too late. Binny was carrying a child.'

'Would Follis really take advantage of someone as young as that?'

'I don't think age came into it, Victor.'

'How do you know that?'

'Remember what Mrs Scawin told us about him. He preyed on women and cast his net wide. One of her female employees chased by him was sixteen.'

'That's immoral.'

'Binny Gale was only a year or two older.'

'Why didn't someone stop Follis?'

'That's a good question, Victor.'

'It's easy to see what he got out of it, but what about the women? Didn't they realise they were being used?'

'Unhappily, they didn't. Binny Gale was a case in point. She was helpless.'

'How can you possibly know that?' asked Leeming.

'You're forgetting something.'

'Am I?'

'Yes,' said Colbeck. 'I went to the house where Follis lodged. I found those letters he kept as trophies. They were declarations of love, Victor. Those women were completely infatuated with him,' he emphasised. 'One of them was signed by someone named Binny. Thanks to Mrs Kendrick, I know the girl's surname now. She was one more victim of the guard's lust. I burned the letter.'

'Why?'

'I didn't want anyone in her family to see it.'

CHAPTER THIRTEEN

Patrick McBride had finally been given some hope. When the crowd had converged on the police station, he guessed what had happened. They had come in support of him. Tom Quinn deserved the credit. He had made the Irish community rally around one of their leading figures. The lawyer had always done his best for McBride. His defence of the man, if not always successful, was strong and well presented. When he was released, McBride vowed to thank Quinn for organising the protest. Somewhere in the crowd had been almost every member of McBride's family. If he continued to be held, he expected Irish communities from other Yorkshire towns to offer their support as well.

One of the policemen in charge of the cells came to see him. He was a big man with the hardened look of someone who had spent many years in the constabulary.

'When are they going to let me go?' asked McBride.

'Soon, I hope,' said the man. 'You're stinking the place out.'

'You can't hold an innocent man.'

'We're not going to, don't worry.'

'I'm being released?' asked McBride, hopefully.

'You'll be remanded to prison to await trial,' said the other. 'As you know only too well, the prison has got high, thick stone walls. Your friends can shout their heads off outside and you won't be able to hear them.'

'I demand to speak to the superintendent.'

'You've done nothing else since you came here.'

'I know my rights.'

'What about other people's rights?' retorted the policeman thrusting his face close to the bars. 'Did you consider them when you burgled their houses? No, of course you didn't. Can't you understand that people have a right to live without fear and to keep what they rightly own?'

'That was in the past,' said McBride, sulkily. 'I paid for my crimes. I've turned over a new leaf now.' The policeman cackled. 'All right, you can mock, but I've been a decent citizen since I was released.'

'Then why didn't you do us all a favour and go back to Ireland?'

'I like it here.'

'You're not wanted, McBride.'

'That's your problem.'

'And it's not just you, it's your whole thieving family.'

'Don't you dare insult them!'

'One of your sons is still in prison, isn't he?'

'Shut your mouth!'

The policeman grinned. 'Like father, like son.'

'Brian made a mistake, that's all. He's paying for it.'

'A mistake,' echoed the other. 'Is that what you call breaking into a shop and stealing all that food? Haven't you ever taught him that there's a difference between good and bad? You failed to educate him, and your priest failed as well.'

'Keep Father Malone out of this.'

'You and your son should have listened to him.'

'That's our business.'

'Father Malone won't be happy when he hears that you've been arrested on a charge of murder.'

'Falsely arrested!'

'Everyone knows that you killed that guard. It's the latest in a series of attacks you've launched on the NER. And this time, you got caught.'

McBride was seething. 'I want to speak to my lawyer.'

'You're asking for the wrong person,' teased the policeman.

'What are you talking about?'

'When you're this close to death, you need Father Malone.'

For most of the time they had worked on the excavation, Nicholas Ewart and his team had enjoyed reasonably good weather. It changed dramatically. Dark clouds formed menacingly, then pounded the city with heavy rain. Ewart and the others pressed on for a short while, but they were fighting a losing battle.

'Stop, everyone!' he called out. 'Or we'll be drowned.'

'What about the trenches?' asked someone.

'Cover them over. We don't want them filled with water.'

The team responded at once, pulling tarpaulins over the two trenches then gathering up their finds and retreating. Ewart was the last to leave. Gazing up at the sky, he made his protest.

'I prayed for fine weather,' he complained.

There was no reply.

Hinton was still in his room when he saw them scurrying towards the hotel. After giving them five minutes or so, he went up to Colbeck's room and knocked on the door. Invited in, he saw that Leeming was there as well.

'I was hoping that you'd come back,' said Hinton.

'Why?' asked Colbeck.

'I have something to tell you, sir.'

'We've got something to tell you as well, Alan,' said Leeming. 'We got caught in the rain on our way back and had to break into a run.'

'What do you have to report?' asked Colbeck.

'I went on a protest march,' said Hinton. 'It was led by a lawyer named Tom Quinn and we all walked to the police station to complain about McBride's arrest. I was the only person there without Irish blood.'

He went on to describe the event and justify his part in it because he had learnt so much. Colbeck was particularly interested to hear about Tom Quinn and decided that he must meet the man at the earliest opportunity. What surprised him was the threat to call in the army.

'That's a weapon of last resort,' he pointed out, 'so it was stupid of the superintendent to use it as a threat. He could have invited the lawyer in to talk it over and that would have been enough to take the danger out of the situation.'

'Mr Quinn dispersed the crowd peaceably.'

'With you among them, I daresay,' noted Leeming.

'I had no choice, Sergeant. I was, literally, swept away.'

'When you joined in,' observed Colbeck, 'you acted wisely. What you've told us explains a lot about Superintendent Nash and his relationship with the Irish community. He's obviously made no effort to be on better terms with them. They're simply a mindless rabble in his eyes.'

'Tom Quinn is a shrewd lawyer. You could tell from the way he spoke. Anyway,' said Hinton, 'what have you been doing?'

'We thought we'd discovered a murder suspect,' said Colbeck. 'The problem is that he was nowhere near the scene of the crime at the time. You take over, Victor. The relevant details are all in your notebook.'

Pleased to be given the task, Leeming took out the book and flipped the pages until he came to the right one. He told Hinton about the anonymous letter, the visit to the market and the encounter with the fishmonger.

'Then we met Mrs Kendrick,' he said.

'Who is she?' asked Hinton.

'She has a haberdashery stall in the market and knows Mr Gale well. When she saw us talking to him before letting him go free, she followed us. The inspector realised that someone was on our tail, so we pretended to split up. That meant I could see who'd been behind us. I pounced on her.' Leeming grinned. 'We ended up in a tea shop with tea and cakes.'

As he listened to the description of the tea party, Hinton burst out laughing. He became more serious when he heard about the poisoned cat and the disappearance of Binny Gale. Despite her limitations, Alice Kendrick had supplied some valuable information.

'Mr Gale sounds like a very nasty character,' decided Hinton.

'That's why I want you to keep an eye on him,' said Colbeck. 'He'd recognise us at once. I want to know more about the disappearance of his daughter. It may turn out to be the motive for the murder of Jack Follis.'

'You told me that Gale was busy elsewhere at the time of his death.'

'He could still have devised the plot.'

'Or even made the bomb that went off,' added Leeming. 'Then, of course, there's the small matter of Mrs Kendrick's cat. He might well have poisoned it.'

'When do I start?' asked Hinton.

'Have a bite to eat first,' said Colbeck, 'then get across to the market. You'll have to borrow an umbrella from the hotel. This rain is in for the day.'

Most of the stallholders were under cover so they were sheltered from the rain. Their customers, however, were soon dripping wet and some of them departed quickly. Alice was back behind the counter of her stall, where her assistant had been selling their haberdashery. She was disappointed to see how many of the other stallholders were giving up and sneaking away. Among them was Owen Gale and his assistants. Having packed everything up, they put it on a cart and Gale drove it off. When he drew level with the haberdashery stall, he brought the horse to a halt so that he could stare accusingly at Alice.

She quivered inwardly. He seemed to know that she had been responsible for setting the detectives on to him.

Back in his home, Ewart dried himself off then examined the day's finds with great care, setting them out on a long table. The barrel padlock stood out from the other items. It was complete and had withstood the passage of time very well. He looked forward to showing it to Miriam Brightwell when she called. The room was his private sanctum, a place where he could have the satisfaction of feasting his eyes on precious artefacts before they went off to the museum. His only regret was that his wife, Charlotte, was no longer alive to share his pleasure. She understood the appeal of archaeology and had worked beside him on excavations.

The morning's haul also included knife blades, spurs, arrowheads, chains, woodworking tools and the remains of a candle holder. He laid them out in what he felt was their chronological order. Put alongside the finds from the previous couple of days, they were an impressive sight. When she came to view them later that day, Miriam Brightwell would feel that the financial support she'd given to him had been an excellent investment.

'When was this?' asked Ben Walters, the railway policeman.

'Some months ago,' said Leeming.

'I'm sorry, Sergeant. I'm so busy, I can't remember what happened yesterday, let alone weeks ago.'

'But it was you who told me where to find Owen Gale.'

'I'd seen the fishmonger's name on display at the market, that's all.'

'That was very helpful to us.'

'So?'

'He had a pretty daughter, apparently. Her name was Binny and she used to work here at the station until Jack Follis spotted her.'

'He spotted every pretty woman,' said Walters. 'It didn't seem to matter what age they were. Wait a moment,' he continued, ransacking his memory. 'Binny Gale. I remember seeing something in the newspaper about a girl of that name. She disappeared.'

'And she's never been found,' said Leeming. 'We've been told that her father caught her talking to the guard outside the station.'

'Then he must have been off duty at the time. Jack wasn't allowed to leave here when he was working.' He narrowed his eyelids. 'Are you telling me that Gale might have some connection with Jack's death?'

'He claims he was nowhere near here at the time. We believe him.'

Walters was curious. 'What brought you to me?'

'I was searching for confirmation. I hoped that you might have seen Follis alone with this girl.'

'Sorry.'

'It would help if someone could tell us more about the row between Follis and her father.' Walters shook his head. 'Let me ask you something else,' said Leeming. 'Have you ever heard of a lawyer named Thomas Quinn?'

'We've all heard of him,' said the other with a knowing grin.

'What sort of person is he?'

'Quinn is the mouthpiece for the Irish community. He can talk the hind leg off a donkey. According to Quinn, his clients are all angels. Well, I'll you this – angels don't vandalise a railway station the way that Patrick McBride and his friends have done here. Quinn is a menace,' he warned. 'Why do you ask about him?'

'Inspector Colbeck has gone to see the man.'

While they went through the niceties, each of them was trying to weigh up the other. Quinn was impressed by Colbeck's appearance and easy assurance. The inspector, in turn, was struck by the lawyer's combative nature and his fierce commitment to his clients. While the office was small and cluttered, it did not diminish Quinn in his visitor's eyes. He could see that the lawyer was far more interested in using the law as a means of defending his countrymen than as a source of money for himself. Only someone with a missionary zeal would do that.

'I thought Nash was leading the investigation,' said Quinn. 'He arrested a client of mine and boasted that he'd solved the case.'

'That was a very foolish boast.'

'Pat McBride should be released at once.'

'I agree wholeheartedly. The legal basis for his arrest is patently unsound.'

Quinn was taken aback. 'I'm glad that you support me.'

'I gather that you led a protest march this morning.'

'How did you know that?' asked the lawyer, suspiciously.

'News travels,' replied Colbeck. 'When you dispersed the crowd, you went into the police station to speak to

Superintendent Nash. My guess is that he refused your demand and sent you packing.'

'I left with renewed determination.'

'That's exactly what I had imagined.'

Quinn was wary. 'Why did you come here, Inspector?' he asked.

'I had the feeling that we were on the same side.'

'You don't sound like an Irishman to me.'

'I was speaking as a former barrister,' explained Colbeck. 'It means that I respect legal detail. There was insufficient evidence for an arrest and we both know it. Since the superintendent refused to act in conjunction with me, he felt impelled to prove that he could solve the case on his own – hence his impulsive arrest of Mr McBride. Like the lord mayor, he is certain the culprit is an Irishman.'

'You obviously don't subscribe to that notion.'

'I've found nothing to support it.'

'Have you challenged Horace Nash?'

'He's too boneheaded to listen to me. Besides,' said Colbeck, 'he chose to act independently in a case we were summoned to handle. That defines the man. He refuses to surrender control.'

'Why don't you put him in his place?'

'There are two reasons. First, I'm too busy working on an investigation that gets more complex by the day. Second, I've taken steps to ensure that the local police will start working with me instead of being in competition.'

'What sort of steps?' asked Quinn.

Colbeck smiled. 'You'll see.'

* * *

For the second half of the journey, Edward Tallis had been lucky enough to travel in an empty first-class compartment. He was therefore able to spread himself out and read his copy of *The Times* without elbowing the passengers either side of him. Pulling on his cigar, he exhaled a cloud of smoke that momentarily obscured the article in front of him. He was in a buoyant mood. Getting out of London was always something of a tonic for him. The trip to York had a special appeal to him.

He would be able to bang a few heads together.

By the time that he set off for the market, the rain had eased slightly but he still had the problem of avoiding the large puddles that had formed in the streets. Hinton thought it unlikely that Owen Gale would still be serving customers in such weather conditions. If the fishmonger had left, Hinton knew where he might find the man because Leeming had been careful to get his address from Alice Kendrick. At the very least, Hinton would have some idea of how close Gale lived to the haberdasher.

When he arrived at the market, he saw that most of the stalls had now disappeared completely. Others stayed on in the hope that the rain would ease off. One of them was Alice Kendrick and Hinton recognised her at once from Leeming's description of the woman. He ducked under the awning of her stall.

'Can I help you sir?' asked Alice, hopefully.

'Actually,' said Hinton, 'I came to buy some fish. I was told that there was a fishmonger here.'

'There was, sir, but he left some time ago.'

'That's a pity.'

'Are you sure that you don't want some cotton or some buttons? Your wife could keep them in her sewing basket until they were needed.'

He was amused. 'I'm not married.'

'A handsome gentleman like you must surely have a sweetheart.'

'Well, yes,' said Hinton, thinking of Lydia Quayle, 'I suppose that I do.'

'Buy something for her, then.'

'It would be a waste of time.'

Bidding farewell, he went off into the rain, smiling at the suggestion that Lydia might sew a button on his shirt for him. She lived in a world where everything was done for her. It was the barrier that kept them apart.

Victor Leeming was talking to the stationmaster when they heard the thunderous approach of a train. Staines abandoned him at once to return to his duties. Like Ben Walters, the stationmaster had been unable to tell the sergeant anything useful about Follis's fleeting relationship with Binny Gale. The only thing he recalled was the sad news about the girl's disappearance. The search for her continued.

The train steamed in and came to a halt beside the platform. Doors were flung open so that passengers could emerge in large numbers. Leeming was about to walk away when he was hailed by a stentorian voice.

'Sergeant!'

'Oh,' gulped the other, turning to see him. 'I forgot you were coming.'

'Good of you to meet me,' said Tallis over the hubbub, thrusting his case into the sergeant's hands. 'Have you made an arrest yet?'

'No, sir . . . not exactly.'

'We'll soon change that.'

'It's all rather complicated, sir.'

'Can't hear you in this confounded din,' shouted Tallis. 'Take me to the hotel. I want to hear why you and Colbeck have made no progress.'

'Oh, we have made quite a bit of progress, sir . . .'

But the words went unheard. Tallis was striding along the platform towards the exit. Leeming had to break into a trot to catch him up.

The first thing that Colbeck noticed when he entered Maynard's office was how much bigger, more comfortable and far tidier it was than the one owned by Tom Quinn. Clearly, the Irish lawyer lacked the resources that Gregory Maynard had at his disposal. One wall of the latter's office was covered by paintings of NER locomotives. Though they were of a high standard, Colbeck didn't think they could match the work of his wife.

'It's good to see you, Inspector,' said Maynard, shaking his hand. 'Dare I hope that you've brought me good news?'

'We haven't made an arrest, if that's what you mean, sir. But I can report progress of a kind.'

'Please tell me what it is.'

'Before I do that, I need to tell you that I've interviewed Thomas Quinn.'

'I see,' said Maynard, bristling. 'Don't trust a word he says.'

'I found him helpful and informative.'

'The man's a thorn in our flesh.'

'My impression was that Quinn was an able lawyer. Did you know that he led a march to the police station to demand the release of Patrick McBride?'

'Quinn is always up to tricks like that, Inspector.'

'I didn't see it as a trick, sir. It was a legitimate protest. From what I've heard, the police had no evidence that McBride was involved in the destruction of the brake van and the death of Jack Follis.'

'Nash is certain that the Irish were involved. If that's true, McBride must bear some of the guilt. Nothing happens without his approval.'

'As things stand, he's under lock and key on a charge of murder. From what I can see, his only crime was that he was born in Ireland.'

'Heavens above!' exclaimed Maynard. 'You're surely not defending the man. McBride has caused immense damage to the NER. The very least that should happen to him is that he is shipped off to Australia.'

'Penal transportation no longer exists, sir. It was abolished – rightly, in my view – some years ago.'

'Really, Inspector! Need you be so exasperating? I brought you to York to solve a murder, not to side with our enemy.'

'That's not what I'm doing, sir.'

'You're starting to sound like Tom Quinn.'

'Then let me be more explicit,' said Colbeck. 'All I ask is that you hear me out before you make a comment. Is that agreed?' Maynard gave a reluctant nod. 'I do not believe that an Irishman was behind that explosion at the station because we have identified another possible suspect and he is as English as you or me.'

'Who is this man?'

'You promised not to interrupt.'

'I'm sorry . . .'

'It was the stationmaster who insisted that the Irish were culpable, and the lord mayor agreed with him. You, however, suggested that anarchists might have been to blame. They have been active elsewhere, you told us. Agreed?'

'Yes,' conceded Maynard.

'Well, I can assure you that the person we have turned our attention to is not an anarchist. He's a man with very strong motive to kill Jack Follis. I'm telling you this in confidence and would ask you to keep your lips sealed.'

'Won't you even tell me his name?'

'No, sir. Just put your trust in us,' asked Colbeck. 'Oh, and one more thing . . .'

'What is it?'

'We have been vexed by the refusal of your police chief to join forces with us in this investigation. I have some good news for you, sir.'

'I could certainly do with it,' said Maynard, ruefully.

'Superintendent Nash may soon change his mind.'

'Impossible! Once he's come to a decision, he always sticks by it.'

Colbeck smiled. 'I don't suppose you'd care for a small wager?'

Miriam Brightwell could never pass the Minster without going into it. She drew great solace from sitting quietly in a pew and thinking about her late husband. Defying the rain, she had come out with an umbrella for her daily walk. It was now propped up in the porch. When she broke off from her reminiscences, she turned to see the dean, talking to the archbishop near the main exit. Their conversation ended and the archbishop came down the aisle towards her.

'It's very brave of you to come out in such inclement weather,' he said.

'Nothing would stop me having my daily exercise, Your Grace.'

'That's an attitude I admire. I wish that I could be as spry as you, but I simply can't find time to go for regular walks.'

'The burdens of office must be very heavy,' she said.

'Fortunately, the dean relieves me of many of them. He's the person who keeps the Minster functioning, after all.'

'I'm aware of that. He is a Trojan.'

'Perhaps we might call him a Viking,' he suggested with a dry laugh. 'They were clearly a breed of men who thrived on hard work. I was fortunate enough to meet Nicholas Ewart in here yesterday. He tells me that things are going well at the site. They've dug up all sorts of fascinating items.'

'Yes,' she said, beaming. 'I know. In fact, I'm going to inspect some of them later this afternoon. I'll get a private viewing and a lecture from a gifted archaeologist.'

'I'm green with envy, Mrs Brightwell.'

'I daresay that you would be equally welcome.'

'My diary is rather full today,' he said, 'but I'll bear it in mind. As for you, enjoy every moment with those Viking artefacts. It will be a glimpse into another world.'

'That's why I'm so excited about it,' she said.

Edward Tallis wasted no time in doing what he was there to do. After booking a room at Scawin's Hotel, he left his case there and set off with Leeming in tow. When they reached the police station, Tallis demanded to see the superintendent.

'And who might you be?' asked the duty sergeant, bossily.

'I am Superintendent Tallis from Scotland Yard and if any of my officers were as badly dressed as you are, Sergeant, they would get a flea in their ear.'

'It hurts,' murmured Leeming, feeling his ear. 'I can tell you that.'

'Superintendent Nash is busy, sir,' said the duty sergeant, straightening his jacket and doing up the top button on his uniform. 'He's talking to the lord mayor. You'll have to wait.'

'Nonsense! I can kill two birds with one stone. Where's the office?'

'It's down that corridor – but you can't barge in there, sir.'

'Oh, yes, I can,' said Tallis, setting off with Leeming at his heels.

They went down the corridor until they came to a door with Nash's rank and name on it in large letters. Tallis grabbed the doorknob, twisted it then pushed hard. He and Leeming surged into the room and startled the occupants.

'How dare you?' yelled Nash, on his feet.

'You've interrupted a private conversation,' said Timms, affronted.

'I've come to be part of it,' said Tallis. 'Introduce me, Sergeant.'

'This is Superintendent Tallis of Scotland Yard,' announced Leeming.

'I don't care who he is,' said Nash, angrily. 'He has no right to come in here uninvited – and neither have you.'

'Listen to me,' ordered Tallis. 'I have come all the way from London to tell you and the lord mayor that this nonsense must end. When I deploy my detectives on a murder case, I expect them to get full cooperation from the local constabulary.'

'We prefer to conduct our own investigation,' asserted Nash, 'and it's a decision supported by the lord mayor – isn't it, Mr Timms?'

'Oh, yes,' said Timms, uncertainly.

'You can go back to London and let us get on with it, Superintendent.'

'I'm giving you an order,' warned Tallis.

'You have no right to do so.'

'The order is not from me – it's from the Home Secretary.' Taking a letter from inside his coat, he held it out. 'I'd advise you to read it, Superintendent. If you don't give my detectives the assistance they require, then you will be forced into early retirement and the lord mayor will be left with a red face.'

Nash and Timms were stunned. They simply sat there with open mouths.

'Read it!' shouted Tallis, putting the letter on the desk. 'The Home Secretary has responsibility for law and order throughout the whole country. He was not impressed at the way that you have behaved.'

Picking up the letter, Nash read it and twitched in pain. He passed it on to Neville Timms. After reading it, the lord mayor tried to salvage some pride.

'Actually,' he claimed, 'I was against the idea from the start. Your arrival here is timely, Superintendent.'

'Indeed, it is,' said Tallis. 'A proper investigation can now begin.'

Leeming followed him out.

CHAPTER FOURTEEN

When the mail was delivered, Madeleine Colbeck was pleased to see a letter from her husband. Watching her read it, Caleb Andrews was worried. He could see that the news was not good.

'What's the trouble, Maddy?' he asked.

She sighed. 'Robert says that the case is becoming more complicated.'

'In other words, he'll be in York for much longer.'

'He's even had to send for Superintendent Tallis.'

'That does sound bad,' said Andrews. 'As a rule, he tries to keep him out of an investigation because he gets in their way. Why would he need the superintendent unless things were desperate?'

'I don't know, Father.'

'Victor is certain to miss his son's birthday now.'

'Don't let's fear the worst,' she said, trying to instil a note of optimism into her voice. 'Robert knows what he's doing. We should remember that.'

'It looks to me as if we need to keep our fingers crossed. I must say,' he went on, brightening, 'it was good to see Estelle today. She's such a nice woman. Did I tell you what she said about her boys?'

'No, you didn't.'

'Estelle told me that they both look up to me. Ever since I took the pair of them around the engine sheds, I've become a sort of hero in their eyes.'

'That's good to hear.'

'At the time, they both swore that they wanted to be an engine driver like me. As a first step, David is now working as a cleaner for the LNWR, but Albert prefers to be a policeman.'

'I'm not sure that his mother approves of that,' said Madeleine. 'She may feel that having one policeman in the family is enough. I know how much Estelle worries about the dangers of police work.'

'Victor has coped very well with them.'

'Albert is not as robust as his father.'

'Give him time.'

'Yes, he's not fully grown yet.'

'That's true,' said Andrews. 'Besides, Albert may change his mind and decide that he wants to be an engine driver, after all – just like me, his hero.'

Madeleine laughed.

It was not often that Colbeck and Leeming were pleased to see the superintendent because they could work more effectively without him. This time was different. At Colbeck's suggestion, Tallis had gone to the Home Secretary and secured the letter that the superintendent had delivered in person to Horace Nash. The police chief had been brought to heel. He was now compelled to take orders from the detectives brought in to lead the investigation.

Leeming was full of admiration for the way that Tallis had behaved.

'We were in and out of there in minutes,' he recalled. 'I've never seen Superintendent Tallis being so forceful. They looked as if they'd been hit by a thunderbolt. He deserves a round of applause.'

'I agree,' said Colbeck. 'He did exactly what I suggested. We must just hope that he doesn't stay in York very long.'

The two of them were in the hotel lounge, discussing what had happened at the police station. Because of the intervention by the Home Secretary, they felt empowered. Colbeck was quick to take advantage of the development.

'I think it's time that I paid a visit to Nash,' he said.

'Do you want me there as well, sir?'

'No, Victor. You stay here until Hinton gets back. See what he managed to find out.' He rose from his chair. 'I'll be on my way.'

'What about Superintendent Tallis?'

'He's gone to see Mr Maynard,' said Colbeck. 'I hope that he's not too hard on him. Maynard is a good man. I'm grateful that he invited us to this glorious city. One day we may even get a chance to look at it properly.'

'Yes,' agreed Leeming. 'Can we start with a visit to Rowntree's cocoa factory?'

* * *

Gregory Maynard was at once impressed and daunted by the appearance of Edward Tallis. While he was delighted to hear of the way that Horace Nash had been brought into line, he found his visitor overbearing. They were in Maynard's office and, with his visitor there, it seemed to have shrunk in size.

'A thousand thanks, Superintendent,' said Maynard.

'It was Colbeck's idea,' replied Tallis. 'It worked perfectly.'

'Even Horace Nash wouldn't dare to take on the Home Secretary.'

'Delivering that letter gave me great satisfaction, Mr Maynard, and it made up for the discomfort of the train journey here.'

'I'm glad to hear that.' Opening a drawer in his desk, Maynard took out a sheet of paper. 'I wonder if you could hand this on to the inspector, please.'

'Yes, of course,' said Tallis, taking the sheet from him. 'What is it?'

'It's a list of recent acts of vandalism at the station. Inspector Colbeck asked me to put them in chronological order.'

'That makes sense.'

'I hope that he finds the list useful.'

'Now,' said Tallis, sitting back in his chair, 'you've answered all the questions I've put to you. Is there anything you wish to ask me?'

'Yes, there is. The inspector told me that he has opened a new line of inquiry. He gave me no details. Do you happen to know what they are?'

'No, I don't and – even if I did – I wouldn't pass them

on to you. Colbeck never does anything without a good reason. I trust his judgement.'

'I would just like a hint of what is going on,' complained Maynard.

'Be patient, sir.'

'I feel as if I'm in the dark.'

'You are,' confirmed Tallis. 'It's a feeling I've had many times when Colbeck and Leeming are in the middle of an investigation. The inspector feeds me enough information to give me an idea that I know what's going on – then he produces something out of the blue that is infuriatingly clever.'

'I'd like less cleverness and a lot more information.'

'It's a feeling with which I'm familiar.'

'Why am I being excluded?'

'Watch and pray, sir.'

'This is my railway company, after all.'

'Then concentrate on running it,' advised Tallis. 'You have your job to do. Give the inspector the leeway to do his. Now that he has the resources of a police force at his command, he will be able to make visible progress.'

The rain had finally stopped, allowing Miriam Brightwell to arrive at the house without need of an umbrella. Nicholas Ewart was delighted to welcome someone he regarded, to some degree, as his patron. No pleasantries were needed. The moment she entered his home, he took her straight into the room where his exhibits were laid out neatly. She was thrilled by the amount and variety of the collection. Knowing how careful she would be, Ewart allowed her to handle whatever she chose.

Miriam cradled a disc brooch in her palms as if it were part of the Crown Jewels. She turned to him with a smile of gratitude.

'This is such a privilege, Nicholas.'

'It's well deserved, Mrs Brightwell.'

'I only wish that my husband could be here to see it all. That goes for Archbishop Thomson as well. When I told him that I was coming here today, he said that he was green with envy.'

'He can visit the museum when everything is on display.'

'I hadn't realised there was so much.'

As they moved from item to item, Ewart kept up a quiet commentary and fielded any questions put to him. He was pleased to see how much his visitor was enjoying the brief tour. When they finally came to the end of the exhibits, she noticed an object under a cloth on a small table in the corner.

'What's that?' she asked.

'It's our *pièce de résistance*, Mrs Brightwell.'

'May I see it?'

'Of course,' he said. 'You'll be as excited as we were when we dug it up a few days ago.' He led her across to the table and took hold of the cloth. 'Are you ready?'

'I'm throbbing with anticipation.'

He lifted the cloth away with a flourish. 'Behold!'

'Oh, my goodness!' she cried.

She stared in wonder at the remains of a Viking skull.

Horace Nash was far more subdued when Colbeck was shown into his office. The police chief had lost his swagger completely. In its place was a resentful scowl.

'I'm glad that we are now on the same side,' said Colbeck. 'I suggest that we forget all about our earlier differences.'

'If you say so,' grunted the other.

'Take your mind back to the sudden disappearance of a young woman by the name of Binny Gale.'

'Who?'

'She's the daughter of a fishmonger, Owen Gale. More importantly, it seems that she developed an attachment for Jack Follis. They became close, it seems.'

'Why are you telling me this, Inspector?'

'It's because I believe that you are following a false trail. You think that the crime was the latest in a series of damaging attacks on the railway station and you immediately arrested Patrick McBride.'

'Quite rightly,' said Nash.

'You are mistaken, Superintendent. Consider, if you will, that the crime was motivated by a hatred of Follis, the guard who was killed in the explosion. He had a weakness for a pretty face. Follis made many friends among the female population but, by the same token, he made bitter enemies.' He studied Nash for a moment. 'Do you have any children?'

'I have a son and two daughters.'

'How would you feel if one of those daughters was involved with a man like Follis?'

'That's impossible!' yelled Nash, indignantly. 'My girls have been brought up properly. They wouldn't let a mere railway guard anywhere near them, especially one with his reputation.'

'Owen Gale felt that his daughter had been properly

brought up as well. Behind her father's back, the poor girl was led astray by Jack Follis.'

'Yes, I remember her disappearing now. It was months ago. We began a search for her.'

'How extensive was it?'

'Our manpower is limited,' said Nash, 'so it was not as extensive as it should have been. But we searched the rivers in case she had drowned herself and we put up posters appealing for help from the public.'

'Was any forthcoming?'

'Not really.'

'What about the father? Did you meet him?'

'Yes, I did. Now you remind me that he was a fishmonger, I recall the stink he brought into this office. Mr Gale was heartbroken.'

'He was also filled with hatred for Jack Follis because he caught the man with his daughter and threatened him with violence.'

'How do you know this?'

'Because I've been looking into Follis's private life. While you were pursuing your vendetta against the Irish population of York, I was wondering if someone was so shocked at the way the guard treated his daughter that he sought revenge.'

Nash shrugged. 'I suppose that Mr Gale had good reason to do so.'

'Exactly,' said Colbeck. 'But we've spoken to him and absolved him of blame. There were other victims of Follis's charms. I discovered that when I searched his lodging.'

'Yes,' said the other, bitterly. 'You got there before me.'

'I feel that the person who planted that bomb was not

an Irishman with a police record. It was someone horrified at the way that Follis had treated a hapless young woman.' He looked Nash in the eye. 'I want you to help me find him.'

The superintendent gave a reluctant nod of agreement.

Miriam Brightwell's reaction was exactly the one that he had expected. As she held the skull in her hands, she had been transfixed. Ewart explained to her that they would now concentrate on finding the bones, slowly building up a complete skeleton. The discovery of the skull had given his work fresh impetus. When she handed it back to him, he placed it gently on the table and stood back.

'The body was first cremated and then buried. You can see the marks of the blaze on the skull. We're lucky that it survived intact.'

'Did it belong to a man or a woman?' she asked.

'One can only guess at this stage, Mrs Brightwell. When we have a full skeleton, we might have a clearer idea.' His face lit up. 'That will be the time to celebrate the fact that we have resurrected our first Viking!'

Patrick McBride was pacing his cell relentlessly. During his time there, he had been angry at his arrest, outraged at his treatment in the police station, then given hope by the protest mounted by his friends. That hope had now faded away to be replaced by something he had never felt before – fear. It coursed through him. Locked away behind bars, he could not look after his family, do his lawful job as a labourer or act as the spokesman for the Irish community. He had been shackled in every way.

Slumping on to the wooden bench, he put his head in his hands. Almost immediately, he sat up straight and shook himself, resolving to show no sign of weakness. It was foreign to his character. He still had friends working on his behalf. They would not rest until he had been released. When he heard a distant door being unlocked, he got to his feet. One of his guards was coming. McBride vowed to ignore the ritual gloating from the man. It could not hurt him.

When the guard unlocked the door and came through it, however, McBride saw, to his surprise, that he was not alone. He was accompanied by Thomas Quinn and by the diminutive figure of Father Malone. The lawyer was grinning broadly, and the white-haired priest was lost in prayer. The guard unlocked the door of the cell.

'We're letting you go,' he said, gruffly. 'This time, anyway.'

Arriving back at the hotel, Hinton was startled to find Superintendent Tallis there, seated in the lounge with Victor Leeming. He cleared his throat and delivered his report. Hinton explained how close Alice Kendrick's house was to the one owned by Owen Gale, and how he kept both dwellings under surveillance for over an hour. There had been no sight of Gale, but the haberdasher had come home at one point and started to unload her stock from the back of her cart.

'She looked nervous,' said Hinton, 'and kept glancing at the fishmonger's house as if expecting him to come charging out at any moment. I felt sorry for the woman. He obviously frightens her.'

'That's what she admitted,' said Leeming.

'How close is the river?' asked Tallis.

Hinton pondered. 'I'd say it was only forty or fifty yards away, sir.'

'Then he could easily have killed her cat and tossed it in the water.'

'I'm not entirely sure that it's dead,' said Leeming. 'We once had a cat that disappeared for ages and—'

'We can do without your reminiscences,' snapped Tallis.

'But I was about to raise a possibility, sir.'

'Let it lie quietly in that vacant area known as your brain. Understood?'

'Yes, sir.'

'Carry on, Constable.'

'That's about it, sir,' said Hinton. 'According to Mrs Kendrick, her cat was poisoned. How does she know that? It could equally well have been battered to death or even killed by the dog.'

'What dog?' asked Tallis.

'The one I heard barking like mad in the garden at the rear of Gale's property. That would have kept any cat away, surely.'

'Mrs Kendrick didn't mention a dog to us,' observed Leeming.

'The woman's memory is clearly at fault,' decided Tallis.

'Be fair, sir. She gave us information that we'd never have got elsewhere. It's the reason she's so scared of her neighbour. When we questioned him at the market, we could see that he was wondering who'd given his name to us.'

'That was because she felt certain he was the killer.'

'Gale is certainly capable of murder,' said Leeming, 'but

he had nothing to do with Jack Follis's death. The inspector and I are agreed on that.'

'Then there's no point in having the fishmonger watched.' He turned to Hinton. 'You did well today, but you need to switch your attention now.'

'Yes, sir,' said Hinton.

'Does that mean you're taking charge of the investigation?' asked Leeming.

'Of course not,' said Tallis, rounding on him. 'I have a mountain of work awaiting me in Scotland Yard. I will be on the first train to London tomorrow.'

'We'll be there to wave you off, sir.'

Leeming ignored the look of utter disdain that was turned on him.

When he came out of the police station, Colbeck was greeted by a lawyer, a Catholic priest, and a grateful Irishman. McBride surged forward to grasp his hand.

'Thank you, Inspector,' he said, pumping away. 'I'm told that you were the person who got me out of there.'

'You should never have been arrested in the first place,' said Colbeck. 'I made that point to Superintendent Nash.'

'So did I,' said Quinn, 'but I was ignored.'

'It took someone from London to put Nash in his place,' decided Father Malone with a chuckle. 'I don't know how you performed such a miracle, Inspector, but you deserve my gratitude.'

'I don't wish to be pedantic, Father Malone,' said Colbeck, 'but I did have some help from the Home Secretary. Indirectly, he was the person who secured Mr McBride's release.'

'Then I'll raise a glass to him,' vowed McBride.

'I might well join you,' said Quinn.

'All things in moderation,' added Malone. 'That's my motto. It's the reason I won't even be having a nip of communion wine.' He turned to McBride. 'Let this be a lesson to you, Patrick. You're free once more. Live a more law-abiding life from now on. People rely on you. Don't sacrifice your liberty again.'

'I'll bear that advice in mind,' said McBride.

'You've said that every time I've given it to you.'

The three Irishmen laughed. Quinn then turned to Colbeck.

'I don't suppose you'd join Patrick and me for a drink, would you?'

'Under other circumstances,' said Colbeck, 'I'd love to have done so. But there is the small matter of a major crime to solve. Please excuse me while I go off to find the real culprit.'

Estelle Leeming was peeling potatoes in the kitchen when she heard the front door open and shut. Her younger son had come home from school. Wiping her hands on a tea cloth, she went into the living room.

'Did you have a good day?'

'No,' said Albert, dully. 'It was boring.'

'I thought you enjoyed your lessons.'

'I do – now and then. Today was different. I kept yawning.'

'I hope none of the teachers saw you.'

Estelle stepped forward to adjust his clothing so that he looked marginally tidier. She stood back to appraise him.

185

Albert looked like a younger version of his father, much more so than his brother did. He had the same tousled hair, the same solid build, and the same cheeky expression on his face.

'When can I leave school?' he asked.

'When you're good and ready.'

'I'm ready now.'

'We'll be the judge of that, Albert.'

'David left when he was my age.'

'Yes, look what happened to him. Now that he goes to work every day, he wishes he'd stayed at school a bit longer. You've seen the state of him when he gets home. He's worn out.'

'I'm stronger than he is.'

'No, you're not,' she said. 'In any case, you're far too young to join the police force. Your father has told you that. He's also told you how important education is. That's why you must pay attention at school.'

'Father told me that being a policeman was a way to educate himself.'

'That's true in some ways, I suppose.'

'Now that he's a detective, he's been all over the country. He even went to America once.'

'I know,' she said with a sigh. 'We missed him so much.'

'Have you heard from him?'

'I've only heard what Mrs Colbeck told me. Your father's in York with the inspector. They're working on a new case.'

'It's my birthday next week,' he reminded her.

'I know, Albert.'

'Does Father know it as well?'

'Yes, of course he does.'

'I'd hate it if he wasn't here on the day.'

'Your father would hate it just as much. He has a good memory for birthdays, and he's never let you or David down before.'

'But he has to obey orders.'

'That's part of a policeman's duty.'

'How can he come home if he's told to stay up there in York?'

'Leave it to Inspector Colbeck,' advised Estelle.

'What's he going to do?'

'One way or another, he'll make sure that we're all together as a family on your birthday.' Albert grinned. 'Now take your hat and coat off and wash your hands. They look filthy. And stop worrying about your father.'

Leeming was alone with Colbeck in the latter's hotel room. The inspector was poring over the list that had been handed to him by Edward Tallis.

'Take a look at this,' he said, offering it to his companion.

'What is it?' asked Leeming, taking it from him.

'It's an inventory of all the damage caused at the station over recent weeks.'

'There's a lot of it, by the look of it.'

'Go down the list, then tell me what you notice.'

Concentrating hard, Leeming went slowly through the list. When he saw one of the crimes listed, he looked up in surprise.

'A fire bucket?' he asked. 'Who would want to steal that?'

'According to Mr Maynard, the thief was an Irishman.'

'How does he know?'

'It's the obvious assumption. Because he had Patrick McBride banned from the station, he believes that the Irish have got together to persecute the NER.'

'Then they'd do something more serious than stealing a fire bucket.'

'Read the list to the end.'

'Sorry. I will.'

Leeming returned to his task, going methodically through line after line. When he had finished, he gave the piece of paper back to Colbeck and shrugged.

'I don't know what I was supposed to see,' he complained.

'What's the difference between a fire bucket and a broken window?'

'I suppose that it would cost more to repair a window than to buy a bucket.'

'You've spotted it at last,' said Colbeck.

'Have I?'

'The damage is in ascending order. It starts with minor acts of vandalism and gets more serious as it goes along. That's why I'm certain this is not the work of the Irish.'

'The stationmaster told us what a nuisance they could be.'

'I've met Patrick McBride,' said Colbeck. 'Admittedly, I caught him in a good mood because I'd helped to get him released from custody. He wouldn't give orders for a fire bucket to be stolen or a pane of glass to be smashed. If he wanted to cause trouble at the station, McBride would choose something much more dramatic.'

Leeming was still none the wiser. 'What are you telling me, sir?'

'This is the work of someone else, Victor. He has a

different sort of grudge against the NER. There's a pattern in that list – a slow escalation. When it reaches its peak, there's only one thing left and that's to destroy the brake van.'

'But there was a guard inside it. That makes it a case of murder.'

'Does it?' asked Colbeck, raising in eyebrow. 'Those earlier doubts of mine are gnawing at me once again . . .'

CHAPTER FIFTEEN

Miriam Brightwell was delighted with her visit to the small exhibition. As she travelled home in the cab, she thought of the immense pleasure she had experienced from seeing – and being allowed to handle – the accumulated finds from the excavation. The room in Ewart's house was a wonderful private museum. If she had dug up any of the relics herself, she mused, she would have been unable to part with any of them. They would have been treasured.

When the cab reached her house, it drew to a halt. After paying the driver, she turned to her front door, which had been opened by one of her servants. She walked past him into the hall.

'Did you enjoy your visit, Mrs Brightwell?' he asked, closing the door.

'It was thrilling.'

'That's good to hear.'

'Mr Ewart showed me the skull of a Viking,' she said, excitedly. 'Just think of that. It's been hidden under the ground for hundreds and hundreds of years. I held it in my hands. It was such a treat for me. I can't thank Mr Ewart enough.'

At the superintendent's insistence, Colbeck dined alone with Tallis that evening. Leeming and Hinton were relegated to a table in the corner. After studying the menu, Tallis glanced at his companion.

'What would you recommend?' he asked.

'Everything we've eaten has been excellent, sir. Scawin's Hotel is noted for its food. It was one of the first things that Mrs Scawin told me.'

'Yes, I met her briefly when I first arrived. It's very enterprising of a woman to run a place like this. I congratulate her.'

'I'll pass that compliment on.'

'I'm glad that you chose this hotel over the much larger one.'

'I remember what happened in Great Malvern,' said Colbeck, referring to an earlier case. 'You stayed in the Imperial Hotel while the sergeant and I went to a very much smaller hotel.'

'Yes,' said Tallis, 'and your choice was much wiser. That dear lady who ran the place gave us the kind of personal service that the Imperial could never match. Be that as it may,' he went on, becoming serious, 'I didn't come to York to discuss accommodation.'

'No, sir, you brought a vital document from the Home Office. It's put the investigation on an even keel at last. Superintendent Nash was holding us back.'

'I'm glad that I was able to restrain that oaf,' said Tallis. 'He struck me as being one of those self-regarding, mindless bullies who give the police a bad name. I was glad to cut him down to size. Right,' he added, slapping the table with his palm, 'let's get down to brass tacks. What exactly is going on?'

'I thought that the sergeant had already given you the basic details, sir.'

'I want a more comprehensive account.'

'Yes, of course.'

'And please don't give me any of your theories,' warned the other. 'Stick to the facts. I find them more reassuring.'

'I understand.'

Colbeck gave him a long, detailed, unvarnished account of what they had done so far and what they intended to do on the following day. After listening carefully, Tallis was only partially appeased.

'Leeming muttered something about a feeling of yours,' he said.

'You asked me not to bother you with theories.'

'I've led many investigations in the past,' boasted Tallis, 'and I always used to get a feeling in the pit of my stomach when I knew that I was on the right path. Have you had a similar feeling about this case?'

'Yes, I have.'

'And?'

'The victim is the key figure. He ran the length of the

platform to get back to the brake van, then locked himself in.'

'So?'

'We know why he was so keen to find some privacy.'

'Really?' asked Tallis. 'How did you acquire this information?'

'A woman came forward, sir. Mrs Scawin persuaded her to speak to me. The woman would only do so on the understanding that she could remain anonymous.'

'Why?'

'She was married, sir.'

'That's appalling!' cried Tallis. 'Did this dreadful man have no respect for marital vows? And did the woman herself have no shame?'

'She was not to blame, Superintendent. While she admitted to being tempted, she did not fall. It was a massive shock to the guard. He was proud of his reputation as a Lothario. Suddenly – for the first time, I suspect – one of his victims changed her mind and resisted. That must have hurt and enraged him,' said Colbeck. 'A woman had finally dared to reject him.'

'I must accept your explanation of his behaviour. As a confirmed bachelor, I have never fully understood the interplay of emotions between the two sexes. If I am honest, I'm not sure that I wish to.'

'Suffice it to say that Follis sprinted to the brake van and got in.'

'Then it exploded.'

'No, sir. There was a gap, according to the stationmaster. In other words,' Colbeck pointed out, 'if the woman in question had welcomed his advances, the guard would still be alive.'

Tallis was befuddled. 'I don't understand what you're telling me.'

'It's quite simple, sir. Was Jack Follis the intended target of that explosion or was he unfortunate enough to be in the brake van at the wrong time?'

'Either way, someone must be held to account for his death.'

'That person will be caught, I promise you.'

'It's a pity that I can't stay here to help.'

'Indeed, it is,' said Colbeck, supporting his lie with the appropriate facial expression, 'but you have already given us great help. An innocent man has been liberated from custody and a wayward police chief has been rightly chastised. I offer you my profound thanks, sir.'

Tallis managed a rare smile.

'More wine, Madeleine?'

'No thank you. I've already had far too much.'

'Let's finish the bottle,' said Lydia Quayle. 'It's a shame to waste it.'

'All right,' agreed her friend, 'but you have most of it.'

Madeleine Colbeck was dining at Lydia's home and contrasting it with her own. It was bigger and more comfortable than her house, but her visitor was not in the least envious. Madeleine had a husband and daughter with whom to share her life. She also possessed a studio where she could develop her talents as an artist and have an independent source of income. Lydia might have more money at her disposal, but she was acutely aware of the emptiness of her life.

'I wish that I could do something, Madeleine,' she said with a sigh.

'You are doing something. You're entertaining a friend.'

'Yes, but when you're gone, I've nothing to do.'

'I thought you were reading that novel I recommended.'

'That keeps me occupied,' said Lydia, 'but that's all it does. It distracts me from the loneliness I sometimes feel. If I could write a novel myself, of course, it would be different. I'd feel I have something to offer.'

'Don't be silly. You already have lots to offer – not least the fact that you're Helena's favourite aunt.'

'But I have no family of my own,' complained Lydia. 'I've been estranged from them for years.'

'You have been tempted to get in touch with them from time to time.'

'Whenever I've tried to do so, I get a lukewarm response.'

'That's very sad.'

'Yes and no, Madeleine. If I feel a sense of loss, I remind myself I've been able to build a new life here in London. That's largely due to you.'

'There is one way to enjoy family life again,' suggested Madeleine.

Lydia wagged a finger. 'Don't tease me.'

'I'm not teasing you. I'm thinking of what you said when Alan was wounded while involved in a case in the Black Country.'

'He was in a terrible state. Seeing him like that really upset me.'

'It only made you feel how much you cared for him,' said Madeleine. 'That's what you told me. You hadn't realised the strength of your feelings for him.'

'It's true.'

'And he is equally fond of you. In fact . . .'

'Don't say it,' whispered Lydia. 'We live in different worlds.'

'Robert and I lived in different worlds once. We made light of them.'

'That's because you were so obviously made for each other.'

'I could say the same about you and Alan.'

'I wish that I could believe it,' she confided, 'but I can't somehow.' Lydia took a deep breath before speaking. 'There's something I've always wanted to ask you, Madeleine, but you might think that it's none of my business.'

'No, I won't. We're friends. Ask whatever you want.'

'Well, I've often wondered how and when Robert proposed to you.'

'If you want the truth,' said Madeleine with a laugh, 'it was not what you might call a proposal. We'd known each other for years and Robert had let me help him with a case involving the theft of a silver coffee pot in the shape of a locomotive. We found ourselves in the Jewellery Quarter in Birmingham. Robert joked that when I had a ring on my finger, I might learn to trust him. And where better to buy one than right there?' Her smile broadened. 'It was like a fairy tale, Lydia.'

When they had finished their meal, Leeming and Hinton decided to take a stroll around the city. They felt that it would be useful if they got to know York in more detail. There was a secondary reason for slipping out of their hotel. It helped them to escape the attention of Superintendent Tallis.

Hinton led the way because he wanted to show Leeming the excavation site in Coppergate. When they got there, they found the trenches guarded by nightwatchmen. The excavations were in too much shadow for them to see anything clearly. All that they could make out in the gloom was the shape of the tarpaulins.

'I was amazed,' said Hinton. 'They were down on their hands and knees, sifting through the earth for something that the Vikings had left behind them.'

Leeming was unimpressed. 'Where's the excitement in that?'

'The man in charge was very excited. They'd found so many things.'

'Is this what he does for a job?'

'Yes, he's a trained archaeologist.'

'Funny way to make a living. At the end of the day, you'll have an aching back, a pain in both knees and filthy hands.'

'But you'll have brought the past back to life,' said Hinton. 'That's what the man told me.'

'I don't see the point, Alan.'

'It's a way of educating people.'

'I'm too old for that kind of thing,' grumbled Leeming. 'Where's that place where you went to find the Irish?'

'Bedern.'

'I'd be interested to see it.'

'It may not be all that safe after dark,' warned Hinton.

Leeming laughed. 'We're from London, Alan. Nothing is as dangerous as some of the streets that we had to patrol.'

'You're right. Besides, there are two of us.'

'Imagine that you're back on the beat in Whitechapel.'

They walked on in silence for a few minutes then Hinton remembered something that puzzled him. He turned to his companion.

'I thought the damage at the station was the work of the Irish.'

'So did I,' confessed Leeming.

'Yet the inspector believes one man was responsible.'

'That's what he claimed when he'd seen the full list of what has happened. He thinks that the Irish had nothing to do with it. They would never have caused that explosion, he says.'

'Why not?'

'Irish people travel by train like everyone else. It's possible that some of them would have been on the platform near the brake van that day. No Irishman would want to wound his fellow-countrymen by planting a bomb that would blow the van apart. The culprit must have been someone else.'

'Why did the lord mayor and the police blame the Irish?'

'Because it's what they do whenever a crime is committed here,' said Leeming. 'The inspector thinks things through. That's why I know we'll catch the killer soon. I just hope it happens before Albert's birthday.'

Most of the people on the railway station platform were waiting for their train to arrive. The man who slipped in through the entrance had another reason for being there. He walked along the platform to the siding where the blackened wreckage of the brake van was still standing. It looked forlorn. He stared at it intently for a long time.

Only when he heard the approach of the train did he move into the shadows and make his way towards the exit.

Nash and Timms met in the superintendent's office. Before going home to dinner, the lord mayor had made time to call on his friend in search of information. After their earlier confrontation with Edward Tallis, both men felt bruised and humiliated.

'What has he said to you?' asked Neville Timms.

'The first thing he did was to demand McBride's release.'

'On what grounds?'

'Legal ones, unfortunately. Inspector Colbeck tied me in knots, to be honest. And since he has the Home Secretary on his side, I had to do what I was told.'

'But you thought that McBride was behind the explosion.'

'I still do,' said Nash, sourly, 'but Colbeck thinks otherwise. He believes that we should be looking for someone with a motive to kill Jack Follis. It turns out the guard had a gift for getting women into bed. One of them was a girl named Binny Gale. I remember her because she disappeared mysteriously. Her father demanded a search.'

'What happened?'

'We did the best we could but found no trace of her. My guess,' said Nash, lowering his voice, 'is that the girl drowned herself when she found out that she was carrying a baby. Binny Gale would have been overwhelmed with guilt. Colbeck reckons that she could never tell her parents what Follis had done to her.'

'I think he's right,' conceded Timms. 'Her father would want to kill him.'

'In this case, the father didn't do anything. Colbeck assured me of that. But there are other women who were tricked into bed by Follis, and they must all have had angry fathers. I've been given a few names of the victims and told to find out details about them.'

'How did the inspector get those names in the first place?'

'That's what annoys me the most,' said Nash. 'He searched Follis's lodging before I had the chance to do so, and he must have found something that set him off in this new direction.'

'What was it?'

'God knows! But I tell you this,' he went on. 'To keep him quiet, I'll do the inspector's bidding. At the end of the day, however, I promise you that I'll be arresting Pat McBride for planting that bomb.'

Owen Gale was seated at the table, staring morosely at the plate of food in front of him. His wife, Margery, a thin, freckled woman with an anxious face, picked at her own meal while keeping one eye on her husband. They were in the kitchen at the rear of the house, a small, musty, crowded room with an undulating stone floor, and a distinct draught was coming in under the door to the garden. An oil lamp provided what light they had.

Margery had been too afraid to speak to the fishmonger. When he was in one of his moods, he was furious if anyone interrupted his thoughts. Eventually, she could wait no longer. Risking a curt rebuff, she reached out to touch his arm.

'Say something, Owen,' she pleaded.

'What do you want me to say?' he demanded.

'Well, you might tell me what happened at the market today.'

'It rained.'

'That was in the afternoon. What about the morning?'

'I sold fish. It's why I go there.'

'You've hardly said a word since you got back,' she reminded him.

'Don't expect an apology.'

'I'd never be that foolish,' she murmured, trying to control her fear. 'You never say sorry – at least, not to me.'

'What are you blathering about, woman?' he asked, concentrating on her at last. 'I haven't eaten anything because I'm not hungry. I haven't spoken because I don't want to. Do you understand?'

'Something happened at the market, didn't it?'

'Be quiet.'

'We have to be able to share our grief, Owen,' she reasoned. 'It's not only you that's suffering. Binny was my daughter as well. I cry myself to sleep thinking about her. I know that you're brooding as well.'

'Shut your mouth!'

'That's a cruel thing to say.'

'Then leave me alone.'

'Owen—'

'ALONE!' he bellowed.

Margery retreated into a hurt silence. Several minutes passed before he spoke. The words were not addressed to his wife. It was as if he were talking to himself.

'Two detectives came to the market,' he began. 'They wanted to talk about what happened to Binny. They treated me as if I was a suspect for what happened at the station. I never touched that man who . . . did what he wanted with Binny. I wish that I had killed him now,' he went on, vengefully. 'Because of him, our lives are not worth living now.'

'Try to forget him, Owen. He's dead now.'

'If there's a funeral for him, I want to be there.'

'Why?' she asked.

'Because I want to dance on his grave!'

After they had finished their meal, Colbeck had lingered over a brandy with Edward Tallis. The superintendent seemed unwilling to let his companion go. He kept talking about his years at Scotland Yard.

'Are you considering retirement, by any chance?' asked Colbeck.

'Of course, not,' replied Tallis, sharply. 'What gave you that idea?'

'During that case in the Malverns, you told us that you were thinking of spending your final years there.'

'I haven't reached my final years yet. I'm as hale and hearty as you are. Why should I walk away from such an important position in the Metropolitan Police Force while I still have so much to offer?'

'I apologise for misunderstanding you, sir. It's just that you struck an elegiac note when you were reviewing your career.'

'It was unintentional.'

'Then let's turn our attention to the case in hand,' said Colbeck. 'Earlier on, you told me that you knew you were close to solving a case when you had a feeling in the pit of your stomach.'

'That was true.'

'I'm in the awkward position of having two such feelings and they're contradictory. Was the bomb planted in that brake van to kill the guard, or was it simply the next stage in a campaign to cause damage at the station?'

'It's your case, Inspector. Make up your mind.'

'What we've discovered is that Jack Follis upset several families. Young women who'd been led astray must have had furious parents. Some of the fathers involved would have wanted to kill the guard.'

'That would have been their immediate reaction,' Tallis observed, 'but they would have been held back by fear of the consequences. They'd have the sense to realise that they'd be sacrificing their own lives.'

'People bent on murder don't usually think rationally, sir.'

'Granted.'

'It may well be that the person who caused that explosion in the brake van didn't realise that, in killing the guard, they would also injure other people. And why did it have to be a public murder?' wondered Colbeck. 'An angry father would have wanted to confront Follis face to face in private.'

'I suppose that's true.'

'Owen Gale admitted that he had the urge to tear Follis apart.'

'He had more reason than most. Are you quite sure that the fishmonger was not involved in the guard's death?'

'I'm certain of it, sir.'

'Then I accept your judgement,' said Tallis, suppressing a yawn. 'Oh, dear! It's time for bed, I think. I'll be off first thing tomorrow.'

'Thank you for responding so swiftly, sir.'

'It was an emergency. A prompt response was needed.'

'You've been a great help.'

'Then stop trying to hustle me into retirement. I have a few years left in me yet.' He rose to his feet. 'As for those conflicting feelings in your stomach, I'll be interested to hear which one turns out to be genuine.'

Bedern was a noisy place after darkness. As they strolled through the area, Leeming and Hinton slowly got used to the abiding stench. They were diverted by the sounds of people clapping in a public house to the sound of a fiddle. From a nearby tenement their ears were assaulted by the noise of a fierce row between a man and a woman. When they moved on, the ear-splitting argument was smothered by the chorus of voices that came from a larger dwelling than most.

'Irish ditties are so catchy, aren't they?' said Hinton.

'And they're always so lively, aren't they?'

'I don't agree. They can be mournful sometimes. I once went to the funeral of an Irish neighbour and the songs at the wake tore at my heart.'

'I didn't realise you were that sentimental, Alan.'

'I was a close friend of the family, that's all. They were lovely people. Whenever we went into their house, they made us feel so welcome.'

'It's in their nature.' Leeming stopped and turned to him. 'I wouldn't say this to the inspector but . . . well, I'm getting worried.'

'Why?'

'If his case drags on, I'll miss my son's birthday.'

'He'll forgive you,' said Hinton. 'If Albert wants to be

a policeman, he'll know that we never have control of our time.'

'I hate letting him down.'

'You haven't done so yet. You could be worrying over nothing.'

'I've got this awful feeling,' said Leeming. 'When you've got children of your own, you'll understand.'

Hinton laughed. 'There's a fat chance of that happening. I'm not married.'

'You will be one day.'

'I'm not so sure, Victor.'

'Be honest, Alan, you've got someone in mind.' Hinton shook his head. 'You may pretend that you don't, but I tell you this. She has you in mind.'

Darkness concealed Hinton's blushes.

Madeleine Colbeck had been enjoying herself so much that she had lost track of time. When she happened to glance at the clock on the mantelpiece, she sat up guiltily.

'Have I been here that long?' she asked. 'I'm so sorry, Lydia.'

'Stay as long as you wish. It's been a joy to have you here.'

'No, I must go. I need my sleep. My days start very early.' They both rose to their feet. 'But I've had such a lovely evening.'

'And so have I. You must come again soon.'

'Thank you.' Madeleine looked around the room. 'I so admire what you've done to the house, Lydia. You've transformed it. You seem completely at home. I could never live alone like this.'

'I'm not alone. I have servants, one of whom is also the cook.'

'That's my point. You're used to having people around you. I'm not. When I moved into Robert's house, I felt embarrassed about having servants. I didn't know how to speak to them. It felt so strange.'

'You seem to have adapted to it very well.'

'Then why do I still have twinges of guilt? If I hadn't met Robert, I'd still have been living with my father in that little house. If he'd died, I'd have had to look for work to support myself. I might even have ended up in service myself.'

'That would have been a terrible waste of your talents.'

'I didn't know that I had any.'

'Stop being so modest,' chided Lydia. 'You've deserved everything that's happened to you. When I first met you, I was struck by how kind and understanding you were. Since then, you've really blossomed.'

'It's kind of you to say so.'

'I owe you so much. And it was all because Robert was investigating my father's murder. It was not the nicest way to meet you, I suppose. To begin with, I was in a very unsettled state. I didn't really know what I wanted out of life. Without realising it, you came to my rescue.'

'You needed help. I was happy to give it you.'

'I'll always remember that.' She kissed her friend gently on the cheek. 'And I can now repay you by doing you a favour. I'll send one my servants out to find a cab for you.'

'Thank you. I'd be grateful.'

'Unless you'd prefer to despatch one yourself.'

'What do you mean?'

'Now that you've learnt to speak to servants,' said Lydia with a grin, 'you should never be afraid to do so. They talk the same language as us, you know. I'll call Sarah in so that you can get some more practice.'

'You're the one teasing me now,' said Madeleine, laughing.

The boy had been driven out of the city that morning by his grandfather. They stopped by a tributary of the Ouse. A keen angler, the old man had used the spot before to catch trout and other fish. The boy walked along the bank to a point where the river narrowed. After checking to see if anyone was watching, he stripped off his clothes and paddled into the river before diving full length. The feel of water on his body was exhilarating. He swam with firm strokes and powerful legs, crossing the river to the opposite bank, which was fringed with reeds.

When his hand went into the reeds, it touched something that felt large and solid. Standing up in the shallow water by the bank, he pushed back the reeds to see what it was. His scream of horror was blood-curdling.

CHAPTER SIXTEEN

Edward Tallis walked briskly along the platform with Colbeck beside him, carrying the superintendent's case. They paused to look at the brake van at the rear of the train, a solid structure of wood and iron.

'It would have taken a powerful blast to blow that apart,' said Tallis.

'Yes, sir. The wonder is that Follis didn't die instantly. By all accounts, he staggered out blindly, then pitched forward on to the platform.'

'It must have been a gruesome sight.'

'One can't help feeling sorry for the man,' admitted Colbeck.

'Save your sympathy for his victims. Their innocence was taken away from them in a way that will haunt them for the rest of their lives.'

'I'm afraid that's true, sir.'

They walked on until they came to an empty compartment. Tallis opened the door and took the case from Colbeck. He issued a warning.

'Keep me fully informed, Inspector.'

'I will, sir.'

'And bring this investigation to a close – swiftly.'

'I can't guarantee that, I'm afraid.'

'Because of me, you now command greater resources. Use them.'

'I intend to, Superintendent. Thank you again for all your help.'

Tallis smiled. 'I enjoyed my visit. Getting here was tiresome but it's always a pleasure to slap down someone who has exceeded his authority.' Hearing a yell, he looked down the platform to see Alan Hinton running towards them. 'What does he want?' he asked. 'Have I left something at the hotel by mistake?'

'It looks as if there might be an emergency, sir.'

'I can't stay in York any longer.'

When he arrived, Hinton was gasping for air, his chest rising and falling. He tried to speak but the words tumbled out incomprehensibly.

'Get your breath back first,' advised Colbeck.

'Has something happened?' asked Tallis. Hinton nodded his head. 'Spit it out, man. What's going on?'

'The body of a young woman has been found,' gabbled the other.

'Where?'

'In a river somewhere, sir.'

'Has she been identified yet?' said Colbeck.

'I've told you all I know, Inspector. A policeman brought the news.'

'What were his exact words?'

'You'll have to ask Sergeant Leeming.'

'Where is the man?'

'He's gone to find out the full details, sir.'

Horace Nash was in his office when Leeming was shown in. The sergeant's arrival reminded him that he had been ordered to cooperate with the detectives, but he was reluctant to do so.

'Thank you for alerting us, Superintendent,' said Leeming.

'This tragedy has nothing to do with your investigation.'

'Do you know that for certain?'

'No,' admitted Nash, 'but my instinct tells me that it was an unfortunate accident. People have been drowned in the river before. In this case, the girl had got entangled in reeds. If someone had not been swimming in that stretch of the river, the body might have lain there indefinitely.'

'Where was it found?'

'Well outside the city.'

'Did you search that far for Binny Gale?'

'No, we didn't.'

'Can you describe the young woman?'

'I haven't seen her myself,' said Nash. 'The body is still being examined.'

'Have you sent word to Owen Gale?'

'Stop hounding me, man. We are following our usual procedure.'

'Then the truth is that you haven't done so.'

'We are making a public appeal for someone to come forward.'

'I think a private one would be more use,' said Leeming. 'We know that Gale's daughter ran away in a dreadful state. Her parents feared she might take her own life. Contact them. It's the first step to take.'

'I don't take orders from you, Sergeant.'

'This could be bad news, I fancy.'

'An untimely death like this is always bad news.'

'You're afraid, aren't you?' said Leeming.

'Of course, I'm not.'

'You still believe that McBride was involved in the murder?'

'That's my business.'

'You'll have to accept that someone else killed Jack Follis. In other words, you arrested the wrong man. Far be it from me to give you advice, sir, but I'd say that McBride deserves an apology at the very least.'

'Good day to you, Sergeant,' snapped Nash.

'Bear in mind that we have a right to be informed.'

'I accept that – but you'll have to wait.'

'Will you get in touch with the Gale family?'

'We will . . . consider that possibility.'

'That's all I wanted to hear,' said Leeming with a grin. 'Thank you for seeing me at short notice. The inspector and I value your change of heart. Goodbye, sir.'

'Get out!' roared Nash.

Alice Kendrick was checking her stock of haberdashery when she heard horses' hooves clacking on the road outside. Looking through the window, she saw the policemen stopping outside the fishmonger's house. She guessed why.

'Poor Binny!' she said, crossing herself.

Returning to the hotel, Leeming told his colleagues what he had found out. Hinton was amused by his account of the conversation with Nash, but Colbeck was considering the implications of the news.

'If it turns out to be Binny Gale,' he said, 'then we may have to take a second look at the father.'

'There was no mention of foul play,' said Leeming. 'She drowned.'

'Someone may have held her under the water.'

'Well, it wasn't the fishmonger. He might have been churlish, but I still think that he was honest with us.'

'I agree.'

'The police think it's a case of suicide. Living in that house must have been an ordeal for her. Perhaps the girl couldn't face it.'

'Will we ever know the truth?' asked Hinton.

'I'm not certain about that. First, let's make sure that Superintendent Nash keeps his word and sends for Gale. Go to the fishmonger's house and see what you can find out.'

'If there's nobody there,' added Leeming, 'you might try Mrs Kendrick. She keeps an eye on what happens to her neighbours.'

'Very good,' said Hinton.

He left the room immediately. Colbeck became pensive. After a short while, he snapped his fingers.

'I should have remembered,' he said. 'It's another reason

that proves the fishmonger didn't plant that bomb at the railway station.'

Leeming frowned. 'What are you talking about, sir?'

'I'd forgotten the description Mr Ewart gave of a man who slipped into the brake van. It doesn't match Owen Gale in any way.'

'Then it was not him, sir.'

'The description we had from Mrs Brightwell was similar. That makes two witnesses, each of them highly intelligent. Neither of them had seen Gale.'

'So why was Mrs Kendrick so certain the fishmonger was the killer?'

'It's because she thinks he committed murder before.'

'Poisoning a cat and blowing up a human being in a brake van are crimes of a very different order. Besides,' Leeming went on, 'we don't know for certain that Patch was poisoned.'

'It's what Mrs Kendrick believes.'

'What do we do now, sir?'

'I'd like to visit the place where the body was found,' said Colbeck. 'Let's go to the police station. Someone will have given a statement about the discovery. I want the exact location.'

Nicholas Ewart was at the site before any members of his archaeological team. He pulled back the tarpaulins covering both trenches and rolled them out of the way. One by one the others began to turn up. When they were all there, he told them what their mission for the day was.

'We all shared the excitement of finding that skull,'

he said. 'Let's make a special effort to find pieces of the skeleton, shall we? I'm convinced that the bones belonging to that Viking are lying here.'

'How deep do you want us to dig, Nicholas?' asked someone.

'As deep as it takes.' He rubbed his hands together. 'The man I think of as Erik Forkbeard is down there in the darkness. Let's bring him into the light of day.'

When he reached the house, Hinton used the knocker on the front door. Moments later it was opened by Alice Kendrick. She recognised him at once.

'You were that handsome young man who came to the market yesterday.'

'I didn't introduce myself,' he said. 'My name is Alan Hinton and I'm a detective from London, assisting Inspector Colbeck and Sergeant Leeming.'

'Yes, I've met those gentlemen. They were kind to me.'

'The inspector sent me here in search of information, Mrs Kendrick. It's to do with Binny Gale.'

'Yes, I heard about that. It's so sad.'

'Who told you?'

'Binny's mother. When the police told them what happened, they asked for someone to identify the body. Mr Gale went straight off with them.'

'What about his wife?'

'She was in no state to go,' said Alice. 'What she needed was company and I was the person she turned to. Margery – that's her name – wept and wept. I did what I could to calm her down, but it was no use. She's made up her mind that the body must be Binny's and that's that.'

'Where is Mrs Gale now?'

'She's sitting in my kitchen, crying her eyes out. I'd better go.'

'Yes, yes, of course. Before you do that,' said Hinton, 'let me ask one more question. Why did Mrs Gale come to you? I thought you weren't on speaking terms.'

'We weren't,' she said, 'but the other neighbours were unfriendly. Margery came here and I did what any decent person would. I must go. She needs me.'

Hinton did not mind having the door closed in his face. He had found out all that he needed to know. He had also learnt what a kind and compassionate woman Alice Kendrick was. After years of tension with her neighbours, she had taken one of them into her home to offer comfort.

Owen Gale had always tried to keep his emotions under control in the past, but he had never been in this situation before. As he stood outside the room in which a dead body waited on a table, he began to tremble. Praying that it was not his daughter, he gritted his teeth and screwed both hands into tight balls.

'Are you ready, sir?' asked the police doctor.

'Yes,' croaked Gale.

'Then follow me.'

Opening the door, the doctor led the way into the room, then shut the door behind him. Covered by a shroud, the body looked so small and defenceless. As his stomach began to churn, Gale put a hand to his mouth.

'There's no hurry, sir,' said the doctor, 'but you'll appreciate how important it is for a body to be identified by a family member.'

Unable to speak, Gale nodded. Pointing a finger, he indicated that he was ready. The doctor took hold of the shroud and pulled it back gently to expose the face of the cadaver. It was hideously white, and Gale did not recognise her at first. As he stared at her in quiet horror, however, he slowly came to see features that made him certain. It was his daughter. Binny Gale was at peace.

They were in luck. When Colbeck and Leeming went to the police station, they not only learnt where the body had been found, they met one of the officers who had gone out to reclaim it. The man was now driving the vehicle out of the city with the detectives on board. He was a thickset individual in his fifties, proud of having been involved in the recovery the body. He stressed that it was by no means the first time he had done such a thing.

'Must have hauled a dozen or more corpses out of the water,' he boasted. 'Most of them were drunken idiots who fell in by mistake and they were all men. I did help to get two women out as well. One had been in the water for weeks before she was found. The other was the worst case,' he recalled. 'She was a scrawny old woman whose throat had been cut from ear to ear. She was floating along like a piece of driftwood.'

'Did you ever find the person who killed her?' asked Colbeck.

'No, sir. We're still looking.'

'What state was this latest body in?'

'Oh, she was beautiful,' said the man. 'At least, she had been. Not any longer. The river had taken its toll. I daren't think what had nibbled at her during all that time in the water.' He shook his head sadly. 'Why did someone like that choose to end her life in the river?'

'How can you be sure that that's what she did?' asked Leeming. 'You saw no visible signs of violence, but she could have been killed first then put in the water by someone. We've seen cases like that before.'

'There was one thing,' recalled the policeman.

'What is it?'

'Well, there wasn't a mark on the body itself. But as we picked her up, I noticed that both her hands were scarred. They'd been bleeding.'

'That is strange,' said Leeming.

'We won't know the truth until we get a post-mortem report,' said Colbeck. 'Who found the body in the first place?'

'A young lad,' replied the driver. 'He swam across the river and . . . well, bumped into her. It was a terrible shock.'

'What was he doing on that stretch of river?'

'His grandfather took him there, sir. It seems that the lad is a keen swimmer. Whenever the old man goes fishing, he takes him along.'

Colbeck was aware of the irony. If the body turned out to be that of Binny Gale, a fishmonger's daughter, it was only discovered because someone went fishing.

The weather was fine, and the members of the team were enthusiastic. Arriving early at the site, they got to work at once. All sorts of Viking artefacts were soon being unearthed. Nicholas Ewart worked as hard as any of them, ignoring the occasional twinges in his knees and shoulders. Various items came to light before

217

someone unearthed a charred bone. It was handed to Ewart.

'It's a part of an elbow,' he said, examining it with care.

'How do you know?' asked the other.

'Because I've seen so many skeletons. Archaeology is not simply about pots, jewellery and assorted artefacts. You must understand the basics of anatomy as well. What we have here is the burial place of a Viking. Judging by the other things we found, he must have been a man of some importance. He was buried with so many grave goods. Oh,' said Ewart, 'it's so wonderful to work here. Every day brings a fresh discovery.'

'I just wish that the people of York appreciated what we're doing.'

'Ignore them. We're not in York now.'

'Aren't we?'

'Down here, we're in somewhere far more interesting.'

'Where's that?'

'Jorvik.'

They had used a bridge across the tributary to put them on the correct bank. The policeman drove on until he came to the spot where the body had been found. Colbeck jumped down and walked across to the clump of weeds nearby.

'Where exactly was the girl lying?' he asked.

'Round about here,' said the policeman, moving to a spot nearby. 'The body was caught up in the weeds. It was invisible to the naked eye.'

'Was it just bobbing up and down in the water?'

'Yes, Inspector.'

'What was holding it down?'

'I don't follow.'

'When you hauled her out, did you explore what was underneath the water?'

'No, sir, we didn't. We were just anxious to get the body back to the city.'

'Sergeant . . .'

'Yes, Inspector,' said Leeming.

'Help me off with this coat, please.'

'You're not going to—?'

'Just do as I say,' ordered Colbeck.

When his coat had been removed, he handed his hat to the sergeant as well. He then began to take off his shoes. Realising what Colbeck was about to do, Leeming was amazed. He knew how vain the inspector was and how careful he was to protect his clothing. Yet he was taking off his shoes and socks before rolling up his trouser legs. Very slowly, he lowered himself into the water. It came up to his knees.

'Be careful, Inspector,' warned Leeming.

Colbeck was not listening. His attention was focussed on getting a secure footing so that he could make his way through the reeds. He parted them with his hands as he moved along. The water was now well above his knees. Without warning, he gave a sudden yell of pain.

'What is it, sir?' asked Leeming.

'That's a good question,' replied Colbeck.

Bending over, he groped among the reeds, then lifted something up for the others to see. It was a heavy boulder with sharp edges.

'This is how she stayed underwater,' explained Colbeck.

'She must have carried this into the reeds. If she'd put this on her chest, it would have helped her stay under the water. I don't believe that anyone else was involved. It's a case of suicide.'

'Poor girl!' sighed Leeming. 'She must have been desperate.'

'It might explain those marks on her hands.' He dropped the boulder into the water and examined his palms. 'Do you see? I've picked up scratches as well.' He showed them to the others. 'I can't be absolutely certain,' he went on, 'but I think that this is a case of suicide. Binny Gale took her own life.'

'We should have done this,' confessed the policeman. 'We should have done a proper search, but we were too eager to get the body back to the city. We didn't look hard enough.'

As Colbeck made his way gingerly to the bank, Leeming was horrified.

'You're soaked to the skin, sir,' he said.

'Those trousers are not fit to wear,' said the policeman.

'No matter,' said Colbeck. 'Having wet feet is a small price to pay for the discovery we've just made.'

Racked by a mingled grief and guilt, Owen Gale sat in a corner at the police station with his head in his hands. The loss of his only child was enough to bear. What he could not forgive himself for was the way he must have driven Binny to take her own life. Gale was still blaming himself when a hand rested on his shoulder.

'It's time for you to go, sir,' said the duty sergeant, softly. 'Your wife deserves to know the truth.'

Gale looked up. 'What's that?'

'It's a burden you'll have to share with her, sir.' He beckoned to a policeman nearby. 'Take him back home. Be gentle.'

The sight of a bedraggled Colbeck coming into the hotel startled Hinton. He looked at the inspector's sodden trousers in disbelief.

'It was all in a good cause,' explained Colbeck. 'The sergeant and I discovered how the girl was drowned.'

'Did you?'

'I'll give you full details when I've dried out. Meanwhile, the sergeant is going to deliver a report to Superintendent Nash.' About to move off, he checked himself. 'Oh, is there any news?'

'The body has been identified by Mr Gale.'

'I see.'

'But there is good news of a sort,' said Hinton. 'When I went to Mrs Kendrick's house, I discovered that Mrs Gale was there as well. When the police took her husband away, she needed comfort from someone. Because the other neighbours blame her and her husband for what happened to their daughter, she turned to Mrs Kendrick. They've been drawn together.'

'It may be the start of a healing process between them.'

'I hope so, sir. Is there anything else I can do?'

'Yes, you can get out of my way so that I can go upstairs and change these trousers. I've provoked too many laughs already.' As he put a foot on the step, he remembered something. 'There is something you can do. I want you to visit that archaeologist, Mr Ewart.'

'I'll gladly do that, sir. He's so interesting.'

'In response to our appeal for help, he gave the best description of a potential suspect that we have. That was days ago. Some other detail may have surfaced by now. However small, it may be of use to us.'

'Wouldn't he have passed it on to you already, sir?'

'I'm afraid not. Mr Ewart, as you well know, lives in a different world. When he has a Viking culture to explore, he is not going to worry too much about an explosion at the railway station.'

After playing for hours in the nursery with his grand-daughter, Caleb Andrews felt the need for a rest. He came downstairs and joined Madeleine in the drawing room. After taking one look at him, she ordered tea and biscuits immediately.

'You look exhausted, Father,' she said.

'I'll soon recover.'

'Helena has worn you out.'

'That's why I handed her over to Nanny Hopkins,' he said. 'By the way, when I glanced out of the window, I saw the postman arriving.'

'That's right. And before you ask me, I did get another letter from Robert.'

'What does he say? Any arrests yet?'

'He feels that they are making steady progress.'

'I want more detail than that, Maddy.'

'There isn't any,' she said, 'beyond the fact that Superintendent Tallis arrived yesterday and confronted the police chief. As a result, Robert now has the backing of the local police force.'

'I should think so, too!'

'There's also a mention of Victor. He's worried because he's almost certain to be stuck in York when Albert's birthday arrives.'

'Have more faith in your husband,' he said. 'He's the only man I know who can find a needle in a haystack with one eye closed.'

'He's facing a very big haystack this time, Father.'

'That won't worry Robert. He's like me. Nothing defeats us.'

'Except your granddaughter, that is,' she reminded him. 'Helena has really taken the wind out of you today. You were forced to retreat downstairs.'

'It's true,' he groaned. 'I had to hoist a white flag.'

Alice Kendrick was the first to spot them. When she glanced out of the window, she saw her neighbour being driven home by a policeman. She turned to Margery Gale.

'Your husband is back,' she said.

'Is he?' asked the other, leaping to her feet and going to the window. 'Yes, you're right. Owen will know the horrible truth.'

'It's wrong to fear the worst.'

'I just can't believe that Binny is still alive. She would have been in touch.'

'Why don't you go home and learn the truth, Mrs Gale?'

'Will you come with me?' asked the other, anxiously.

'Me?' said Alice in surprise. 'Why do you need me there?'

'It's because you've been so kind. I know that we haven't always got on, but you were good to me when I needed help. Nobody else was. I can't tell you how grateful I am.'

'Then I'll be glad to go with you.'

When they left the house, the police carriage was already leaving. Margery Gale linked arms with Alice, and they walked in step. Before they reached her home, Owen Gale came out and stood there forlornly. All the anger and energy had drained out of him. His wife cried out.

'It was Binny,' she said. 'She took her own life, didn't she?'

Alice had to support her to get her to the house. Gale was puzzled.

'What are you doing here?' he asked, looking at Alice.

'Mrs Kendrick has been wonderful to me, Owen. She's been so kind.'

He looked blankly at his neighbour. 'Thank you,' he said at length. 'You were kind to Binny as well. I'll remember that from now on.'

His wife threw herself into his arms and they hugged each other. Alice went quietly back to her house. She was no longer needed.

'It was Binny, wasn't it?' said Margery.

'Yes, it was,' replied her husband with a shudder. 'We drove her to it, Marge.'

Hinton was delighted to have an excuse to talk to the archaeologist again. He reached Coppergate in time to see Ewart holding up his latest find. It was part of a sword. The rest of his team gathered around him to inspect it. Hinton had to wait a couple of minutes before Ewart noticed him.

'I wonder if I might have a word with you, sir?' asked Hinton.

'Yes, of course.' After wiping his hands on a rag, Ewart

climbed out of the trench and joined him. 'Have you come for another lesson about the Viking culture?'

'That will have to wait, sir. When we met before, I told you that I would only be in York for a short while. You are connected to the reason I'm here.'

'Really? How can that be?'

'You've already met Inspector Colbeck and Sergeant Leeming. My name is Alan Hinton and I'm a detective constable working with them.'

'Well,' said Ewart, 'that is a surprise. I took you for something else altogether. Anyway, it's good to see you again.'

'Thank you, sir. The inspector was grateful for the description you gave him of a man who was lurking near the brake van on that day. He just wonders if any new detail has popped into your mind since then.'

'No, I can't say that it has. I was happy to help your colleagues but, since then, I've been rather preoccupied.'

'Yes, I can see that.'

'I'll try hard to recall the man I saw,' promised Ewart, 'and, if anything does pop up in my mind, I'll let the inspector know at once. But I'm afraid that I'll have to disappoint him.'

'That's a pity, sir.'

'Have you made any progress in the investigation?'

'Yes, we now have your police helping us instead of setting themselves up as our rivals. That's a big improvement. Oh, yes,' added Hinton, 'and a young woman drowned herself in the river. We believe that her death is somehow linked to that explosion at the railway station.'

'I'll be interested to hear if that's the case. Meanwhile,

however . . .'

'Yes, yes, I won't keep you from your work any longer, Mr Ewart.'

'I have to say that I'm upset to hear about the suicide of a young woman. Only someone who has been pushed to the very brink would do such a thing. My sympathy goes out to her family.'

'I feel the same, sir.'

'What was her name?'

'Gale – Binny Gale.'

Seated at the table in the kitchen, they stared at each other. Neither of them could find words to express their sense of loss and their feeling of guilt. Owen Gale realised that he had been far too hard on his daughter when he caught her with Jack Follis. From that moment on, he'd treated her as if she had committed a terrible crime. Margery's sympathy for her daughter was tempered with disapproval. She was shocked that Binny had been unable to confide in her. The bond between mother and daughter had been severely damaged.

All that they could expect now was a life of continual regret. There would be public disgust to endure and there might well be friends who would drift away from them, but they could cope with that. What they could not begin to address was the terrible feeling that they had let their only child down. As parents, they had failed abysmally. Another fear was lapping at their minds. When they were given details of the post-mortem report, it might well contain another shock.

* * *

Leeming was amazed at the transformation. When he went to Colbeck's hotel room, he gaped at the change.

'You look as good as new, Inspector,' he said.

'Thank you, Victor. I'm glad that I'll no longer provide amusement for anyone who looks at me.' He adjusted his frock coat. 'How did you get on at the police station?'

'I told Superintendent Nash what you had found among the reeds, and he refused to believe that you had actually gone into the water.'

'I have a pair of wet trousers to prove it.'

'He was also annoyed that his own men hadn't done the same thing,' said Leeming. 'When they found the body, they simply brought it back here.'

'Then they would never have established how the girl died. Suicide or murder? We are now certain that Binny Gale was not held under the water by someone else. She took her own life.'

'Her parents will never forgive themselves.'

'It will be a heavy cross to bear, Victor.'

'What do we do now, sir?'

'The first thing,' said Colbeck, 'is to call on Mr Maynard. There was a letter waiting for me when I got back. He's had claims from people who had luggage or goods in that brake van when it burst into flame.'

'That's his problem, not ours.'

'It's a matter of great interest to us,' said Colbeck. 'All the witnesses who were there at the time talk of a big explosion. If we know exactly what was inside that brake van, we may discover what caused it.'

CHAPTER SEVENTEEN

Olive Cusworth stood in the middle of the room and looked around it with a nostalgic smile. They would never find a lodger like Jack Follis again. He had brought real joy into her life. As she looked at some of his belongings, she wondered if anyone would come to claim them. He must have had relatives of some sort, she believed. When the news of his death reached them, it would surely prompt one of them to come forward. Until then, she could keep the room as a kind of shrine.

She felt an upsurge of affection. Olive was so lost in her memories that she didn't hear her husband arrive in the open doorway.

'What on earth are you doing?' he asked.

'Oh!' she cried, turning to see him. 'I didn't realise you were there.'

'Jack has gone. He's not coming back.'

'It's cruel of you to remind me of that, Simon.'

'He was my friend as well as yours,' he reminded her. 'I played cards with him sometimes. I miss those evenings.'

'I miss talking to him. He was always so cheerful.'

'We both have wonderful memories of him, Olive, but we mustn't just wallow in them. Jack wouldn't have wanted that. To start with, I think we should find another lodger as soon as we can.'

'No!' she exclaimed. 'We can't do that.'

'It's a waste not to use this spare room,' he argued. 'We'll put an advertisement in the newspaper. Lots of people would be interested, I'm sure.'

'This is Jack's room,' she insisted, 'and that's what it must stay.'

'It's unhealthy to think that way, Olive.'

'No, it isn't.'

'We must try to forget him.'

'Never!' she protested. 'He brought so much joy into this house.'

'But he's dead now. We may have liked him but someone else hated him so much that they blew him up in his brake van. Why would anyone do that?'

She was confused. 'What are you trying to tell me, Simon?'

'There must be a part of his life we knew nothing about.'

'That's not true. He always talked to me about his work.'

'What about the time when he wasn't working?' he asked. 'Think of those evenings when he got back very late. Where had he been?'

'Jack was entitled to a private life.'

'How did he spend it? That's what I want to know.'

'I can't believe you're being so unkind,' she said, sharply. 'We're mourning the loss of a dear friend. We should be remembering all the good things he brought into our lives.'

'I do remember them. I think of him every day.'

'And so do I. It's the reason I want this room kept exactly as it is.'

'Let him go,' he urged. 'Forget him.'

She was outraged. 'How can you say such a thing!'

'Because I don't want him casting a shadow over our lives, Olive. I know that he gave us both a lot of pleasure but there was a dark side to Jack that we never saw. It got him killed,' he emphasised. 'Always remember that.'

'I'll mourn him my way, Simon – and I'll never forget him.'

'Then I'll have to get used to it,' he said, shoulders sagging.

'What do you mean?'

'While he was alive,' he croaked, 'you belonged to Jack. He made you happy. Now that he's gone, I hoped I'd have my wife back again. But there's no chance of that. In your mind, this room will always be his.' He gave a hopeless shrug. 'I've lost you forever.'

When the detectives went to his office, Gregory Maynard gave them a warm welcome and offered each of them a seat. He picked up a sheaf of papers from his desk.

'These are some of the claims,' he explained.

'Are you expecting any more, sir?' asked Colbeck.

'Oh, yes, and I daresay there will be a few bogus claims as well. These, however,' he went on, passing the sheaf to him, 'are all perfectly genuine.'

'Thank you.'

While Colbeck studied the claims, Leeming changed the suspect.

'Have you heard that a young woman was found dead in the river?'

'Yes,' said Maynard, 'but I've no idea of the details.'

'Her name was Binny Gale and she was a friend of the guard. In fact, we believe that she was a very close friend,' he said, knowingly. 'That's why we've taken such an interest in her. She may be linked to the murder of Jack Follis.'

'What do you know of this young woman?'

'We know the most important thing,' said Leeming. 'She committed suicide. Inspector Colbeck confirmed that by wading into the water near the spot where she was found.'

'That was very enterprising of you,' said Maynard, turning to Colbeck.

'It was important to find out the truth, sir,' said the other. 'Turning to these claims, I see that someone had four large tins of paraffin in that brake van. And there seem to be other combustible items.'

'What about the tins of cocoa that were in there?' asked Leeming.

'That's irrelevant,' said Colbeck.

'Not to me, sir.'

'The man who placed a bomb in there could not possibly have known that he would cause so much damage. My guess is that he had no idea what was in that brake van. How could he?'

'He could have put everything there deliberately,' said Leeming.

'Then why are the items in question the subject of claims from seven or eight different people? Are you suggesting a conspiracy between them and Follis?'

'Well, no, not really.'

'Remember what Mr Ewart told us. The man he saw was only carrying a small bag. It must have contained the bomb. If he'd been carrying four large tins of paraffin, I think that the archaeologist would have noticed it.'

'That's true,' conceded Leeming.

'What do you deduce from those claims, Inspector?' asked Maynard.

'I believe that we jumped to a wrong conclusion.'

'And what's that?'

'The bomb may not have been put there deliberately to kill the guard,' said Colbeck. 'It was there simply to cause an explosion and inflict limited damage. With so many combustible items in the van, it created a bonfire. Jack Follis was unlucky enough to be caught in the middle of it.'

'You've had your doubts from the start,' Leeming reminded him.

'Yes, I have. I couldn't see how the bomber could know the exact time when the guard would get into the brake van.'

'If he simply wanted to cause minor damage, he didn't need to know.'

'That's right, Sergeant.'

'I'm not sure that I understand the implications of what you're telling me, Inspector,' said Maynard.

'We have to look at the case from a different angle, sir.'

'You raised that possibility once before.'

'I didn't have the evidence to support it then.'

'Can it really be that the explosion was the work of

someone whose aim was merely to give us a scare and cause limited damage?'

'Yes, sir,' replied Colbeck. 'The intention, I suspect, was a brazen act of vandalism. Unfortunately, the result is a murder case.'

'Then there's an obvious suspect.'

'Is there, sir?'

'Perhaps Superintendent Nash arrested the right man, after all.'

When he was released from custody, Patrick McBride had celebrated with his friends in their favourite pub. He was now anxious to get compensation for the time he spent behind bars. Having been assured by Thomas Quinn that he deserved a payment of some kind, he went to the lawyer's office to see if there had been any response from the police. Quinn lifted a letter from his desk.

'Nash denies arresting you by mistake,' he told McBride. 'The most he is offering you is a fulsome apology.'

'Damn his apology!' howled McBride. 'I suffered in there, Tom.'

'I know you did.'

'It wasn't just being locked up. I'm used to that, so I am. It was the abuse I got almost every hour of the day and night. They treated me like dirt and jeered at me through the bars.'

'You have caused them a spot of bother in the past,' said Quinn.

'Aye, and I'll cause a lot more now I'm free.'

'That would be a big mistake, Pat.'

'They goaded me on purpose.'

'Yes, but nothing would please them more if they caught you trying to get your revenge on them. You must be a model citizen from now on. It's a point I'll raise with Nash.'

'I'd like to raise the point of my boot against him.'

'Then you won't get a penny in compensation.'

McBride grimaced. 'We need the money, Tom.'

'I'll keep pressing as hard as I can. You have my word. Meanwhile . . .'

'Yes, I know,' sighed the other. 'I go back to labouring. Sure, it's no effort for me but there's something strange about money that I earn legally. It doesn't give me the same thrill.'

'Get out!' yelled Quinn, laughing. 'I'll pretend I never heard that.'

Alan Hinton lingered at the site for the sheer pleasure of watching Nicholas Ewart. Though he was in charge of the excavation, the archaeologist worked shoulder to shoulder with the young men in his team. If one person found something of interest, they all gathered around him. What really impressed Hinton was that Ewart did not talk down to him. Treating the detective as an equal, he had been affable and informative. Ewart was also a gifted teacher who knew exactly how to impart knowledge.

When he broke off for a brief rest, Ewart noticed that Hinton was still there. He was both pleased and amused.

'Are you under orders to watch us?' he asked.

'I wish we were,' replied the other. 'I could watch you all day.'

'You're welcome to join us down here in the trench.'

'I'd love to, sir.'

'What's stopping you?'

'I'm supposed to be on duty. If I go astray, I'll be on the next train to London. Inspector Colbeck doesn't allow slacking. He brought me here to work.'

'Then I'll let you get on with it, Constable Hinton.'

'Don't forget what I said.'

'I won't, I promise you. I'll try my best to remember any additional details about the man I saw at the station. It may take time, however,' he warned. 'For the rest of the day, I'm firmly locked away in the world of the Vikings.'

It was only when she had left the house that Olive Cusworth was able to reflect on what her husband had told her. Jack Follis had replaced him in her affections. An old man with a variety of physical handicaps could not compete with a much younger one who showered Olive with compliments. While Simon liked their lodger, he felt that his wife's interest in him went beyond the bounds of mere affection. Whenever the couple had been alone together, she talked endlessly of Follis, relishing the pleasure of saying his name repeatedly.

She had left the house to visit a friend. On her way back home, Olive felt pangs of guilt. Simon's complaint was a fair one. He had been edged out whenever Follis was there. She had neglected her husband badly. Olive vowed to make amends. She also tried to view her relationship with their lodger honestly. When he first appeared, she felt a maternal affection for him but, as time went by, it developed into something else. Thinking about it made her come to a dead halt. Had she betrayed her husband by succumbing to an urge to get closer to their lodger? Had she done something of which she ought to be ashamed?

Setting off again, Olive was in a state of confusion. She did, however, come to one decision. The spare room would certainly not be kept as a shrine. They would find another lodger. Jack Follis would no longer exercise control over her.

Arriving back at the house, she was admitted by one of the servants.

'I'm glad you've come, Mrs Cusworth,' said the woman.

'Why?'

'You have a visitor.'

'We weren't expecting anybody.'

'Mr Cusworth said I was to show you straight into the drawing room.'

'Oh, I see.' Removing her hat and coat she handed them to the woman. 'I can find my own way, thank you.'

'As you wish, Mrs Cusworth.'

Olive walked to the drawing room and opened the door. Her husband was seated in his armchair and a woman in mourning attire was on the sofa. When they saw Olive, they rose to their feet.

'I'm so glad you're back, my dear,' said Simon. 'Allow me to introduce our visitor.'

'I'd rather do that myself,' said the woman, confidently. 'It's good to meet you, Mrs Cusworth. My name is Maude Follis.'

'Oh, I see,' said Olive. 'You must be related to Jack.'

'I'm his wife.'

After leaving Maynard's office, Colbeck decided to call on Superintendent Nash. It was hours since the body of Binny Gale had been discovered. A post-mortem would be under way. As usual, he was given a cold welcome.'

'What's brought you back, Inspector?' asked Nash.

'I have a favour to ask.'

'I hope that it's nothing to do with Binny Gale. That case belongs to us. I don't want you trespassing on it.'

'It could be relevant to the explosion at the station.'

'I don't see how.'

'The young woman was attracted to Jack Follis. That's a polite way of saying that, having noticed her working at the station, he selected her as his next victim. Someone who saw the way he exploited her might have felt that Follis deserved punishment.'

'Her father would certainly have good cause.'

'We questioned him. Mr Gale didn't plot his death. That much is certain.'

'The other certainty,' said Nash, expansively, 'is that the fate of this young woman is our business. You are intruding. Goodbye, Inspector,' he added with a sneer. 'Unless you happen to have another letter from the Home Secretary.'

'Don't mock, Superintendent.'

'As far as this case goes, we rule the roost.'

'Then try to handle the case professionally,' said Colbeck. 'When your officers reclaimed the body, they didn't bother to examine the area where she was found. We did search it and confirmed that Binny Gale drowned herself. Instead of trying to crow over me, you should discipline your men for being so inefficient. If they belonged to the Metropolitan Police Force, they would have been given a stern reprimand and a threat of dismissal.'

'I'll . . . speak to them myself,' mumbled Nash.

'Before you do that, please answer the question that brought me here.'

'What's that?'

'The body must already have been examined.'

'So?'

'Something must have become apparent, Superintendent.'

'The answer is that Miss Gale was not with child.'

'Did you tell that to her father?'

'No, Inspector. He was here before the post-mortem took place.'

'Then I'll take it upon myself to pass on the news.'

'That's our job,' asserted Nash.

'You'll be too busy dealing with the bungling officers who hauled the body from the river. I know the exact details of how their daughter died,' said Colbeck, 'and I don't need your permission to pass them on.'

'You're interfering.'

'It's my right to do so, Superintendent.'

'That's debatable.'

'If you feel aggrieved,' said Colbeck, 'you must write to the Home Secretary. He'll remember that you interfered in our investigation – so prepare yourself for a dusty answer.'

Olive Cusworth needed time to adjust to the shock. Having assumed that Jack Follis had been a bachelor, it never occurred to her that he might have a wife, especially one as blunt as this one. Maude was a beefy woman in her late thirties. She was attractive in her own way but there was an earthiness about her that Olive found troubling. She wondered why her lodger had never once mentioned that he was married.

'I can see you're surprised,' said Maude, looking at her. 'You're asking yourself where I sprang from, aren't you? The answer is Lincoln. We lived there so that I can look after Mother. When Jack was offered a job here, we agreed that he'd move to York, keep in touch with me by letter and visit us whenever he could.'

'I see,' murmured Olive.

'Mrs Follis has been telling me how religious Jack used to be,' said Simon. 'It seems that he always tried to go back to Lincoln on a Sunday so that he could take his wife and mother-in-law to the local church.'

'That was good of him,' said Olive. 'We didn't really see that side of him.'

'Jack was so grateful to you both,' said Maude. 'He kept saying how kind you both were. His letters were full of things you did for him.'

'It was a pleasure to have him here, Mrs Follis,' said Simon.

'Yes,' agreed Olive. 'We tried to make him feel at home.'

'It was a comfort to know he had such good friends,' said Maude. 'I daresay you want to know how I heard what . . . happened to him. Someone sent me a cutting from one of your newspapers. I couldn't believe it at first, and neither could Mother. Jack was so good at looking after himself, see. He'd done some boxing when he was younger. It gave him that jaunty way of his.'

'We'll always remember that about him,' said Simon.

'I cried and cried when I heard the news,' recalled Maude, 'and Mother was so upset, I had to fetch the doctor. We could afford it. Jack gave me money regular. And when I did see him, he brought presents.'

'Why did you come to York, Mrs Follis?' asked Olive.

'I wanted to know the truth,' replied Maude, clearly offended by the question. 'It's my right. Jack was my husband. We meant everything to each other. Then, of course, there's his belongings.'

'Ah, yes.'

'They're mine now.'

'If you want to know how he died,' said Olive, 'you'll need to go to the police station.'

'I felt I had to come here first. This house was special for Jack.'

'I'm glad that he felt like that,' said Simon. 'But I must correct my wife. Instead of going to the police station, you must get in touch with Inspector Colbeck. He's a detective from Scotland Yard and took charge of this case. We've met him. He's a very nice man, isn't he, Olive?'

'Yes, he is,' she said.

'Where will I find him?' asked Maude.

'He's staying at Scawin's Hotel next to the railway station.'

'I'll get over there once I've collected Jack's things.'

'Yes, of course,' said Olive, standing up.

Simon pulled the bell rope and a maid soon appeared. He asked her to conduct their guest to the spare room. After a flurry of farewells, Maude left with the maid. Olive lowered herself into her chair with relief.

'Well,' said her husband. 'That was a surprise, wasn't it?'

'A rather unpleasant one,' she sighed.

'Who would have thought that Jack was married? He was so free and easy that I assumed he was a bachelor. As

240

for going to church, I can't ever remember him doing that here. Can you, Olive?'

'No, I can't.'

'Mrs Follis was an interesting woman, wasn't she?'

'No,' she said. 'I thought she was common.'

Owen and Margery Gale sat in their living room in complete silence. Neither of them could find words of comfort. The shock of their daughter's disappearance had been profound, but the confirmation of her death was even worse. They both knew that there would be criticism to weather. People would blame them for driving Binny to kill herself. Several would shun the couple. It would also affect the fishmonger's trade. Instead of serving a host of regular customers, he would have to survive on a few. Pointed out in the market, he'd be the target of malicious gossip.

Margery eventually found something positive to say.

'Mrs Kendrick was the only one to care,' she said.

'What's that?' he asked, startled out of his gloom.

'There was nowhere else to go, Owen. The other neighbours have turned against us. It's almost as if we killed Binny ourselves.' She used a handkerchief to stem the tears that began to trickle. 'In a way, they're right. We let her down. We should have looked after her proper. We were in the wrong.'

'I know,' he confessed.

'Yet Mrs Kendrick took me in. She'd seen you go off with the policemen and guessed what must have happened. She knew how I must be feeling. That's why she let me in. She loved Binny as much as we did.'

'I don't want to hear about Mrs Kendrick,' he growled.

'We've been unkind to her, Owen.'

'I know.'

'She just wants to be friends with us.'

'Forget her. I only want to talk about Binny.'

'All right,' she said. 'Do you want some tea?'

'No. Just be quiet.'

He lapsed into a brooding silence and his wife soon joined him. They were impervious to the sound of the cab as its wheels scrunched on the road outside. When there was a knock on the door, they were jerked out of their reveries.

'Don't open the door,' he said. 'Let them go away.'

'It might be Mrs Kendrick.'

'We don't need her right now.'

'She knows we're in, Owen.' Margery went to the window and peered out. 'It's not her. It's a gentleman.'

'Why is he bothering us?'

'It might be important.' There was another knock on the door. 'Now that he's seen me, he's not going away.'

'Right,' he said, hauling himself out of the chair. 'I'll deal with him, Marge. Don't say a word. Leave the talking to me.'

Victor Leeming was waiting at the hotel when Hinton returned. They found a private corner in the lounge. Hinton told the sergeant about his conversation with Nicholas Ewart and how much he admired the man.

'He works on the excavation from dawn till dusk,' he said.

'More fool him!'

'It's important work, Sergeant.'

'It takes second place to what we do,' said Leeming. 'Dealing with vicious criminals means that we face danger every day.'

'We haven't found any vicious criminals in York.'

'That's beside the point, Alan. Our job is to keep people safe. All that Ewart does is to dig up the earth like a child playing in the sand on a beach.'

'Now that's unkind!' protested Hinton. 'He's very brainy. When they've finished at Coppergate, he's going to write a book about Viking life.'

'Well, I'm not going to read it,' said Leeming. 'All I want to know is if he remembered any other details about that man going into the brake van?'

'No, he didn't.'

'So much for being brainy!'

'But he did promise to get in touch with us if he did recall something. Anyway,' said Hinton, 'what have you and Inspector Colbeck been doing?'

'We went to see Mr Maynard. He had some news for us.'

Leeming went on to describe their visit and how they now knew what had been in the brake van when it was blown up. Hinton was intrigued to hear the information.

'The explosion wasn't meant to kill anyone?' he said in disbelief.

'That's what the inspector thinks. It was just bad luck that there were so many things in the van that it caught fire immediately.'

'What if there'd been no paraffin and so on in there?'

'Then the bomb would have gone off, given everyone a fright but caused very little damage. If the guard had been

243

inside at the time, he'd have got away with a few scratches. Instead of that . . .'

'He was killed.'

'I feel sorry for him. Jack Follis sounds as if he was a threat to the young women of the city, but I still pity him. There'll be people who say that he got what he deserved,' said Leeming, 'but that's unfair. According to the stationmaster, Follis was good at his job. It's what he did in his spare time that caused the trouble.'

'What did the inspector think about this new information?'

'In a way, he almost expected it.'

'How could he possibly do that?'

'From the start, he thought there was something funny about this case. Now we have some idea what it was.'

Owen Gale was angered by the sight of Colbeck on his doorstep. He resented the way that the detectives had come to the market and treated him as a possible suspect for the murder of Jack Follis. Yet he could hardly close the door in the man's face. He let their visitor in then led him into the sitting room.

'This is Inspector Colbeck,' he told his wife. 'He's trying to find out who killed Jack Follis.'

Margery was roused. 'It had nothing to do with us,' she cried.

'I know, Mrs Gale,' said Colbeck, softly. 'That's not why I'm here. This is a very awkward time for you, I realise that, but I have information regarding your daughter that I felt you should hear.'

'What sort of information?' asked Gale, suspiciously.

'When the police found her body, they made no effort to establish exactly how she died. That left open the possibility that she might have been murdered.'

'She wasn't, was she?' said Margery with a shudder.

'No, Mrs Gale. I took it upon myself to visit the place where Binny was found. Under the water was a heavy boulder. I'm almost certain that she used it to keep herself under water.'

'Would it have taken long?' she asked.

'What does it matter?' said Gale, sadly. 'Our daughter took her own life. We were to blame.'

'That's not true, sir,' Colbeck pointed out. 'Her friendship with Jack Follis had something to do with it.'

'Binny was such an honest girl until she met him,' said Margery. 'We were very close. She told me everything. All at once, she stopped. I should have known something was wrong.'

'I'm as much to blame,' admitted Gale.

'Well,' said Colbeck, 'I won't add to your distress. I came here to pass on news that might bring you a crumb of comfort.'

'What is it?'

'A post-mortem is being conducted.'

'They're not going to cut Binny open, are they?' howled Margery, standing up in alarm. 'I couldn't bear that.'

'It's standard procedure, Mrs Gale. Something of interest to you and your husband has already been established.'

'What is it?' demanded Gale.

'Your daughter was not carrying a child.'

'Thank God!' he exclaimed.

'I felt that you should be made aware of that, sir.'

'Thank you, Inspector.' Gale turned to his wife. 'Hear that, Marge? It was our worst fear. Binny was not . . .' Overcome with relief, his wife nodded. 'It was good of you to take the trouble to let us know, Inspector. We're very grateful.'

Gale went across to his wife and hugged her. Having brought them some consolation, Colbeck stole quietly out of the house.

Olive Cusworth was feeling hurt and betrayed. She had allowed herself to believe that her friendship with her lodger had forged a bond between them. Jack Follis had paid her compliments in a way that her husband had never done. She now realised that she had been tricked. Follis had not only wormed his way into her affections so that he could exploit them, it transpired that he was a married man. Moreover, his wife was a woman to whom Olive had taken an instant dislike.

'How much longer is she going to be?' she said, irritably.

'Give her time, Olive,' said Simon. 'Sorting through Jack's things must be very upsetting for her.'

'Having her here is very upsetting to me. I'm not waiting any longer.'

Hurrying out of the room, Olive went straight upstairs to the one that had belonged to their lodger. She rapped on the door then opened it. Maude Follis was sitting on the bed, going through a pile of clothes and other items, examining each one before putting it into the case she had brought. She gave Olive a hostile stare.

'He was mine,' she said with pride. 'Whenever you think of Jack, remember that he was all mine.'

CHAPTER EIGHTEEN

Madeleine Colbeck was delighted when her friend turned up at the house without warning. As she stepped into the hall, Lydia Quayle raised both hands in apology.

'Don't worry,' she said. 'I'm not staying.'

'You'll be more than welcome to do so.'

'I've brought you a present, Madeleine.'

'That's very naughty of you,' scolded the other with a smile of gratitude. 'You're always giving me presents.'

'You've given me something far more valuable than any gift.' She handed over a package. 'I was in a bookshop when I happened to notice this.'

'What is it?'

'Open the package and see for yourself.'

Madeleine tore off the brown paper and held up her gift. 'Oh, this is lovely, Lydia! It's a book about York.'

'Yes, and it's full of beautiful illustrations. Since you can't be with Robert in person, you can look at the sights that he is enjoying.'

'Oh, I don't think he'll have any time to enjoy a tour of York. When he's involved in a case, he never has a moment for anything else. But thank you so much, Lydia. What a kind thought of yours!'

'The book spoke to me.'

'I'm glad that you listened to it,' said Madeleine with a smile.

'Is there any news?'

'Robert's letter came this morning. He and Victor are still working hard on the case – and so is Alan, of course.'

'I hope that he comes back in one piece this time.'

'I'm sure that he will, Lydia. If you're worried about him, you could always take a train to York to find out for yourself.'

'Alan would never forgive me!'

'Then go in disguise.'

'You're a bad influence, Madeleine Colbeck,' said Lydia with a giggle.

'You miss him, don't you?'

'Yes, I do. But you must miss Robert very much. That doesn't give you the urge to race off and be with him.'

'I'd be in the way.'

'The same is true of me.'

'At least admit that it's a tempting idea, Lydia.'

'I've warned you before. You must stop trying to push us together.'

'Don't you feel in need of a gentle nudge?'

'I prefer to let nature takes its course, Madeleine. What's the rush, anyway? We're both still young,' Lydia pointed out. 'If anything is going to happen, it will do so in the fullness of time.'

'Then I'll say no more.' Madeleine held up the book. 'I'll really enjoy reading this and looking at the illustrations. Robert says that the Minster is magnificent – but he's only managed to have a glimpse of it.'

'What a shame!'

'It's a murder investigation. He's completely tied up in it.'

'When you write to him, please send my love.'

Madeleine grinned. 'Who is it intended for – Robert or Alan?'

'You're being wicked again.'

'I'm sorry to tease you. In view of this lovely present you bought, it's unkind of me. I just want you to be as happy as I am.'

'I'm happy in my own way,' said Lydia. 'Do you understand?'

Colbeck arrived back at the hotel to discover that somebody was waiting to meet him. He found the woman in Sarah Scawin's office, seated in a chair and talking to the owner of the hotel. Seeing her mourning wear, Colbeck guessed that she might be someone from the Follis family. When he learnt that she was, in fact, the guard's wife, he was taken aback.

'We had no idea that he was married,' he admitted.

'Well,' said Maude, 'you ought to have known. Jack wore a wedding ring. He swore that he'd never take it off.'

'I didn't meet him when he was . . . still alive, Mrs Follis.'

'In that case, I forgive you.'

Colbeck had never met any widow who was quite so

forthright. In the wake of their husband's unexpected death, most wives would have been unable to leave their house, still less go on a train journey. Maude Follis clearly loved and missed her husband deeply, but she was not going to let bereavement hold her back from doing what she felt was necessary.

'Mrs Follis has already been to her husband's lodging,' said Sarah as she moved to the door. 'Feel free to make use of my office for as long as is necessary.'

'Thank you, Mrs Scawin,' said Colbeck.

Sarah left the room and he turned to Maude Follis with a polite smile.

'How may I help you?' he asked.

'I'd like to hear the truth about the way Jack died,' she said. 'I spoke to a Sergeant Leeming, but I had the feeling he was holding something back. Please don't do the same thing, Inspector. I'm a strong woman. I won't faint.'

'You're entitled to a full account, Mrs Follis.'

'I'll not leave until I've had it,' she warned, crisply.

'Your sense of purpose is commendable.'

'And I'd rather you didn't use big words. Talk proper.'

'I'll do my best.'

Colbeck gave her a simple, straightforward account of what had happened, and how he and his colleagues had been gathering evidence from various sources. What he was careful not to mention was his theory that Follis might have been killed by accident. Nor did he mention the fact that her husband had taken an interest in other women, and that he would certainly have removed his wedding ring when he met them in private. He did not wish to damage her memory of him in any way.

250

Showing no emotion, Maude listened carefully throughout.

'Thank you,' she said when he had finished. 'Why couldn't that sergeant of yours have told me all that?'

'I daresay that Sergeant Leeming was trying to spare your feelings.'

'I have a right to know, Inspector.'

'Most wives in your position are not quite as robust as you, Mrs Follis.'

'I did my crying when I read about Jack in a newspaper cutting,' she told him. 'He wouldn't have wanted me to be weak and helpless. In any case, I need to be strong for Mother. She takes a lot of looking after.'

'Who is with her now?'

'We have good neighbours. But I didn't come here to talk about me and Mother. I want to know if you'll catch the man who killed my husband.'

'We'll catch him,' promised Colbeck.

'When?'

'I can't give you an exact time, Mrs Follis.'

'I see,' she said. 'Well, now that you've told me what happened, I want to reclaim Jack's wedding ring. It means the world to me.'

'His effects are being kept at the police station. I'd be happy to take you there and introduce you to Superintendent Nash.'

'Yes, please.'

'Then let's go,' he said, moving to the door.

After looking around the office for a moment, she followed him out.

* * *

Olive Cusworth was ashamed of herself. She knew that she had behaved badly towards Maude Follis. When the woman turned up out of the blue, she shattered Olive's image of her lodger. Why had he never told her that he had a wife? It was cruel of him. Olive was shocked to realise that she had been having impure thoughts about a married man. She had disliked and resented Maude Follis on sight, making no allowance for the fact that she was the widow of a man who had been cruelly murdered. Instead of showing her the sympathy due to her, Olive had been cold and unfriendly. She now felt a searing guilt.

Leaving the house, she walked in the direction of the Minster, determined to pray for forgiveness. It was the only way to make amends for her behaviour. Before she could enter the building, however, she saw a friend of hers coming out. It was Miriam Brightwell, gliding along with a serene smile on her face. They knew each other well because they sat together on one of the many committees associated with the Minster.

'Good afternoon, Mrs Brightwell,' said Olive. 'How are you?'

'I'm very well, as it happens, but you don't look as if you're in the best of health. Is there a problem of some sort?'

'Yes, there is,' admitted Olive, 'and it's the reason I'm here.'

She told her friend what had impelled her to come and why she felt so guilty about her treatment of Maude Follis. Miriam was sympathetic.

'Don't be too hard on yourself,' she advised. 'The person to blame is your lodger. He deceived you cruelly. When his wife turned up, you were caught off balance. Given the circumstances, your behaviour is understandable.'

'I should at least have been courteous to the woman, but she made that difficult for me because she had such an unpleasant manner.'

'Make allowances for her situation.'

'That's what I failed to do and I'm here to confess it. However,' she went on, 'enough of my troubles. I'm glad to see you looking so well and happy.'

'It's because I had a wonderful treat, Mrs Cusworth.'

'Oh?'

'Have you seen the excavations in Coppergate?'

Miriam went on to describe the progress being made by the archaeological team and how she had been given a private exhibition of some of their major finds. She was still excited at being allowed to hold a Viking skull.

'It was so kind of Mr Ewart,' she said.

'I'm not sure that I would have done that,' Olive told her. 'I might look at a skull if it was in a museum but touching it . . . no, I'd find that creepy.'

'I thought it was a huge privilege. It . . . inspired me.'

'Why dig people up like that? They should be allowed to rest in peace.'

'But we can learn so much about our past,' argued Miriam. 'You must talk to Nicholas Ewart. He has such a passion for the history of this city.'

Some days were better than others. Viking artefacts came to the surface in abundance. Today was less productive. Despite their intensive work, the team had unearthed far less than usual, and none of the items was in any way special. Nevertheless, they soldiered on, lifted by Ewart's encouragement.

'When we finally come to an end of our work on this site,' he promised, 'we will have a celebration at my house. I think we all deserve it.'

There was general delight and agreement.

Horace Nash was both surprised and interested to meet Maude Follis. Aware of the guard's reputation, he could not believe that the man was married, especially to a woman like the one who had come into his office with Colbeck. He was, however, considerate towards her and responded to her request. Nash summoned an officer and sent him off with Maude to the room where her husband's effects were kept. When they had gone, Nash turned to Colbeck.

'That was a big surprise,' he said.

'It came as a shock to me and, I daresay, to his landlady.'

'There's not much for the wife to reclaim, I'm afraid. His clothing was burnt and so were most of the things in his wallet. The coins in his pocket survived, however.'

'Mrs Follis is only interested in one thing, Superintendent.'

'What's that?'

'His wedding ring.'

'I don't think that we ever found one,' said Nash. 'I was not directly involved in dealing with the body, mind you, so I could be wrong.'

'When will it be released?'

'I'm not sure yet, Inspector.'

'Mrs Follis will need to make arrangements for the funeral.'

'As soon as I know the answer, I'll get in touch with her.'

'Thank you – and thank you for dealing with the lady so sympathetically.'

'I'm like you, Inspector. I've had a lot of experience of dealing with grieving wives. Not that Mrs Follis is anything like the others,' he added. 'She is . . . very unusual.'

'I agree.'

Colbeck had been in the superintendent's office before. This visit was different. He reflected that it was the first time they had met there without having an argument. It was a sign of progress.

When she came out of the Minster, Olive Cusworth felt that her fervid prayers had to some extent absolved her of blame. Miriam Brightwell's comment had comforted her. It was Jack Follis who was responsible for the way that she had behaved. He had deceived her. He had told her that he preferred the life of a bachelor and she had never seen him wearing a wedding ring. Olive knew that the house would seem empty without him. That was why they had to acquire a lodger in his place as soon as they could. Instead of taking in a man who might tell her lies, however, she resolved that they would seek a woman this time.

Maude Follis was unusually silent when Colbeck took her back to Scawin's Hotel. Eventually, he tried to find out why.

'I'm sorry there were so few effects left,' he said.

'Most of the things that mattered were at his lodging.'

'The fire must have destroyed the things he had on him at the time.'

'It did,' she agreed, 'but his wedding ring had escaped damage.'

'I'm glad to hear that, Mrs Follis.'

'What surprised me was that he wasn't wearing it on his hand.'

'Then where was it?' asked Colbeck.

'According to the policeman who showed me his effects, it was on a chain around his neck.' She was mystified. 'Why on earth did Jack carry it like that?'

Alice Kendrick had fallen asleep in her chair with her knitting in her lap. When she did finally wake up, she thought that she heard a noise. She went from room to room on the ground floor but was unable to locate what had made it. In the end, she opened the front door and peeped out. On the doorstep was a little box containing half a dozen eggs. There was no need to wonder who had left them there. Alice knew at once that they had come from the Gale family.

It was a peace offering. She was overjoyed. Alice's life would be different from now on. In losing Binny Gale, she had, by way of recompense, won the friendship of the girl's parents.

Edward Tallis was working at his desk when there was a knock on the door. A policeman came into the office with a telegraph for him.

'This is from Inspector Colbeck,' said the man.

'About time, too,' grumbled Tallis. 'Thank you.'

The messenger left and the superintendent read the telegraph. It informed him that Jack Follis had been married and that his wife had now arrived in York.

'Heavens!' he cried in disgust. 'Not only a Casanova – a rampant adulterer as well!'

Though Colbeck invited her to dine with him at the hotel, Maude Follis declined the invitation. She preferred to be alone. On the following day, she was to have a meeting with the solicitor used by her husband. She felt that he would be able to deal with the police on her behalf and supervise the transfer of the body to Lincoln. Maude suddenly looked tired and confused.

Colbeck therefore dined with his colleagues. As they reviewed the case, he asked each of them to give his opinion. With his son's birthday creeping closer, Leeming was downcast, fearing that they would still be in York when the date finally arrived. Alan Hinton, by contrast, took a more hopeful view. He had a feeling that they were getting closer to an arrest but had little evidence to sustain his theory. What he did ask was a question that had been troubling him ever since Colbeck had suggested that the crime might have occurred by accident.

'There's one thing I don't understand, sir,' he said.

'What is it?' asked Colbeck.

'If this really was an accident,' said Hinton, 'why didn't the person responsible come forward?'

'Would you have done so in his position?' asked Colbeck.

'I'd consider it, sir.'

'Then you are exceedingly honest.'

'Why do you say that?'

'Because I don't think that anybody else would do so, Alan. If he confessed to the crime of causing minor damage in the brake van, he wouldn't be absolved of a charge of murder because he could not prove that his confession was true. In other words, he'd be putting his head in a noose. No, Alan,' Colbeck went on, 'the most we could hope for is that he might contact us anonymously to explain what had happened.'

'The man was a criminal,' said Leeming. 'He'd never own up.'

'Doesn't he have a conscience?' asked Hinton.

'No, he doesn't,' said Colbeck. 'Besides, if my theory is wrong, then the explosion was designed to kill, after all. If that's the case, someone is still toasting his success at getting rid of a person he really hated.'

Patrick McBride was in a pub with his friends. Beaming with pleasure, he raised his tankard of beer for a toast.

'To Tom Quinn, Esquire!' he said.

'Tom Quinn,' his friends repeated.

'The cleverest lawyer to come out of Ireland.'

'If he was that clever,' said someone, 'you and your son wouldn't have spent time in prison.'

'Tom got years cut off our sentences,' asserted McBride. 'I won't hear a word against him. The man is a genius.'

'How well does he know you, Pat?'

'Sure, there's only one man alive who knows me better and that's Father Malone, God bless him! He's looked into my soul.'

'Have you confessed all your crimes to him?'

McBride guffawed. 'I'm not that stupid!'

* * *

Margery Gale had cooked a meal but neither of them had an appetite. Sitting in silence, they just picked at the occasional item on their plates. From time to time, each of them glanced at the empty chair at the table, the one always occupied before by the other member of the family.

'Don't blame her,' pleaded Margery. 'Whatever she did, Binny was still our daughter. Try to remember all the good things she did.'

'I don't blame, Binny,' he said, quietly. 'I blame myself. I should have noticed the signs. She was a good girl, but she had no defence against a man like Jack Follis. He would have spotted that at once and moved in to tempt her. I tried to rescue her, but it was too late.'

'You brought her to her senses, Owen.'

'Did I?'

'She realised how badly she'd let us down.'

'Binny never told me that. All I saw was a daughter who turned away from me because I was strict with her. What she did was wrong. I had to keep reminding her of that.' He heaved a sigh. 'I think I yelled at her once too often.'

'That wasn't why she ran away, Owen,' insisted his wife. 'She was ashamed. She told me that she had no purpose in living any more. What a terrible thing for a girl of her age to say! I felt as if she'd thrust a knife into my heart.'

'There are hard times ahead, Marge,' he warned. 'Wherever we go, people will point us out. We're the parents whose daughter drowned herself. Because of that, Binny can't have a Christian burial.'

'There's one thing to hold on to,' she said.

'I don't see it.'

'Binny was not carrying a baby outside wedlock.'

'We know that,' he said, 'but nobody else will believe it. Tongues are wagging already. I'm dreading the next market day.'

'We should have thanked that inspector proper,' she mused. 'He went out of his way to help us. He brought us some comfort. I'll always remember Inspector Colbeck. He was good to us.'

Gale looked across at her. 'There won't be many people like that.'

Alan Hinton was the first of them to retire to bed. Colbeck and Leeming were soon leaving the dining room. Sarah Scawin came across to them.

'Thank you for advising Mrs Follis to spend the night here,' she said.

'It seemed the sensible thing to do,' replied Colbeck. 'She's a woman in distress. If she needed us, we'd be under the same roof.'

'Being in a crowd unsettled her. She asked a favour of me. Since she wanted to be alone, she wondered if she could have a meal in her room. Ordinarily, I'd have refused,' she said, 'but this was a special case.'

'That was very considerate of you, Mrs Scawin,' said Leeming.

'I was not only thinking of Mrs Follis.'

'Why do you say that?'

'For reasons you know only too well, Jack Follis was banned from this hotel. But his memory remains fresh, especially in the minds of my female staff. I didn't want one of them to make an incautious remark about Follis in front of his wife.'

'That would really upset her,' said Colbeck. 'If we keep her ignorant of gossip about him, she'll still be able to preserve fond memories of her husband.'

Sarah was honest. 'It's more than I'm able to do!'

Ellie Duckett was the first of the servants to come downstairs that morning. She was a pretty, fair-haired young woman who loved working at the house. Well treated by Miriam Brightwell, she made light of the many duties she had to perform. When she came into the kitchen, she was about to put water in the kettle when she noticed a faint chill. Looking around, Ellie saw that a window was slightly ajar. It gave her an instant feeling of alarm. When she inspected it, she realised that the window had marks on it that showed it had been forced open.

For a few moments, she just stood there and dithered. Then she ran up the stairs and knocked on the door of Miriam's bedroom. Flinging it open, she went into the gloom and crossed to the bed.

'Mrs Brightwell,' she gasped, touching the woman's arm. 'I think we've been burgled.'

Getting no response, she put her hand on Miriam's shoulder and shook her. Instead of waking up, the woman simply lolled sideways. Ellie was terrified.

Her scream echoed throughout the whole house.

* * *

By the time that Horace Nash reached the house with two policemen in tow, Ellie had calmed down a little but was still close to tears. She gave the newcomers a garbled account of what had happened. After examining the kitchen window, Nash and his men were taken upstairs and into Miriam's bedroom. The curtains had been drawn back to let the light in, and the bedsheet had been drawn up to cover the dead woman. Nash turned it back and saw the bruising on Miriam's neck.

'Someone strangled her,' he concluded. 'She was too weak to put up a fight.' After pulling the sheet back over the face of the corpse, he turned to the servant who had brought them into the bedroom. 'Was anything taken from the house?'

'Yes,' said the man, opening a wardrobe. 'The safe has been emptied.'

The police stared at the open door of a safe that peeped out from under the dress hanging above it. A key was in the lock.

'Where was the key kept?' asked Nash.

'Mrs Brightwell always had it with her, Superintendent,' said the servant.

'Has the house ever been burgled before?'

'No, but someone did try to get in one night.'

'When was this?'

'Three or four months ago,' said the other. 'We heard noises and came down to see what was causing them. We must have frightened the burglar away.'

'I wish that you could have done the same last night. Right,' said Nash, 'let's move Mrs Brightwell out of here.' He turned to one of the policemen. 'Go and fetch the undertaker. Warn him that she must be handled with great care.'

'Yes, sir,' said the man before leaving.

Nash looked at the body. 'She was a dear lady,' he said with genuine fondness.

'Mrs Brightwell did so much for York. We are going to miss her badly.'

Colbeck was having breakfast with Leeming and Hinton when the message came. A policeman told him about the murder and said that Superintendent Nash had asked him for his opinion. Abandoning his food, Colbeck collected his hat and went out of the hotel to a waiting cab. On the way there, the policeman gave him a very brief account of what had happened.

'Has the body been moved?' asked Colbeck.

'Yes, sir.'

'That's a pity.'

'The superintendent wanted it out of the way, sir. When word spreads, there'll be a crowd outside the house. Mrs Brightwell's body will be spared all that attention.'

'It can be unseemly at times,' agreed Colbeck. 'Friends and well-wishers will be there, but so will the ghouls who are somehow drawn to get a glimpse of murder victims. The killer himself might even come to gloat.'

When the cab reached the house, there was a small cluster of people outside. A policeman was on duty to keep them on the opposite side of the road. Colbeck went into the house and met Nash in the drawing room.

'Thank you for sending for me,' he said.

'You're here on one condition, Inspector.'

'What is it?'

'This is our case,' emphasised Nash.

'I accept that.'

'But I'd value your help.'

'Thank you,' said Colbeck.

Nicholas Ewart was working at the site in Coppergate when a man came running towards him. Ewart recognised him as one of the servants from Miriam Brightwell's house. He was puzzled by the man's appearance and sense of urgency. Taking the archaeologist aside, the servant passed on news of the murder. Ewart was so shocked that he looked as if he were going to fall over. He had to steady himself with a hand against a wall. When he had recovered, Ewart told the members of his team to carry on working without him. Then he and the servant hurried away from Coppergate.

Nash had been thorough. He had worked out the route that the intruder had taken before he let himself into the bedroom occupied by Mrs Brightwell and took Colbeck along it step by step. When they entered the bedroom, he pointed out the safe visible through the open door of the wardrobe. Colbeck went to examine it. Since it had been made at the Chubb factory, he knew that it could not have been opened without the key or combination. It was too heavy for a man to remove it on his own.

'Whoever the killer is,' said Colbeck, 'we can be sure of one thing.'

'What's that?'

'He's been in this house before. I suggest you ask for a

list of tradesmen who have worked here over the past year. That includes those who worked in the garden. Where do the staff sleep?'

'In the attic,' said Nash.

'It's the kind of information that would have been very easy to get without arousing any suspicions. Someone working on the roof, for instance, would be aware of the rooms in the attic. Or a casual word with one of the servants would establish where he and the others slept.'

'Why did he have to kill the poor woman? He could have knocked her unconscious, emptied the safe and taken whatever he wanted.'

'Mrs Brightwell would be a witness,' said Colbeck. 'Left alive, she would remember details that might lead directly to his arrest. It was not a risk he was prepared to take.'

'I see.'

'What was she wearing when she was found?'

'Her nightdress,' replied Nash. 'That's all.'

'If I'd found her, I'd have left her there so that she could be examined at the scene of the murder.'

'I did what I felt was right,' said Nash, sounding a note of warning. 'I do things my way, Inspector.'

'It was not meant as a criticism.'

'I hope not. Is there anything else you need to see?'

'I'd like to talk to the servants in turn,' said Colbeck, 'starting with the young woman who made the grisly discovery. After that, I want to prowl around the garden for a while.'

'Why? This is where the murder happened.'

'Yes, but it was planned by someone who knew what time Mrs Brightwell went to bed. He watched her window until the light went out. He would look at the attic windows as well,' he continued, 'and had probably done so on previous nights, so that he could follow the sleeping patterns of all the occupants.'

Nash chuckled. 'You sound as if you've been a burglar yourself,' he said.

'Preparation is everything.'

'How would he know that Mrs Brightwell had a safe?'

'The sheer size and grandeur of the house would tell him that it was owned by someone with wealth. A safe would have been almost obligatory. We once arrested a prolific burglar,' recalled Colbeck, 'who had lawful employment in a jewellery shop. He was in the ideal place to gauge the wealth of any clients he met, as well as their taste in precious stones. He took big risks because he knew that he could expect a large haul.'

'How did you catch him?'

'With the greatest difficulty,' confessed Colbeck.

Before the conversation could continue, a policeman interrupted them.

'There's a gentleman downstairs who insists on speaking to you, sir,' he said. 'He claims to be a close friend of the victim.'

'What's his name?' asked Nash.

'Nicholas Ewart.'

'I know him,' said Colbeck. 'He gave us the best description we have of a potential suspect for the explosion at the railway station. He's an archaeologist by profession.'

Nash gave a nod. 'Then let's see what he has to say.'

* * *

Nicholas Ewart was waiting impatiently in the drawing room. He was oblivious to the beautiful ornaments all round him, and to the fine paintings that decorated the wall. Pacing up and down, he reached for a handkerchief as more tears threatened.

When they entered the room, Colbeck could see that the man was in a state of agitation. Ewart was surprised to find him there.

'Why are you here, Inspector?' he asked. 'This case has nothing to do with the explosion at the station.'

'Superintendent Nash was kind enough to invite me here,' said Colbeck.

'That's right,' agreed Nash. 'I'm never too proud to take advice.' He looked at Ewart. 'I'm told that you were a friend of Mrs Brightwell, sir.'

'Yes,' said Ewart, 'and a very grateful friend. The project that I'm leading would have been impossible without a generous grant from her.'

'When did you last see the lady?' asked Colbeck.

'The day before yesterday. Mrs Brightwell came to my house to view some of the Viking artefacts we dug up in Coppergate.'

'Ah,' said Nash, 'so you're one of those people on his knees with a trowel. I must have seen you when I walked past.'

'Forget about me,' said Ewart, with a dismissive wave. 'I want to hear about Mrs Brightwell. One of her servants broke the news to me. Daniel gave me very few details. I want to know everything.'

'We're still at an early stage, Mr Ewart,' said Nash. 'Besides, I'm not going to release information about the murder yet, least of all to someone who has no right to hear it at this stage.'

'But I do have the right!' claimed Ewart. 'We were close friends.'

'In that case,' said Colbeck, intervening, 'I'd like to hear more about the lady. Superintendent Nash is leading this investigation so we can let him get on with it. We, meanwhile, could have a quiet chat.' He looked at Nash. 'Is that acceptable to you?'

'It is,' said the other. 'I know that I can rely on your discretion, Inspector.'

Colbeck did not need a warning. He was not going to disclose precise details of the murder to a person who was not involved in the investigation. When Nash moved away, Colbeck indicated the sofa.

'Why don't we sit down, sir?' he asked.

'I'm not sure that I can,' said Ewart. 'I feel so restless.'

'In that case, stand there while I sit down.' As he settled down on the sofa, he glanced around. 'This is such a beautiful room.'

'I felt that every time I came here.'

'How much do you know about this case, sir?'

'Not enough, Inspector. That's why I'm so desperate. In some ways, Mrs Brightwell was like a mother to me. I can't believe that she . . .'

'Take your time, sir,' advised Colbeck. 'When you feel ready, tell me what the servant has already told you. That way, I'll know where to start.'

While having breakfast together, Leeming and Hinton speculated on where Colbeck had gone when he was summoned. The fact that a policeman had come in search of him at least proved that the local constabulary were at last cooperating with them. That was a source of relief. When they left the dining room, they were spotted by Sarah Scawin. She came over to them.

'You've just missed Mrs Follis,' she said. 'She has an appointment with her husband's solicitor.'

'What sort of mood was she in?' asked Leeming.

'She was very subdued, Sergeant.'

'We heard that she was a resolute woman.'

'Mrs Follis is much quieter today,' said Sarah. 'She was also rather nervous.'

'Why?' asked Hinton.

'She thought that one or two people were giving her strange looks. Word must have got out that she was married to Jack Follis. The sooner she gets home to Lincoln, the safer she'll be.'

'I think you're right. Finding out the truth about her husband would be a frightful shock.'

'Perhaps you can help us, Mrs Scawin,' said Leeming. 'Before he could have his breakfast, Inspector Colbeck was hauled out of the hotel by a policeman. Have you any idea why?'

'I can only hazard a guess, Sergeant.'

'What is it?'

'Well, a guest came in not long ago and said that someone was murdered during the night. I don't know the details.'

'They don't matter,' said Leeming, disconsolately.

'I'd have thought you'd take an immediate interest in the case.'

'Inspector Colbeck has already done that. I feel sorry

269

for the victim, but I feel sorry for my younger son as well.'

'Why?' she asked.

'It's his birthday in a matter of days,' explained Leeming. 'I promised to be there. That would have been unlikely if we had only one crime to solve. If we have another murder case on our hands as well, I could be trapped here till doomsday.'

CHAPTER NINETEEN

Seated on the sofa, Colbeck listened to an account of the murder that Daniel had given Nicholas Ewart. It veered more towards sensation than fact. The inspector realised why the man had been so upset. In return, Colbeck gave him a more measured account.

'In essence,' he said, 'what appears to have happened is this. Ellie Duckett, one of the servants, came downstairs this morning to make a cup of tea for Mrs Brightwell. The girl felt a draught and saw that it came from an open window in the kitchen. She also saw marks on the frame that showed the window had been forced open. Flying into a panic, she ran upstairs to rouse Mrs Brightwell and found that she was dead. You can imagine how she felt.'

'What exactly did she find, Inspector?'

'I've just told you. Her employer was dead.'

'Yes, but how?' pressed Ewart. 'Had she been stabbed, smothered, beaten to death? I need to know.'

'Then you'll have to wait until the Superintendent releases the information.'

'You already have it.'

'I'm not in a position to divulge the details, sir.'

'I'll be very discreet,' promised Ewart. 'You have my word for it. I'd just like to know how the intruder killed a dear friend of mine.'

'Does it really matter, sir?'

'It matters a lot to me, Inspector.'

'Why?'

'Because I'm afraid of what happened before Mrs Brightwell was killed. We had a murder in York over a year ago. An older woman, another widow, disturbed a burglar one night. He not only knocked her unconscious,' said Ewart, 'he . . . took advantage of her when she was in no position to defend herself. Once he'd had his pleasure, he slit her throat.'

'Nothing like that occurred in this case, sir, I can assure you.'

'That's a relief!'

Colbeck was firm. 'But that's all I'm prepared to tell you.'

'Daniel, the servant who came for me, was largely incomprehensible. He was still suffering badly from shock.'

'If you don't mind my saying so,' said Colbeck, 'the same could be said of you, Mr Ewart. The news has come like a thunderbolt.'

'It has. I admit it freely.'

'Then let's turn to another subject. It may help to clear your mind a little. Sit down and tell me about your excavation in Coppergate.'

Madeleine Colbeck was tidying up her studio when there was a tap on the door and her father entered. He looked around in amazement.

'What's happened?' he asked.

'I thought it was time to give the place a clean from top to bottom.'

'If you did that, it wouldn't be your studio any more, Maddy.'

'Yes, it would.'

'No,' he argued. 'You work best with a complete mess around you. Why put those frames in a tidy pile like that? And why isn't the floor covered in all the usual rubbish? You're an artist. You're not supposed to bother about clutter.'

'Well, I do this morning, Father.'

'Why?'

'I suppose that I felt ashamed of the place.'

'So?' he said with a shrug. 'You're the only person who ever sees it.'

'No, I'm not. You come in here as well.'

'I used to – when you let me, that is. But I'm not coming here again if it's as spick and span as this. It's not you, Maddy.'

'Oh, I see,' she said, stopping to look around. 'It is very different, I suppose.'

'Why on earth did you open that window?'

'I wanted to let in some fresh air, of course.'

'The smell of that oil paint is wonderful,' he said. 'Don't you miss it?'

'Well . . . I suppose that I do.'

'Then put down that duster and pass me the brush. I'll take them downstairs so that you can turn your studio into a tip again.' She laughed. 'I'm serious. When I popped in here yesterday, I knew at once you were an artist. Today, you're acting like one of the servants.'

After handing him the duster, she reached for the brush and passed it over.

'I suppose it's too early for the mail?' he said.

'Yes, it is.'

'When it comes, let me know what Robert says.'

'I'm afraid that his letter will be like to the one I had yesterday,' she said. 'No matter how hard they work, progress is very slow. It's depressing.'

'Robert will make an arrest in the end. He usually does.'

'I know.'

'Then you'd better start a new painting and go back to your bad habits.'

'What bad habits?' she said, offended.

'Dropping things everywhere and being unable to find them. Leaving those frames all over the floor so that you trip visitors up. Forgetting to clean your brushes properly. In other words,' he said with a grin, 'for behaving more like the daughter I love. Next time I come in here, please let this studio say "Maddy" to me.'

'I promise,' she said, hugging him.

'Once in a while, I do give good advice.'

* * *

274

The reward posters had been up for days now but there were still people coming in from time to time with information they considered useful. Details had been collected by Ben Walters, the railway policeman. He weeded out anyone who had clearly invented a story in the hopes of getting the reward money, while passing on the names and addresses of those he felt might be of use. Leeming and Hinton went off to find a man whose story had impressed Walters.

The detectives found themselves standing outside a large, rambling house with three storeys. Leeming studied it.

'One thing is clear,' he decided. 'Mr Godfrey is not after the reward money. If he can afford a place like this, he doesn't need it.'

'That means we'll be talking to an honest man,' said Hinton.

He rang the bell and, soon afterwards, a maidservant opened the door. When they explained who they were, she had clearly been told to expect a visit from the detectives. Inviting them in, she took them down a passageway to a sizeable drawing room with a low ceiling. When the woman left, they glanced around, noting the sense of luxury.

Paul Godfrey entered the room and introduced himself. Leeming gave their names and ranks. Godfrey was a well-dressed man in his sixties with wispy grey hair and a wrinkled face. The detectives were invited to sit down, but Godfrey remained on his feet, looking like a vicar about to give a sermon. He had a high, reedy voice and a habit of jabbing a finger in the air as he spoke. He also kept blinking.

'I hope that you haven't come on a fool's errand,' he said.

'We heard what you said at the station, Mr Godfrey,' replied Leeming, 'and we feel that your evidence may be of value.'

'I do hope so, Sergeant. As I explained to that railway policeman, I was on the train delayed by that deafening explosion. We were held up afterwards for a long time. The passengers in my compartment were very restive.'

'I'm not surprised, sir,' said Hinton, taking out his notebook.

'One of them was so angry that he tore up his ticket and went home.'

'You obviously had more patience.'

'I had to go to London,' said Godfrey. 'My daughter and her family were expecting me. In addition to that, I had business in the city.'

'What sort of business, sir?'

'I own property there.'

'I see.'

'Perhaps we could move on to the evidence you gave,' said Leeming, keen to avoid being diverted into the man's private life. 'We've been told that you saw someone hovering near the brake van. Please describe him.'

'Well,' said Godfrey, 'he was a rather shabby fellow with a cap pulled down over his face, yet there was something about him that interested me. He had the look of a gentleman somehow. I'd put him close to your age, Sergeant, but he had a much slimmer build. What caught my attention was the way that he kept walking to and from the brake van, as if wanting to get into it yet changing his mind at the last moment.'

'Where were you at the time, sir?' asked Hinton.

'I was in the coach nearest the brake van. I had a clear view of the man.'

'How far away would you have been?'

'Oh, I don't know – twenty yards or so, I suppose.'

'Were you shaken by the explosion?'

'I was terrified, like everyone else in my compartment. Porters came to help us on to the platform. It was only when the fire in the brake van had been put out, and it had been towed away that it was deemed safe for us to board the train again.'

'What was the journey to London like?' asked Leeming.

'Much too long and very fretful. I was so glad to arrive in one piece.'

'Did you wonder what had caused the explosion?'

'Yes, I wondered if it had been the work of anarchists. Some of them use a bomb as a trademark.'

'That idea was considered, Mr Godfrey.'

'It was considered and discarded,' said Hinton.

'Go back to this man, sir,' said Leeming. 'You saw him acting suspiciously. Did he get into the brake van at any point?'

'I think that he must have,' said Godfrey. 'All of a sudden, he vanished as a group of people walked past him. When I looked again, he was striding towards the exit as fast as he could.'

'Would you recognise him if you saw him again?'

'I'm certain that I would.'

'Yet you were at least twenty yards away.'

'I have good eyesight, Sergeant,' said the other, 'and there's something I haven't told you.'

'What is it, sir?' asked Leeming.

'I'm fairly certain that I've seen the fellow before.'

'That's interesting.'

'It could mean that he lives here in York. To put it another way,' said Godfrey, jabbing a finger at them, 'the killer may be right under your noses.'

Inviting the archaeologist to talk about his work turned out to be an ideal way to calm the man down. Colbeck not only learnt a great deal about the work being done in Coppergate, he discovered how close Ewart and Miriam Brightwell had been. They sat together on the Board of Trustees at the museum, and both were involved in activities at the Minster. It was clear that Miriam had used Ewart as a kind of private tutor. He had advised her which books to add to her library and donated a couple that he had written himself.

When the man was sufficiently soothed, Colbeck told him to return to the excavations and carry on with his work. Sad to leave, Ewart agreed.

'When will I learn the full details of . . . what happened?' he asked.

'Superintendent Nash will release them when he feels ready to do so.'

'I'm sorry to have bothered him.'

'He understands, sir. Mrs Brightwell had great importance in your life.'

Ewart nodded. Rising to his feet, he left the room, leaving Colbeck free to speak to the servants. He found them waiting in the library and was delighted to see the well-stacked bookshelves against three walls. Of the servants, Ellie was still gibbering about what had happened, and Daniel was as pale of a sheet. Nan, the cook, a chubby middle-aged woman with eyes full of fear, was almost afraid to speak. It was the same with the others. They felt guilty that their employer had been murdered while they were still asleep, and they worried about an uncertain future.

Colbeck talked to them one at a time, hearing the same information and abject apologies again and again. Until the previous night, the Brightwell home had been a happy and comfortable place in which to work. At a stroke, that life had ended. When he had been through the domestic staff, Colbeck went into the back garden and examined the kitchen window from the outside. He then inspected the other windows at ground level.

The garden was large and well-tended. There were plenty of trees and bushes behind which an intruder could lurk while studying the house for the best mode of entry. Colbeck explored every inch before he went back indoors. Horace Nash was waiting to welcome him.

'Well,' he asked, 'what have you found?'

'I discovered what a delightful garden Mrs Brightwell had,' said Colbeck. 'Then I tried to look at the house through the eyes of a burglar.'

'And?'

'I wondered why he decided to steal nothing more than the contents of the safe,' said Colbeck. 'I know that the most valuable items were kept in there. To get at them, however, he would somehow have to wrest the key from Mrs Brightwell. There was a big risk involved. Before he overpowered her, she might have screamed for help. He could easily have avoided that possibility.'

'How?' asked Nash.

'By remaining downstairs,' Colbeck told him. 'There are rich pickings here. You must have noticed the cabinets filled with expensive items. Then there are the ornaments on display in all the rooms. Each one would bring him a pretty penny. With everyone fast asleep,' he continued, 'there was little danger of discovery.'

'I see what you're getting at, Inspector,' said Nash. 'The burglar didn't just come to steal. His real intention was to kill Mrs Brightwell.'

'The theft was secondary and intended to distract us.'

'It's an interesting thought.'

'You might bear it in mind,' said Colbeck. 'Thank you for inviting me here, Superintendent. I won't get under your feet any longer.' He remembered something. 'Oh, incidentally, Mr Ewart has apologised for trying to badger you.'

'There was no need. Emotion got the best of him, that's all.'

'I managed to soothe him eventually.'

'Good,' said Nash. 'And thank you for your advice about the burglar. In a previous life, I fancy you might well have been one.'

Colbeck smiled. 'Is that a compliment or a reproof?'

On their long walk back to the hotel, Alan Hinton made sure that he decided on the route. Both detectives felt that their visit to Paul Godfrey's house was worthwhile.

'His description of the suspect,' said Hinton, 'was like the one that you got from Mr Ewart.'

'That's true,' agreed Leeming.

'According to your notes, Ewart said that he looked like a tradesman.'

'He also told us that the man was carrying a little bag. There was no mention of that from Mr Godfrey.'

'Perhaps he didn't see it.'

'Or perhaps it wasn't there.'

'I don't understand, Sergeant.

'Mr Ewart is much younger and more observant than Mr Godfrey,' said Leeming. 'There was more detail in his description. What we heard today was interesting, but I wonder if it's completely reliable. Mr Godfrey is old and – from the way he kept blinking at us – it was obvious that his eyesight was not all that good.'

'I still think he may have seen the killer.'

'I hope you're right. If the man lives in York, it would be a great help to us if Mr Godfrey happened to bump into him in the street.'

Hinton laughed. 'There's no chance of that.'

'Wait a moment,' said Leeming as he looked around, 'this isn't the way that we came. Why are you taking me on a different route?'

'It's because I'd like another glimpse of that excavation in Coppergate,' admitted Hilton. 'Mr Ewart will be there. We can give him a wave as we pass.'

'What's the inspector doing now, I wonder,' said Leeming.

'Helping to solve another case.'

'Ours is the more important one, Alan.'

'Yes, of course.'

'We're not at the behest of Superintendent Nash.'

'Perhaps not,' said Hinton, 'but the fact that he's asking

for help shows that he now has some respect for Inspector Colbeck.'

'I want the inspector to concentrate on the case we came her to solve.'

'Are you still hoping to get home for your son's birthday?'

'Hoping is no use,' said Leeming. 'I've got to the stage of praying.'

As soon as Colbeck returned to the hotel, he was intercepted by Sarah Scawin. She took him into her office for a private conversation.

'I'm not prying,' she said, 'but my guess is that you were summoned earlier on because of the murder that took place in the night.'

'That's correct, Mrs Scawin.'

'May I ask who the victim was?'

'It was a lady by the name of Mrs Brightwell.'

Sarah was shocked. 'Surely not!'

'I'm afraid that it's true. The house was burgled, and she was found dead. That's all I can tell you.' He studied her anxious face. 'From your reaction, I assume that you know the lady.'

'I'm not acquainted with Mrs Brightwell, but I know of her. Her name is often in the newspapers because she's given money to various good causes. Also, I know her by sight. She is such a dignified woman.'

'The search for the killer has already begun,' he told her. 'May I ask if there is any news about Mrs Follis?'

'Yes, she will be on her way back home very soon. I spoke to her when she came back from the solicitor. He seems to have put her mind at rest.'

'That's good.'

'I thought it was very brave of her to come here so soon after Jack Follis's death. Having been through the experience of losing a husband,' she confided, 'I know what a crippling blow it is.'

'Mrs Follis had the additional shock of learning that he'd been murdered. Very few wives could have adjusted so quickly to that. A moment ago, you described Mrs Brightwell as a dignified woman. In her own way,' said Colbeck, 'I believe that Mrs Follis had dignity. It was allied to a fierce sense of her duty as a wife.'

'It's a pity that her husband had no sense of duty towards her,' said Sarah.

Colbeck pursed his lips. 'Sadly, that's all too true.'

Maude Follis was in the compartment of a train that had left the city behind it. Sitting upright with her hands clasped in her lap, she reflected on the kindness and sympathy she had met in York. Inspector Colbeck had been gentle with her, as had Sarah Scawin. The only person less than considerate towards her had been Olive Cusworth, the landlady of whom her husband had spoken so well. It troubled her.

As she thought about her future, the full sense of loss flooded her mind, and made her grit her teeth. The other passengers in the compartment kept glancing across at her, struck by the way she was holding her head high instead of being hunched in grief. What they could not see, however, was that, behind her veil, tears were streaming down her face.

* * *

Olive Cusworth was still feeling guilty. Despite her visit to the Minster the previous day, where she had been on her knees for a long time, she could not shake off the memory of discovering that Follis had been married. It had been wicked of him to pose as a bachelor and, in a sense, lead her on. She had entertained ideas about him that were decidedly improper. Had she known more about the character of her lodger, she would not have allowed him over the doorstep.

But it was her treatment of his wife that continued to cause the pain. Maude Follis was a woman in a dreadful predicament, losing a husband she had known and loved for many years. If he had died in an accident, it would have been bad enough. To learn that he had probably been murdered must have been devastating. His widow deserved the utmost care and support. Yet Olive had somehow been unable to provide it. Even after his death, Follis had a hold on her. She feared that vivid memories of him – and of his wife – would live in her mind forever.

Colbeck was interested to hear their report of the visit to Paul Godfrey. The man's description of a possible suspect was close to the one given by Nicholas Ewart.

'I spoke to him earlier,' Colbeck told them.

'We saw him working away in Coppergate,' said Hinton.

'I'm glad to hear it, Alan. It's what I advised.'

'When did you meet him, sir?' asked Leeming.

'At the murder scene,' said Colbeck.

They were seated in the lounge at the hotel, comparing notes of their respective activities. Colbeck gave them details of the murder and of his advice to Superintendent Nash. Leeming was very upset. He could not believe that anyone would wish to kill Miriam Brightwell.

'She was such a lovely woman,' he said. 'I remember her telling me what she'd seen on the day of the explosion at the station. Mrs Brightwell was so well spoken.'

'The lady was a close friend of Mr Ewart,' said Colbeck. 'That's why he arrived at the house in such a state. The poor man was shaking all over. When I'd calmed him down, I urged him to go back to work because he needed something else to occupy his mind.'

'I hope that you're finished with that case now, sir,' said Leeming.

'Yes and no.'

'It's nothing to do with you. We should concentrate on our own case.'

'And we will do, Victor. But there is a link between the two crimes.'

'Is there?'

'Mrs Brightwell gave us valuable information about a suspect in the other case,' said Colbeck. 'If I can be of use to the investigation into her death, I'll be happy to do so.'

'But that will mean you neglect the murder of Jack Follis, sir,' Hinton reminded him. 'Are you leaving us to proceed with that?'

'Not at all. It just means that I may give the superintendent the benefit of my advice from time to time. Our next step is quite simple. Now that we have three similar descriptions of a suspect,' said Colbeck, 'we can introduce him to the public.' He turned to Leeming. 'I want you to go back to Mr Godfrey to confirm the details he gave you, and to ask if he would allow an artist to come into his house.'

'But we don't have one, sir,' said Hinton.

'We soon will. I discussed the possibility earlier with Mr Gregory. He told me that the police use an artist who does this kind of work for them. We'll give him the three testimonies that we have and see if he can conjure the suspect up on paper.'

'What about Mr Ewart?' asked Leeming.

'There's no need to approach him,' said Colbeck. 'I'm certain that he will do anything to help us. Mrs Brightwell, alas, is no longer here to make her contribution but we have her description of the man.'

'What must I do, sir?' asked Hinton.

'Go to the police station. Get the name and address of the artist, then track him down. Explain what we want, then bring him here. Meanwhile,' he continued, 'I'll speak to Mr Maynard. He had those reward posters printed very quickly for us. I hope that he can do the same with the artist's impression.'

'What will our appeal say, sir?' asked Leeming.

'We'll keep it simple,' said Colbeck. 'It will be in block capitals – DO YOU KNOW THIS MAN?'

Alice Kendrick was relieved that the hostility between her and the Gale family had now disappeared. However, she regretted that it had taken the suicide of their daughter to bring it about. There was an immediate gain. If she happened to see Owen or Margery Gale when she was outside her house, she would get a friendly wave rather than a dark stare. That morning, she had even been able to exchange a few words with the fishmonger as he drove past on his cart.

Their new relationship, however, was not entirely

harmonious. The death of her cat continued to give her pain, and she still believed that Patch had been killed by Owen Gale. How could she find out the truth? Would there ever be a time when the two families were on such a footing that she felt able to discuss the fate of her cat? Alice doubted it.

Having got the address of the artist, Hinton left the police station and walked to a property near a wharf. Looking at the small, dingy, neglected house, he realised that Hugh Verrall, the artist, was struggling to make a living. Because the downstairs curtains were closed, Hinton was unable to peer in through the window. He used the knocker and waited. There was no sound of movement within the house. When he knocked ever harder, there was a muffled yell. Not long after, a man opened the door a few inches.

'What d'you want?' he snapped.

'Are you Mr Verrall?'

'Yes, I am.'

'I'm Detective Constable Hinton and I'm here to take part in the investigation of the explosion at the railway.'

'Then why are you bothering me?'

'We need your skills as an artist,' said Hinton. 'I've just come from the police station. They told me that you're very good at your job.'

'Yes, I am!' Verrall's tone became more polite. 'Well, if there's money involved, you'd better come in.'

He opened the door wide to reveal that he was wearing nothing but a ragged dressing gown. Verrall was a skinny man in his forties with long, stringy hair and a black beard salted with grey. He beckoned his visitor into the house and closed the front door. When they went into the front room, there was another shock for Hinton. A buxom young woman was standing in the corner, wearing a flimsy dressing gown over her naked body. Completely at ease, she gave Hinton a smile.

'Hello,' she said.

'This is Phoebe,' muttered the artist, indicating her. 'My model.'

Hinton was keenly aware that she had a closer relationship with the man than that. Artist materials were scattered everywhere but there was no easel up in readiness. What caught the eye was a rumpled daybed in the corner. Clearly, Hinton had interrupted the couple at an awkward moment. Phoebe was dispatched with a nod from Verrall. After she'd tripped out of the room, the artist turned to his visitor.

'How much are you offering?' he asked.

'You'll be well paid, sir.'

'I'd better be.'

Hinton explained what they wanted from the artist. Verrall, meanwhile, flung off his dressing gown to reveal a hirsute body. Unperturbed by the presence of a stranger, he slowly dressed himself. Hinton glanced around the room and was impressed by some of the paintings propped up against the walls. Most were portraits. One featuring Phoebe showed her posing naked and holding a small bird on the palm of one hand. There was a curious innocence about it.

'Right,' said Verrall, tucking a sketch pad under his arm. 'Let's go.'

* * *

Colbeck was waiting in the lounge when Leeming returned to the hotel. The sergeant reported that Paul Godfrey welcomed the idea of using the services of an artist and urged them to come to his house at any time. It was not long before Hinton returned with Hugh Verrall in tow. The artist was introduced to Colbeck and Leeming. He was less interested in helping to solve a major crime than in establishing his fee.

'Which one of you will pay me?' he asked.

'None of us,' said Colbeck. 'Mr Maynard will take care of that. He's the managing director of the NER.'

'I don't work for nowt.'

'We understand, Mr Verrall.'

'Where's this description, then?'

'I've got two of them,' said Leeming, taking out his notebook, 'and Constable Hinton has the other one in his notebook.'

'Give me the most detailed one,' said Verrall.

After flicking to the correct page, Leeming handed over the account given by Nicholas Ewart. As soon as he'd read it, Verrall produced a few swift preliminary sketches. They were astonished at how quickly he worked. The artist had even included part of the station in the background.

'That was just for practice,' he said. 'I'll give you more detail next time.'

Colbeck and Leeming were mesmerised. Their colleague was also impressed by the artist's obvious talent. In his case, however, Hinton was thinking about the nude portrait of Phoebe and her bird.

* * *

Newspaper reporters had descended on Miriam Brightwell's house. Horace Nash had to break off to give them a statement. Refusing to answer any questions at that stage, he went back to his interrogation of the servants. Ellie Duckett had recovered a little from the shock of seeing her employer lying dead in her bed. What she feared was that the image would haunt her forever.

'She was the kindest person I've ever met,' she told the superintendent. 'When I started here, I could barely read and write. Mrs Brightwell made me have an hour each day for lessons. Now and then, she taught me herself.'

'Did you ever see her wearing much jewellery?'

'Once or twice, that's all.'

'Then why did she have so much of it in her safe? One of the other servants showed me a list of what was in there. Why have such a collection when she so rarely wore any of it?'

'Mrs Brightwell did wear it when her husband was alive. Mr Brightwell always gave her a necklace or a ring for her birthday and at Christmas. He was very generous. When he died, she stopped wearing the lovely earrings he bought for her.'

'Which jewellery shop did he go to?'

'Oh, it was always Wymark's, sir,' said Ellie. 'Mr Brightwell believed they were the best in York.'

'I wouldn't know,' admitted Nash. 'Never had much call to buy jewellery. Apart from you and the other servants, who would have known what was locked away in that safe? In other words, did Mrs Brightwell ever show it to a friend?'

'She might have, sir.'

'But you can't be sure.'

'No, I can't.'

'Thank you, Ellie. It's brave of you to answer my questions. I know you must be very upset by what happened. That's all for now.'

Glad to escape, she headed for the door. Suddenly, she turned round.

'Oh, I've just remembered. There was someone she showed the jewellery to.'

'Who was it?'

'Archbishop William.'

Since he had been fascinated by the excavation in Coppergate, Hinton was given the task of speaking to Nicholas Ewart. The archaeologist broke off from his work.

'Is there any news?' he asked, breathily. 'Have they identified a suspect for the murder?'

'I'm sorry, sir,' apologised Hinton. 'I know nothing about the latest murder. I came here to talk to you about the explosion at the station.'

'Oh . . .' Ewart was deflated.

'Someone else has come forward with a description of the man you saw near the brake van. We've found an artist to draw a rough portrait of him, based on the new evidence. Can I show it to you?'

'Yes, of course.'

'Here we are, sir.'

Hinton showed him the first of the two sketches that he was carrying. Ewart studied it with great interest. Eventually, he shook his head.

'It's like the person I saw,' he said, 'but it's not him. I

remember the cap he wore whereas this man has a very different hat. And where's the little bag I saw?'

'The artist was working from a description provided by a gentleman who was in the coach next to the brake van. He watched the man for some time. Now,' said Hinton, putting the second sketch beside the first one. 'The artist read the statement that you gave us, and this is the result. Is this anything like the man you saw?'

'It's much closer to him,' replied Ewart, scrutinising it. 'He was taller, perhaps, and he was bent forward much more but well, this is a reasonable likeness.'

'Compare the two of them, please. There are similarities.'

'There are also differences. He was dressed as a tradesman. I remember that clearly. This man's attire is too neat and tidy. Yes, I know it's only a sketch, but I fancy that the person who gave you this description was looking at a totally different person.' Ewart handed the sketches back. 'I'm sorry. I'm only being honest.'

'Of course, sir,' said Hinton, hiding his disappointment.

'If you'll excuse me, I'll get back to work.'

Ewart turned away abruptly and joined his team.

Paul Godfrey gave a more positive response to the two sketches. When he visited the man, Leeming took the artist with him so that he could make any changes necessary.

'I congratulate you, Mr Verrall,' said Godfrey. 'With a few deft strokes, you've captured the essence of the man I saw. There are, however, a few things that need to be altered.'

'I'll do what you like,' said Verrall, 'as long as I get paid.'

'You will,' promised Leeming. 'You're happy with the

figure based on your evidence, Mr Godfrey,' he went on, 'but what about this other sketch that we've brought?'

He placed the portrait based on Ewart's account beside the other one. Godfrey blinked continually as he studied it, glancing at the earlier one occasionally. Having been impressed by the first sketch, he was clearly having doubts.

'We both saw the same man,' he decided at length, 'but we've remembered him differently. I didn't see any bag in his hand, for instance, and he was not wearing a cap like this one. Yet there's something about him that reminds me of the person I saw.' He turned to the artist. 'Let me suggest a few alterations.'

'Suggest as many as you like, sir,' said Verrall. 'When I know I'll get my fee, I'll make all the changes you want.'

'This is not about money,' said Leeming, sharply. 'It's about catching someone who caused the death of a guard and inflicted untold damage at the railway station. Don't you care about that?'

'Yes, of course. I want him caught as much as you do, Sergeant. There's just one thing I need to know.'

'What is it?'

'If my sketch helps to catch the man,' asked Verrall, 'do I get a bonus?'

CHAPTER TWENTY

As soon as Colbeck was given the final version of the suspect, he was impressed with the detail that the artist had incorporated. On the advice of Paul Godfrey, a couple of other figures had been sketched in lightly in the background. Despite his age, Godfrey's memory seemed to be functioning well. With great care, Colbeck added the wording to the poster. After consulting Gregory Maynard, he took it to the printers and placed an order. It was given immediate priority.

When he returned to the hotel, he was surprised to find a request from Horace Nash. Colbeck responded at once, taking a cab to Miriam Brightwell's house. There was less of a crowd outside it this time. The uniformed policeman guarding the front door recognised him at once and ushered him into the house. Nash was alone in the drawing room, staring at a sheet of paper. Seeing Colbeck, he jumped to his feet at once and crossed over to him.

'Thank you so much for coming, Inspector,' he said. 'I've no right to drag you away from your investigation, but I wanted to ask you a favour.'

'Have you encountered a problem?'

'Take a look at this,' said Nash, handing him the sheet of paper. 'It's an inventory of what was in Mrs Brightwell's safe when it was plundered.'

'Good gracious!' said Colbeck, glancing at the list of items and noticing their value. 'This is a substantial amount of jewellery.'

'Yet, since the death of her husband, Mrs Brightwell never wore any of it. I asked one of the servants if her mistress ever showed the jewellery to anyone else.'

'What was the response?'

'The one person who was allowed to see it was the archbishop.'

'That is strange,' said Colbeck. 'Have you questioned him about this?'

'No,' admitted Nash, almost sheepishly. 'I was hoping you might do that for me. I'm never at ease talking to anyone from the Minster. The one time I tried to have a conversation with Archbishop William, I was almost tongue-tied. I don't know why. I'm sure that you could talk to him without feeling . . . well, out of place in the Minster.'

'Archbishop William is not always there. As you know, he lives at Bishopthorpe Palace to the south of the city.'

'Either place makes me nervous.'

'How necessary is it, Superintendent?'

'Something tells me that it's important,' said the other.

'As a detective, you will have had the same feeling as I did. A stray clue falls into your hands, and you just know that you must follow it up.'

'Or find someone else to do it,' said Colbeck with a smile.

In a sense, he was glad that Nash had approached him. It showed how much the superintendent had learnt to trust his rival. For a man as big and fearless as Nash, it had taken a real effort to confess to a weakness.

'Very well,' agreed Colbeck. 'But I can't go immediately.'

'I can wait. All I ask is that you don't tell anyone why you need to speak to Archbishop William. It would make my officers look at me askance, if they knew that I was afraid of a harmless man in rich vestments and a mitre.'

'I daresay that he takes the mitre off when he's at home.'

Nash offered his hand. 'Thank you, Inspector.'

'I'll let you know what happens,' said Colbeck.

Their handshake was firm and meaningful. They could never bring themselves to like each other but at least they could work effectively together. Colbeck now had enough policemen as he wished to call upon. Talking to an archbishop was the least that he could do in return. Besides, he was very much looking forward to it.

Once the reward posters had been printed, Leeming collected them and asked for the invoice to be sent to Gregory Maynard. The sergeant then enlisted Hinton and the two of them put up the posters at the railway station on top of the ones already on display. Passengers with keen eyesight would notice that the reward had been increased. Leeming gave Hinton his orders.

'That's enough work for us, Alan,' he said. 'Let the police put up the rest of the posters. They'll know the best places to display them.'

'They're ready to help us now,' said Hinton, 'so why not make use of them?'

'Exactly.'

'By the way, what did you think of the artist?'

'Verrall was an interesting character. I liked him – though I wish that he didn't keep talking about money.'

'He lives in a small house in a rough area. Every penny counts for him.'

'Artists can't all be rich and famous,' said Leeming. 'When you went to his studio, did you see any of his paintings?'

'Yes,' replied Hinton, recalling the one of Phoebe. 'They're very . . . striking.'

'Then good luck to him. Verrall did exactly what we asked of him. I just hope that his poster catches people's attention.'

'I'll take the rest of them around to the police station,' said Hinton. 'It's good to have them on our side at last.'

Bishopthorpe Palace was an impressive country house standing on the banks of the River Ouse. Set in a wooded area, it included a gatehouse, stables, a brewhouse and a brewer's cottage. When he saw the front elevation, Colbeck realised that it was a house with medieval origins. He alighted from his cab and headed for the entrance.

Since he knew how busy the archbishop would be, the most he expected was an appointment in the future. On hearing that he had a visit from a Scotland Yard inspector, however, Archbishop William sent for him immediately. Colbeck was taken to a large study.

'Good day to you, Inspector,' said the archbishop, rising behind his desk. 'This is an unexpected pleasure.'

'It's an honour to meet you, Your Grace. I'm ashamed to say that in all the time we've been here, I've yet to step inside the Minster.'

'Your work has obviously preoccupied you.'

He indicated two chairs, either side of a low table. They sat opposite each other. Colbeck glanced around the room.

'This must be a wonderful place to live,' he observed.

'It has its drawbacks, I'm afraid. Some of the rooms are akin to igloos in the winter, but we've learnt to live with that. The problem with a house so old and large is that it does give one a sense of undeserved importance.'

'In your case, I suspect that it's well deserved. However,' said Colbeck, 'I won't take up any more of your time than is necessary. I came in connection with a murder investigation.'

'Yes, I'm very much aware of what happened at the railway station.'

'I'm talking about the murder of Mrs Brightwell earlier today.'

'Heavens!' exclaimed the other. 'What a tragedy! Word reached me while we were having breakfast. I've not been able to touch a morsel of food ever since.'

'I understand that you knew the lady well.'

'I knew and admired her, Inspector. She was a remarkable person in every way. Mrs Brightwell was among the first people to invite us to her home when my wife and I came to York. One only had to look at her,' he went on, 'to realise that one was in the company of a true Christian.'

'I had the same feeling, Your Grace.'

'Do the police have any suspects in mind?'

'Not yet, but Superintendent Nash is working hard on the case. He showed me the inventory of what was kept in her safe. Its contents were all stolen, I fear, but at least we know what they were. That will make tracing some of them much easier.' He paused for a moment to measure his words. 'I understand that Mrs Brightwell once showed you some of the jewellery she kept in her safe.'

'She was kind enough to hand over the most important item,' said the other. 'We had been invited there for that express purpose. My wife and I had the most delicious meal, I must say. Afterwards, Mrs Brightwell conducted us to a room with a large table in the middle of it. Several items were on display but there was only one that caught my attention.'

'What was it, Your Grace?'

'It was a most beautiful crucifix, encrusted with diamonds. The dear lady wanted to donate it to the Minster. It's now on the altar in one of the side chapels. I was absolutely thrilled,' he went on. 'My wife, however, was equally thrilled by the jewellery laid out on the table. It was of the highest quality.'

'I gathered that.'

'We were therefore surprised to be told that she had never worn any of it since the death of her husband. It seemed such a shame to us. Why keep such treasured items hidden away in a safe? They deserved to be on display and giving pleasure to the person wearing them. Then,' continued the archbishop, 'Mrs Brightwell said the most surprising thing. I thought at first that she was joking, but she was quite serious.'

'What was it that she said?' asked Colbeck.

'That she had always dreamt of being married in the Minster.'

'I daresay that many ladies have shared that dream.'

'In their cases, it would simply be a fantasy. For Mrs Brightwell, it was more of an ambition. She wondered if I would consent to take the marriage service.'

'Did she have a second husband in mind?'

'No, but she hoped that one might come along in due course.'

'If it's not a rude question,' said Colbeck, 'had wine been served during dinner?'

'Oh, yes, and Mrs Brightwell had more than her share of it. But I don't believe you can explain away her declaration by saying that she was inebriated.'

'Were you given a reason why she wished to remarry at some point?'

'We were, indeed – and it rather shocked us.'

'Why was that?'

'Well, since you've met her, you know what a poised lady she was.'

'I'm told that she was poised and sophisticated,' said Colbeck, approvingly. 'It would have been a pleasure to meet the lady.'

'Mrs Brightwell was not poised on that occasion, Inspector. She told us that she would consider getting married for a second time because she would be able to wear her jewellery once again.' He spread his arms. 'Don't you find that strange?'

* * *

As he delivered the rest of the reward posters to the police station, Alan Hinton was given a surprise by the desk sergeant. After peering intently at the face on the poster, the man snapped his fingers.

'I think I know who this is,' he said. 'Adam Tranter.'

'Where can we find him?'

'I'll give you his last known address, but he's unlikely to be there.'

'Then where will he be?' asked Hinton.

'Who knows? Since he came out of prison six months ago, he's kept out of trouble. That suits us. Tranter has been spotted doing odd jobs around the city, so maybe he wants to live an honest life at last – until he runs out of money, that is. Then he'll go back to his old trade as a burglar.'

'Are you sure that he's still in York?' asked Leeming.

'Oh, yes. This is his territory. Tranter would never leave.'

'Is he the sort of man who'd bear a grudge against the railway station?'

'He bears a grudge against everything and everybody,' said the duty sergeant. 'Tranter is one of those people born to hate.'

Colbeck was careful to choose his words when he met up with Horace Nash again. He explained that he had seen Archbishop William at his palace and found him eager to help them. When he described the display of jewellery on a table, he stressed that it was the jewelled crucifix that impressed the visitors most. He told Nash that Mrs Brightwell made a light-hearted reference to a second marriage.

'That surprises me,' said the superintendent. 'There was nothing at all light-hearted about the lady. She was always so serious.'

'Apparently, she had been drinking.'

'That, too, is out of character.'

'You know the lady better than I do, so I'll defer to your judgement. On the other hand,' he went on, 'I did get the impression that she had a lot of unfulfilled ambitions. Like so many women, she was thwarted by lack of opportunities.'

Nash smirked. 'Is that such a bad thing, Inspector?'

'Yes, I think it is.'

'Then we must disagree. There's a man's world, like the one you and I live in, and there's a woman's world. That's as it should be.'

'I take issue with you on that score,' said Colbeck. 'Women are unfairly held back.'

'Would you trust one of them to work alongside you?'

'In theory, I would.'

'Then what happens if they face an angry crowd as I did when Tom Quinn had the gall to organise that march? No woman could have stood up to them the way that I did.'

'I agree,' said Colbeck. 'She would have solved the problem by other means.' He went on quickly as Nash started to bluster. 'But let's not fall out over the role assigned to the female members of our population. You have a murder to solve and so do we.'

'That's true. Arguments will get us nowhere. At least I now know why the jewellery was shown to the archbishop and his wife. Thank you for your help, Inspector. You did something that I was very uneasy about.'

'Archbishop William is only human, just like you or me.'

'Then why does he scare me a little?'

'Perhaps he makes you feel guilty,' said Colbeck with a grin.

'You could be right,' confessed Nash.

'At all events, you can take his name off your list of suspects. There's one thing of which I can assure you, Superintendent. Whoever killed Mrs Brightwell and stole her jewellery, it was certainly not Archbishop William.'

Giving him a farewell wave, Colbeck left the house.

'And this is the Minster,' said Madeleine, turning over the page to show her visitor a photograph. 'It says here that it's the second largest Gothic cathedral ever built.'

'It looks enormous.'

'I daresay that Victor might get a chance to go into it.'

'I doubt it,' said Estelle with a laugh. 'The only thing that will interest him in York is one of the cocoa factories. He's still a boy at heart, really.'

Madeleine had been surprised when her friend turned up at the house. Unlike her, Estelle Leeming could not afford to hail a taxi whenever she needed one. Getting to the Colbeck residence involved a long and tiring walk. Estelle had made the effort to see if there was good news about the investigation. When told the information that came that morning in a letter from York, Estelle had been depressed. Madeleine had tried to cheer her up by showing her the photographs in the book given her by Lydia Quayle. It had provided a distraction for a short while, but Estelle was not really concentrating on what she was seeing.

'I suppose that I should prepare for the worst,' she sighed.

'Don't be downhearted, Estelle.'

'Murder cases always take such a long time.'

'That's not true,' said Madeleine. 'They've been lucky more than once. And they now have the police force working with them at last. That will make a huge difference.'

'It's such bad luck that Victor is so far away from London.'

'A fast train might get him back in an afternoon.'

'But he's not free to catch it, Madeleine, is he?'

'I'm afraid not.'

'Albert will get over it in time,' said his mother, 'but it's going to upset him. It will upset David as well, of course. He's dying to see his father back home.'

'Helena Rose is the same. She asks about Robert every day.'

'Maybe it was our fault for marrying policemen.'

Madeleine smiled. 'I've never regretted it for a moment,' she said.

'Neither have I. Look,' Estelle went on, reaching out to grasp her friend's arm, 'if, by any chance, you do get to hear better news . . .'

'Then I'll make sure I pass it on to you immediately. I'm not having you walking all the way here again. I'll find a way to get a message to you, Estelle.'

'Thank you, Madeleine.'

And I'm going to insist on paying for a cab to get you safely home again.'

'Oh, I couldn't let you do that.'

'Try stopping me!'

* * *

Colbeck decided to visit Coppergate so that he could see how Nicholas Ewart was getting on. The archaeologist had reacted to the news of Miriam Brightwell's death as if she were a member of his family. When the cab dropped him off, Colbeck walked to the site, almost certain that he would find Ewart immersed in his work in one of the trenches. In fact, there was no sign of him. It was worrying.

Colbeck summoned the oldest member of the team at the site. He was a lanky man in his thirties with an intense stare.

'Where is Mr Ewart?' asked Colbeck.

'He's had to go home, sir. Nick had some very bad news.'

'Yes, I know about that. I advised him to come back here but he is obviously unable to concentrate. Are you in charge?'

'Yes, sir,' replied the man. 'Nick took some of the day's finds home with him. When it's time to leave the site, I'll gather up everything that's come to light since he left. He wanted it delivered to his house.'

'And where exactly is that . . . ?'

After the trudge back from the police station, Leeming and Hinton were looking forward to a rest at the hotel. When they got there, however, there was a message for them. It was delivered by Henry Kemp, the duty manager.

'I was asked to pass on some information by the stationmaster,' he said.

'What is it?' asked Leeming.

'He'd like a word with one of you.'

'Did he say why?'

'He didn't say anything,' replied Kemp, 'because he

didn't come in person. One of the porters delivered the message by word of mouth.'

'That's good enough for me,' said Hinton. 'Thank you for telling us.'

He and Leeming set off for the railway station at once. A summons from the stationmaster meant that he had something important to tell them. The fatigue in their legs had disappeared now. They were almost skipping along. As they entered the station, they looked around but saw no sign of Frederick Staines. It was only when a train pulled away from a platform that they realised the stationmaster had been behind it. He gave them a friendly wave.

Hinton was certain that they were about to hear something useful, but Leeming was wary. He said that it was better to lower their expectations and save themselves the pain of disappointment. But his advice failed to remove the broad smile on Hinton's face. Because Staines was hurrying towards them, they quickened their own pace. When they met, the stationmaster was panting.

'You sent us a message,' said Leeming.

'It was intended for Inspector Colbeck, really,' Staines told them.

'Is it good news?' asked Hinton.

'It could be.'

'Then please tell us what it is.'

'Them posters you put up earlier aroused a lot of interest. Passengers arriving and leaving took a good look at them. One gentleman reckoned that he knew exactly who the man was.'

'And who was he?'

'It was someone called Adam Tranter.'

'I knew it!' said Hinton in delight.

'Was this man certain it was Tranter?' asked Leeming.

'Oh, yes. There was no question about it. The gentleman had good reason to remember him.'

'Why was it?'

'Four or five years ago, Tranter tried to burgle his house.'

Armed with directions, Colbeck soon reached the house. When he saw how close it was to the Minster, he promised himself that he would take a peep inside it. For the moment, Ewart took precedence. Colbeck used the doorbell and was soon looking into the face of a servant.

'Mr Ewart is not seeing visitors today,' the man told him. 'He is unwell.'

'He looked in good health when I saw him earlier. Perhaps you could tell him that Inspector Colbeck wishes to see him.'

'Oh, I see . . . In that case, please step inside.'

Colbeck was left standing in the hall while the servant disappeared. In what seemed like only a few moments, Ewart himself came into view, full of apologies. He led his visitor into the drawing room, and they sat down.

'The servant took my orders too literally,' said Ewart. 'When I said that he must turn people away, I should have told him that there were honourable exceptions. You are one of them, Inspector.'

'I'm gratified to hear that, but sorry to learn you're unwell.'

'It's the sickness that comes with grief, I'm afraid. If you went to find me in Coppergate, they'll have told you I was simply unable to do anything. My body had turned to jelly.' He flicked a hand. 'However, my problems are not important.' He leant forward. 'Have you brought any news?'

'I suppose that you could call it that, sir.'

'Then tell me – please tell me.'

Colbeck explained that Superintendent Nash had asked for his help, though he made no mention of the latter's discomfort in the presence of the eminent prelate. He went on to tell Ewart what had happened when Archbishop William and his wife had been invited to dinner by Mrs Brightwell. Ewart was curious.

'That's odd behaviour for Mrs Brightwell,' he said. 'She and her husband were so well matched that I couldn't imagine her letting another man anywhere near her. As for the display of jewellery, however, Archbishop William and his wife were not the only visitors allowed to see it. My wife and I dined there once, and Mrs Brightwell insisted that her husband showed us what he had bought for her over the years. Each purchase represented a birthday, an anniversary, or a special date of some sort. He was in no way showing off,' emphasised Ewart. 'He just wanted us to see how much he adored his wife.'

'What did Mrs Ewart think of the display?'

'Charlotte was envious, of course, and may even have wished she'd married someone with greater wealth than I will ever have. But it was Mrs Brightwell's reaction that interested her.'

'In what way, sir?'

'Well, we were aware that she and her husband were known for their philanthropy. They were genuine benefactors with a natural desire to help others. But

308

Charlotte saw a glint in our hostess's eye that really shocked her. She told me afterwards that it was as if Mrs Brightwell was gloating over her jewellery. In truth,' said Ewart, 'I saw no indication of it, but women have keener instincts.'

'I agree with you wholeheartedly.'

'Until now, I'd quite forgotten that dinner party,' admitted Ewart, 'but Mrs Brightwell's bearing on that occasion did show her in a slightly different light. It didn't affect my admiration of her in any way, mind you. She remained an important figure in my life. But the fact is,' he concluded, 'that what Archbishop William and his wife must have regarded as unexpected behaviour had been seen by us years ago.'

Leeming and Hinton had returned to the hotel. Their excitement at hearing that a second person had identified the face on the reward poster as that of Adam Tranter was diminished by the fact that the man in question had left York on business.

'Nevertheless,' said Hinton, 'we've had another person who identified him. We may have a few more tomorrow.'

'Thanks must go to Mr Godfrey.'

'And to the other witnesses.'

'It was Mr Godfrey who provided some crucial details. He sat beside Verrall as the artist did one version after another.'

'Have you ever wanted to have a portrait of yourself, Sergeant?'

Leeming laughed. 'Who'd want to look at a picture of my ugly mug?'

'Your wife and children would.'

'They prefer to see me in the flesh.'

'Then you could have a portrait with your clothes off,' teased Hinton. 'Verrall is very good at drawing figures in the nude.'

'Well, he's not going to have me as a model,' said Leeming, huffily.

They were seated in the lounge and were soon joined by Colbeck, who swept in and removed his top hat before sitting opposite them. He studied Leeming.

'Your cheeks are looking rather red, Victor. Have you been running?'

'No, but we had a brisk walk back from the police station.'

'Why did you go there?'

'We were following a lead, sir,' said Hinton. 'When I delivered those posters to the police station, the duty sergeant thought he could identify the man. His name is Adam Tranter. And a second person has picked him out.'

'That sounds promising,' said Colbeck.

Hinton went on to explain what they had been doing in the inspector's absence. When he heard that the second man who provided the suspect's name was now on his way to London, Colbeck was disappointed.

'Let's start with the police,' he suggested. 'Since this man is well known to them, they are much more likely to find him than we are. Go back to the police station, Alan, and ask them to institute an immediate search for Tranter.'

'What if the superintendent objects, sir?'

'Oh, there's no chance of that happening.'

'How can you be so sure?' asked Leeming.

'It's because I've done him two favours,' said Colbeck.

'I not only offered him free advice about the latest murder, I saved him from the ordeal of talking to Archbishop William.'

'Was it such an ordeal?'

'It was for him, Victor. In fact, I had a pleasant conversation with the archbishop. Without realising it, he told me what to do next.'

'And what's that?'

'While Alan is organising a search for Adam Tranter, you and I are going to one of the city's jewellery shops.'

Everyone knew Bobby Bray. He was a wizened old man with a white beard, and he played his violin at the railway station in the hope that passengers might drop money into the upturned cap he left on the platform. He had a limited repertoire, but his lively jigs were very popular. Coins had been flicked into his cap regularly. When his arms started to ache too much, he abandoned his work and gathered up his money. Bray had been wondering why passengers had been stopping to look at some new posters that had been put up. With his violin under his arm, he sauntered across to one of them and peered at it through milky eyes.

'Jesus!' he cried.

Turning on his heel, he scuttled out of the station and went into a maze of streets. When he arrived at a dilapidated house, he let himself in and went upstairs. Bray knocked on the first door he came to.

'Who is it?' growled a voice from inside the room.

'It's me,' replied Bray. 'It's old Bobby.'

'What d'you want?'

'I've come to warn you, Adam.'

'Why?'

'Open the door and I'll tell you.'

The door was unlocked and flung open. Adam Tranter peered at him. He was a sturdy, middle-aged man with eyes that seemed to carry a permanent threat in them.

'What's this about a warning, Bobby?'

'Don't go anywhere near the station.'

'Why not?'

'They've put up a poster with your face on it.'

'Eh?'

'There's a price on your head, Adam.'

'You're pulling my leg,' said Tranter, dismissively.

'I wouldn't dare do that. We're friends.'

'Sometimes.'

'Go and see for yourself,' advised Bray, 'but go in disguise. If I can recognise you when I'm half-blind, then other people may do the same. In your position, I'd get out of York as fast as my old legs'd carry me.'

'But you're not me, are you?' said Tranter.

'No, I'm not, Adam.'

'Nobody frightens me away.'

'I'm just trying to do you a favour. Don't I get any thanks?'

By way of reply, Tranter went into the room and slammed the door shut.

They went to the premises of Joseph Wymark and Son, a long-established business that specialised in expensive jewellery. It was in a narrow, twisting, cobbled street. Leeming looked enviously at the display in the front window of the shop.

312

'I wish I could afford to buy something from here, sir.'

'Then you'll have to find another job,' said Colbeck. 'The Metropolitan Police Force is not known for the generosity of its pay scales.'

'Look at those rings – they're beautiful!'

'There are much better and more expensive ones inside, Victor. No jeweller puts his finest ware in the front window where it might be the victim of a smash and grab raid. Anything of real value will be locked away in a safe. It would only be taken out to show to trusted customers – like Mr and Mrs Brightwell.'

Leeming was puzzled. 'Is that why we're here?'

'Yes, it is.'

'But we weren't sent to York to solve a murder that involved stolen jewellery. We're investigating an explosion at the railway station.'

'What if there's a connection between the two cases?'

'There's no evidence to support that idea.'

'Then why do I have this strange feeling?'

'Oh, no!' moaned Leeming. 'Those strange feelings of yours always mean that we take much longer to make an arrest. Why can't we just solve one crime and go home?'

'All will become clear in due course, Victor. Come on,' said Colbeck, reaching for the doorknob. 'Let's go into the shop and talk to them about Mrs Brightwell.'

After a gesture of despair, Leeming followed him.

Horace Nash was seated in the drawing room at the Brightwell house, going through his notes carefully. When a policeman interrupted him, the superintendent was annoyed.

'I told you to leave me in peace,' he snapped.

'There's someone who wishes to speak to you, sir,' said the other.

'If it's Inspector Colbeck, let him in. If it's anybody else, tell them that I'm too busy to see them.'

'But the gentleman insists that he has information for you.'

Nash screwed up one eye. 'What sort of information?'

'He didn't say, sir.'

'What's his name?'

'Mr Ewart.'

'Ah,' said Nash, getting to his feet. 'You'd better send him in.'

Moments later, Nicholas Ewart entered the room. He apologised for barging in but felt that he had to come. The archaeologist looked far more composed than he had been when he first burst into the house. It seemed as if he had mastered his grief enough to think clearly about what had happened.

'I had a visit from Inspector Colbeck earlier on,' said Ewart.

'Why did he come to you?'

'He wanted to talk about Mrs Brightwell's jewellery. I remembered an incident that took place when I and my late wife, Charlotte, were invited to dinner at this house. Mrs Brightwell's husband was alive at the time. He showed us a display of the jewellery he'd bought his wife. Charlotte was envious, of course, but she was also realistic. There was no way that I could afford to buy such things. Besides, Charlotte and I had never been acquisitive.'

'Is there a point to this story, sir?' asked Nash, politely.

'I'm just coming to it.'

'Good.'

'Inspector Colbeck's visit jogged my memory,' said Ewart. 'Until that point, I'd been unable to think straight. After the inspector had gone, I remembered Mrs Brightwell telling me that she never wore any of the jewellery locked away in the safe, but that she took it out from time to time so that she could polish and admire it. In the privacy of her bedroom, she admitted, she loved to wear some of it and stand in front of her mirror. Frankly,' he went on, 'I was shocked. Mrs Brightwell had always struck me as being above such things. To begin with, she was a devoted churchgoer, much more likely to read the Bible than adorn herself with jewellery.'

'None of her servants mentioned this habit,' said Nash.

'It was her secret, Superintendent. She was an intensely private woman.'

'Why did she confide in you?'

'I like to think that it was because she trusted me. After all, we had a mutual interest in treasure,' said Ewart. 'Mrs Brightwell's came from a jewellery shop and mine came from beneath the earth. Vikings were not averse to precious items, you know. We've found several ornamental brooches.'

'What are you suggesting, sir?'

'I'm convinced that I was not the only person taken into her confidence. Other people might have been told about her passion for jewellery, even shown a display of it. I'm not pointing a finger at anyone,' said Ewart, swiftly, 'but what if one of those people found the temptation irresistible?'

'It's possible, I suppose.'

'All I'm suggesting is that you might look more closely at Mrs Brightwell's close friends. Clearly, none of them would be able to steal the contents of that safe themselves. However,' said Ewart, 'as you know better than anyone, there are burglars for hire in this city.'

'We've arrested a few of them, sir.'

'Then you may have to arrest another one – along with his paymaster.'

After a few moments, Nash gave him a nod of gratitude.

'I'll need the names of Mrs Brightwell's circle,' he said.

When he arrived at the police station, Alan Hinton was met with a disappointing response. The duty sergeant told him that he had no power to authorise a major search for Adam Tranter. What he could do, however, was to give them the services of one man. Hinton was shocked.

'What use is that?' he said.

'Wait until you meet Constable Shawcross,' advised the duty sergeant. 'He has a great reputation for finding crooks.'

'We expected more help.'

'Len is all you need.'

When the constable was summoned, Hinton was less than impressed. Leonard Shawcross was a grizzled veteran, close to retirement age. His body was slack, and his eyelids were barely apart. Given his orders by the duty sergeant, he looked at Hinton then gave him a lazy smile. The two of them left the police station.

'Have you any idea where to find Tranter?' asked Hinton.

'No, I don't,' confessed the other, 'but I know someone who does.'

'Who is he?'

'Bobby Bray. He plays a violin at the railway station.'

'Is that where he is now?'

'No, he'll be at the White Lion, probably. We'll start there.'

Hinton was faintly reassured. Shawcross led him towards an area of the city that had ugly, terraced housing and an assortment of public houses. The White Lion stood on a corner as if leaning against its neighbour for support. The two of them went into the building to be met by a noisome fug. It took them a few moments to adjust to it.

'Who are you after this time, Len?' asked the barman.

'Bobby,' said Shawcross.

'He's next door.'

'Good. I thought he might be.'

With Hinton at his heels, Shawcross pushed his way through the crowd and went into a smaller and even smokier room. Seated in the corner was Bobby Bray with his violin on the table in front of him. After a swig from his tankard, he gazed up at the newcomers.

'Are you looking for me?' he asked.

'No,' replied Shawcross, 'but we're looking for a friend of yours.'

'Who's that?'

'Adam Tranter.'

'He's got no friends,' said Bray, sourly.

'Where is he, Bobby?'

'How should I know?'

'It's because you do him favours now and then,' said Shawcross. 'You're the only man in York who can bear him, and you know where he lives.'

'Well, he's not here any more,' protested Bray. 'I can tell you that. His face is on a poster that's been put up everywhere. There's a big reward offered. Adam must have seen the poster. He's probably a hundred miles away from here by now.'

Wearing a hat to conceal most of his face, Adam Tranter walked slowly into the railway station and looked around to make sure that he was unobserved. He then drifted across to the poster on the wall nearby. It shocked him. Bobby Bray's warning had been timely. Tranter was the target of a manhunt. He left the station at once.

CHAPTER TWENTY-ONE

Nobody was as acutely aware of Robert Colbeck's unique skills as Edward Tallis. Over the years, the superintendent had watched him solve murder after murder, often by the strangest means. His admiration of the inspector, however, was shadowed by what he saw as the man's defects. Chief among them was his maddening habit of being economical with the facts. When the superintendent wanted a full report, he was often fobbed off with a few lines. Colbeck had not even managed that today. He had sent a telegraph so terse that it was almost derisory. After reading it through again and again, Tallis cast it aside in dismay.

'What does he mean by helping the police?' he cried. 'I went all the way to York to ensure that the police were helping *him*.'

He broke off to reach for the cigar glowing in his ashtray.

After putting it into his mouth, he inhaled deeply then sent a cloud of smoke rising to the ceiling.

'Our sole interest in being in York,' he said, 'is in solving the crime reported to us by the North Eastern Railway. Why isn't he obeying orders?'

It was a rhetorical question. Tallis knew only too well that Colbeck was likely to disobey any orders that restricted his freedom to act independently. Most of the time, the inspector's departures from correct procedure yielded good results. On this occasion, however, there seemed to be no hope of that. Colbeck had apparently set one murder case aside so that he could assist someone who was struggling with another one. As Tallis's temper began to rise, his teeth were clenched, and his heart began to pound.

There was only one way to provoke Colbeck into action and to get regular accounts of his progress sent to Scotland Yard. Taking a sheet of paper from his desk, Tallis wrote three words on it.

Joining you soon.

When the message arrived in York in the form of a telegraph, Tallis knew that he would get the response that he wanted. It was a justified act of dishonesty.

'That will light a fire under you, Inspector,' he said with a chuckle.

Colbeck was wary. He and Leeming were back at the hotel when he received a message from Horace Nash. It made him sigh. The superintendent was asking to meet him as soon as possible. There was a note of urgency in his letter. Colbeck's immediate response was to say that he was unavailable until the evening. Second thoughts then began to surface. He reminded himself that there were, in his opinion, links between the two investigations.

'Superintendent Nash needs me,' he said.

'Let him solve his murder on his own,' counselled Leeming.

'I daresay that he only wants my advice.'

'You know what mine is, sir. Stay well clear of him.'

'I'm sorry, Victor. It could be important.'

'So is my son's birthday,' said Leeming under his breath.

Colbeck left the lounge and walked to the nearest cab rank. It was not long before he was arriving at the Brightwell house. Nash was waiting for him in the drawing room.

'What were you doing in that jewellery shop?' asked the superintendent. 'My men have sharp eyes. You and the sergeant were spotted going into the shop owned by Joe Wymark and his son.'

'It's where every item of Mrs Brightwell's collection was bought. I was interested to learn more about the lady and her husband.'

'Then you've come to the right place, Inspector.'

'Have I?'

'Yes,' said Nash. 'I had a visit earlier from Mr Ewart. The initial shock of learning about the fate of his close friend has worn off a little. Now that he's able to think straight, he's been wondering about Mrs Brightwell's jewellery, and he came up with an interesting suggestion.'

He went on to tell Colbeck what the archaeologist had said. At first, Nash confessed, he thought that Ewart's suggestion was worthy of consideration. On reflection, however, he had dismissed it.

'You made a sensible decision,' said Colbeck.

'Did I?'

'Both of us agreed that the burglar came to kill before he stole. Surely, nobody in Mrs Brightwell's circle would countenance a murder. One of them might lust after her jewellery, but I can't really see that he would have the urge to steal it if a violent attack were involved. The risk would be far too great.'

'Are you saying that Mr Ewart's suggestion had no value at all?'

'It sounds like the idea of a man who is desperate to help,' said Colbeck. 'Mr Ewart was, to some extent, in awe of Mrs Brightwell. News of her murder knocked him almost senseless.'

'We both saw that,' agreed Nash.

'Now that he is recovering slightly, he has been casting around for a means of identifying the killer. This idea popped into his mind. I daresay that others will do so as well. Bear with him, Superintendent,' advised Colbeck. 'The man is in pain.'

'I feel sorry for him.'

'As for the visit to Wymark's, it was more than worthwhile. I not only learnt a great deal about Mr and Mrs Brightwell, I discovered that there had been a burglary at the shop a month or so ago.'

Nash was offended. 'Then why weren't we called in at once?'

'Don't take it so personally,' said Colbeck. 'If news of a burglary at a jewellery shop spread, it could deter potential customers from patronising the place. The owners prefer – wisely, in my view – to exercise discretion. I've only told you because I know that you will respect their decision.'

'Well, I suppose I do . . . to some extent. What was stolen?'

'The jewellery was untouched.'

'Then why go to the trouble of breaking into the premises?'

'The burglar took something that may prove to be extremely valuable.'

'And what was that?'

'He opened a locked cupboard that contained the files. Every client was listed in alphabetical order, along with a record of their purchases. The Brightwell file was among those taken away,' said Colbeck. 'Do you see what this means?'

'Yes, I do,' replied Nash. 'He knew exactly what was in her collection and how much each item cost.'

'All that he had to do was to find out where it was kept, and how he could best get to it. The crime was planned well in advance and the necessity of killing Mrs Brightwell was accepted.'

'What about the shop's other clients?'

'The customers whose files were stolen have already been warned,' explained Colbeck, 'so they'll have taken additional security measures. Nobody wants a spate of burglaries in York.'

'We certainly don't,' said Nash, grimly.

Under duress, Bobby Bray led them through the streets. He kept complaining that he should be at the railway station, earning money with his violin. Constable Shawcross ignored him, but Hinton wanted to know more about the man.

'How long have you played the violin?' he asked.

'Seems like a lifetime,' grumbled Bray.

'You must have seen a lot of changes happening in York.'

'Changes are what other people notice. They pass me by. My days are just the same now as they were sixty years ago.'

'Except that there was no railway station then.'

'True.'

'Yet that's where you play every day. I'd say that was a big change.'

Bray looked at him. 'I'm a musician,' he said. 'I play the same tunes now that I played when I first learnt how to hold my fiddle.' He came to a sudden halt. 'This is as far as I go.'

'Why?' asked Hinton.

'Because I don't want Adam to see me with a policeman.'

'You told us he'd have disappeared,' Shawcross reminded him.

'I'm taking no chances.'

'Where's the house, then?'

Bray gave them directions, then added a heartfelt plea.

'If you do nab him, you won't tell him that I brought you here, will you?'

'No,' promised Shawcross.

Leaving him there, the two of them went around the corner to a row of houses in a dreadful state of disrepair. Windows were cracked, slates had fallen off the roof and there was a woebegone air to the whole terrace. They went to the address they'd been given and found the front door unlocked. Shawcross clambered up the staircase with Hinton at his heels. The policeman turned to him.

'Tranter always puts up a fight,' he warned.

'I'll be ready for him,' said Hinton.

Shawcross raised a fist to pound on the door but, as soon as he hit it, the door swung open. The room was small, filthy and noxious. Apart from the table and one chair, the only thing there was the badly stained mattress in the corner. There were obvious signs of a swift departure by its former occupant.

'How can anyone live like this?' asked Hinton in disgust.

'He's gone,' said Shawcross. 'Must have seen his face on that poster.'

One of the first things that Colbeck did when they arrived in York had been to arrange with the nearby telegraph station to deliver any messages for him to Scawin's Hotel. Leeming was in the lounge when he saw one of the clerks come into the building. He went off quickly to intercept him.

'Is that for Inspector Colbeck?' he asked.

'Yes,' said the clerk.

'I'm Sergeant Leeming. I'll pass it on to him.'

'Very good, sir.'

After handing the telegraph to him, the clerk went back to the station. Though he was dying to read the message, Leeming knew that he would have to bide his time. Less than ten minutes later, Colbeck came in through the front door. Leeming went across to him.

'This came for you, sir,' he said, handing the telegraph over.

Colbeck opened the envelope and glanced at the message. 'It's from Superintendent Tallis,' he said.

'What does he say?'

'See for yourself.'

Leeming read the three words and beamed. 'He's coming soon,' he said. 'That will speed things up. The superintendent will make sure that we spend all our time on the crime we were sent here to solve.'

'He's just trying to scare us, Victor.'

'Well, I'm not frightened. To be honest, sir, I'm delighted.'

'Your delight is short-lived, I fear. This threat of a second visit here is in response to the rather short telegraph I sent the superintendent earlier today. He will soon receive a much more detailed report in the letter I sent yesterday. As soon as he reads that,' said Colbeck, confidently, 'he will decide to stay where he is.'

Having spent twenty minutes with the commissioner, Edward Tallis returned to his office to find that the mail had been delivered. As he sifted through it, he dropped some of the letters straight in the wastepaper basket. He then recognised Colbeck's elegant hand and tore open the missive to find that he was holding a five-page report on events in York. Tallis gave a knowing smile.

'You're a cunning, old devil, Colbeck!'

There was no point in questioning him any more. It was clear that Bobby Bray had no idea where the suspect was. The old man liked to think that he was Adam Tranter's friend even though he was often treated by him with contempt. When he heard what had happened, Bray concealed the fact that he was glad that Tranter had escaped in time. Hinton was disappointed but Shawcross remained hopeful.

'He'll be back before long,' he predicted.

'Where is he now?' asked Hinton.

'He's got bolt-holes all over the place.'

'Adam likes to keep on the move,' said Bray, knowledgeably. 'I haven't a clue where he'll turn up next.'

'Wherever it is,' said Shawcross, taking him by the scruff of his neck, 'I want to know at once. Do you understand?' Bray nodded. 'Don't let me down, Billy, or I'll make your life a misery.'

'I hear you,' said the old man.

'Then remember what I said.' Shawcross pushed him away. 'I'm able to have you banned from the railway station.'

Bray was panic-stricken. 'You can't do that!'

'I don't make idle threats, Bobby.'

'No, no, sir, I realise that.'

'Then disappear and keep your ears peeled for any news? Got it?'

'Yes, Constable Shawcross. As soon as I hear anything, I'll be in touch.'

Anxious to get away, he broke into a little trot. Hinton watched him go.

'Did you believe what he just said?'

'Of course not,' said Shawcross with a hollow laugh. 'Bobby Bray will lie through his teeth all day long – and play that fiddle of his while he does so.'

The warm sun had lured Madeleine Colbeck out into the back garden. Seated on the patio, she divided her time between reading her husband's latest letter and watching her father playing with his granddaughter. Andrews was tossing a ball to Helena Rose then trying to catch it when it came back. He usually dropped it, sending the girl off into peals of laughter. After picking the ball up from the lawn a couple of dozen times, Andrews was puffing hard. He signalled to the nurse to take over from him, then walked up to the patio. When he plopped himself down beside his daughter, he gave a sigh of relief.

'That girl will be the death of me,' he said.

'It was your idea to teach her how to catch a ball,' said Madeleine.

'Then I must have been mad. Once she caught it, she didn't just toss it back. Helena Rose threw it straight at me.'

'You should have moved further away from her.'

'I agree, Maddy. I gave her too much of a target.' He noticed the letter in her hands. 'What does Robert say?'

'It's one of the most curious cases he's ever had.'

'Why?'

'Well, he's in charge of one murder investigation but keeps being asked for advice about another one. It was very distracting at first, but he thinks differently now.'

'Why is that?'

'Robert doesn't really know,' she said. 'The cases are quite different, but he feels that there may be a link between them. The trouble is that he has no idea what it is. It's not often that he admits to being baffled. He's a bit like you in that respect.'

'What do you mean?' demanded Andrews.

'Well, you'd never admit that you were confused.'

'That's because I never was!'

She laughed. 'You're doing it again, Father.'

'Doing what?'

'Refusing to accept that there are some things you just can't do. Running around the garden is one of them. Those days are over for you.'

'Don't make me feel even older than I am, Maddy,' he told her. 'Forget about me. I want to hear about Robert. Did he really say that he was baffled?'

'Not in so many words,' she replied, 'but that's what he meant. He also said that he had every confidence in solving both murders – in due course.'

Alice Kendrick felt as if a great weight had been lifted off her. Instead of having to cope with the burden of Owen Gale's hatred, she could now step outside her front door with impunity. Binny Gale's suicide had changed things for the better. Some of the neighbours had blamed the parents for what the girl had done and turned away from them. Alice felt that that was unfair. They had loved their daughter very much and sought to protect her from a man who had a hold over Binny. Alice felt that that should be remembered. During a moment of crisis, she'd taken Margery Gale into her home and given what comfort she could. She liked and sympathised with the woman. While she still had a vestigial fear of the fishmonger, it disappeared whenever he waved to her. As he'd driven his cart past her house that afternoon, he saw Alice through her front window and raised his cap to her. Doubt had been planted in her mind. Could a decent, caring, hardworking man like that really have killed her cat?

Back at the hotel, Hinton delivered his report. Colbeck was quiet and meditative throughout. Leeming was disappointed to hear that Tranter had fled before Hinton and Shawcross reached the house.

'If you'd managed to arrest him,' he said, 'we could have handed him over and booked our return tickets to London.'

'That's what I was hoping would happen,' said Hinton. 'We came close but not close enough.'

'At least we know who the man we're after is.'

'Do we?' asked Colbeck.

'Yes, of course,' said Leeming. 'His name is Adam Tranter. Three different people gave us a description of him. They saw him near the brake van.'

'They saw someone, Victor, but it may not have been Tranter. Since we've been here, I've seen over a dozen people who looked like the man on the poster we had printed. It is, after all, only an impression. It's not a photograph.'

'I thought you believed that we'd finally identified him, sir,' said Hinton.

'I did for a short while,' said Colbeck. 'Then I asked myself what possible motive he might have to plant that bomb.'

'Constable Shawcross had the answer to that. Tranter is one of those people who are burning with hatred. They get their pleasure from destruction.'

'Then why didn't this man disappear, Alan? Anybody else who committed a crime like that would want to get as far away from the city as possible. Yet we know that Tranter stayed in York. You even found someone – Bobby Bray – who knew where he'd been living.'

'It was a foul den,' said Hinton.

'Tranter has to be our man, sir,' asserted Leeming. 'Mr Ewart recognised him from that sketch the artist drew, and

330

Mr Godfrey was even more certain. Then there was Mrs Brightwell. If she'd still been alive, I'm certain that she would have said that we had the right person as well.'

'How close did she ever get to him?' asked Colbeck.

'About thirty yards – that's what she told me.'

'What was she doing at the station in the first place?'

'She didn't say,' admitted Leeming. 'She was such an imposing lady that it seemed rude to press her for details.'

'Yes,' agreed Colbeck, 'she was the sort of person who would stand out in any crowd. That being the case, why wasn't she noticed by Mr Ewart? They're friends, after all. Both were close to the brake van at the same time.'

'Mr Godfrey was even closer,' said Hinton.

'I'm more interested in the other witnesses, Alan. We know that Mr Ewart was there to wave off his sister, but we have no idea what reason Mrs Brightwell had for being there. It's too late to ask her now,' said Colbeck. 'We may never know.'

'What do we do next, sir?' asked Leeming.

'I'd like you to question the stationmaster. He's not the most prepossessing man but he does his job well and has a good memory. If Staines caught a glimpse of Mrs Brightwell on the day in question, he'd be certain to remember it.' Leeming's face was dominated by a frown. 'Did you hear what I said, Victor?'

'What?' asked the other. 'Oh, yes. I must speak to Mr Staines. But something else popped into my mind.'

'What was it?'

'Well, as soon as we put up those reward posters, we had a quick response. Mr Ewart joined the queue early on and gave us the most accurate description of a suspect that we had.'

'Mrs Brightwell gave you one that was fairly similar.'

'Yes, but she took a long time before she came forward.'

'Perhaps she didn't see the reward posters?' said Colbeck.

'They were put up everywhere, sir. Besides, if she was such a close friend of Mr Ewart's, then he'd have told her how important it was to help the investigation by telling us what she saw that morning.'

'That's a good point, Victor.'

'I should have thought of it before.'

'There's one way we might be able to answer that question,' said Colbeck. 'I'll speak to Mr Ewart directly.'

'What would you like me to do, sir?' asked Hinton.

'You can go to the station as well. Put some pressure on that old man playing the violin. He clearly knows more about Adam Tranter than he's admitted. See if you can get more information out of him.'

'I'll do my best. Constable Shawcross had to bully him into helping us. I'll try a more friendly approach. It sometimes works.'

He and Leeming took their leave and went straight to the railway station. Left alone, Colbeck took out his notebook and checked the exact sequence of events since they had been there. The germ of an idea began to form in his mind.

As the lord mayor, Neville Timms was obsessed with the idea of giving the city an attractive image. Two murders in a matter of days had badly scarred that image. He called on Horace Nash to express his fears.

'York is getting a bad name,' he warned. 'People will think twice about coming here if they feel that it's unsafe to do so.'

'We'll sort it out,' promised the superintendent.

'But you can't concentrate all your resources on Mrs Brightwell's murder. You've now been forced to help Inspector Colbeck.'

'That works both ways.'

'I don't see how.'

'The inspector has been helping me in return.'

Nash told him how he'd sought Colbeck's advice and been impressed by what the latter had suggested. Even though he was working hard on his own investigation, the inspector had found time to visit the jewellery shop favoured by the Brightwell family and discovered something relevant to the case.

'I should have thought of doing that,' confessed Nash.

'Why didn't you?'

'Frankly, it never occurred to me.'

'Then it's just as well that Colbeck used his initiative.'

'Fair play,' said Nash. 'He's been very helpful even though Mrs Brightwell's murder must be a distraction for him. At least, that's what I thought. I now get the impression that he thinks the two cases might be connected.'

'That's nonsense!' exclaimed Timms. 'One was a direct assault on the railway company while the other was an appalling murder of a dear lady whose jewellery was stolen. I can't see the slightest similarity between the two cases.'

'Inspector Colbeck can.'

To speak to him, Bobby Bray had to be interrupted. The old man was in the middle of playing a lilting melody when Hinton stood in front of him and waved his arms. Bray stopped immediately and bristled with anger.

'Couldn't you wait until I'd finished?' he yelled.

'Keep your voice down.'

'I'm trying to earn money.'

'That makes two of us, Mr Bray,' said Hinton. 'If I don't do my job properly, I won't get paid. To be honest, I didn't want to interrupt you because I was enjoying that tune you were playing. If I'd been a passenger, I might even have dropped something into your cap. You have a gift.'

Bray was mollified. 'Well, thank you . . .'

'I just need to have a quiet chat with you about your friend, Adam Tranter.'

'He's not really a friend.'

'Then how do you keep track of him?'

'Playing my fiddle here is safe,' explained Bray. 'Before I got this spot, I had to play in the street and that was dangerous. People used to mock me and some of them tried to grab the money in my cap. The worst time was when a couple of drunks threatened to hit me. Adam happened to come along,' he recalled. 'He saw what was happening and rescued me by knocking the pair of them out. I was grateful and said I'd do him favours from time to time. That's what I did.'

'When did you move here?'

'It was when the man with the barrel organ died. He owned this spot from the moment the station opened over twenty years ago. I was the first person to jump in to take his place. Now then,' he went on, eyeing Hinton, 'what is it you want to know about Adam . . . ?'

Because the stationmaster was so busy, Leeming had to wait some time before he could question the man. When

Staines eventually went back to his office, the sergeant followed him in.

'If you have a question,' said Staines, 'please make it a quick one. I'm still on duty and the next train is due to arrive in minutes.'

'You must remember every detail of what happened on the morning of the explosion,' said Leeming. 'Do you recall seeing a lady named Mrs Brightwell here?'

'No, I don't.'

'Do you know who I'm talking about?'

'Yes, of course. Nobody would forget Mrs Brightwell. She's so grand and is always dressed like royalty. And I can tell you for the second time that she wasn't here that morning.'

'Then why did she tell me about the man she saw loitering near the brake van? She gave me a full description.'

'I can't pick out everyone in a crowd,' said Staines, 'but some people stick out a mile. She was one of them.'

'Would you swear that she was not here?'

'I'd bet my house and my two greyhounds on it.'

When a visitor arrived unexpectedly, Nicholas Ewart was surprised but he responded gracefully. He took Colbeck into his study, offered him a seat, then asked if he wanted refreshment of any sort. After declining the offer, Colbeck looked around the room. Ancient tomes were stacked on the shelves alongside more recent publications. A few Viking artefacts were on the desk, cushioned in cotton wool.

'I'm sorry to interrupt your work,' said Colbeck.

'I was just trying to occupy my mind, Inspector. If I work at the site, I simply can't stop thinking about Mrs

335

Brightwell. Every so often, my eyes fill with tears. If that happened in public, it would be embarrassing.'

'Understandably.'

'Now,' said Ewart, 'is there any news?'

'There's news about the suspect for the explosion at the railway station, sir. You saw that artist's impression of him.'

'That's right. The artist excelled himself.'

'Someone identified the suspect as Adam Tranter,' said Colbeck. 'Does that name mean anything to you, sir?'

'It's . . . vaguely familiar, but that could be because I saw the name in a newspaper report. Has he been in trouble with the police?'

'Tranter has spent a lifetime doing just that, Mr Ewart. Anyway, let's put him aside, shall we? I wanted to ask you about Mrs Brightwell. When you went to the station to see your sister off that morning, did you happen to notice the lady?'

'I'm afraid that I didn't,' said Ewart. 'I was too busy talking to Ellen.'

'You may have missed Mrs Brightwell, but I find it hard to believe that she would have missed seeing you. Surely, she'd have come across to you?'

'Yes, she would. Mrs Brightwell would consider it rude not to speak to me.'

'Then why didn't she do so?'

'Are you quite sure that she was there, Inspector?' asked Ewart.

'We have a record of it, sir.'

'Really?'

'When we began to interview people who'd been there at the time, Mrs Brightwell turned up at the very end.

Sergeant Leeming took her statement. She claimed to have been close to the brake van,' said Colbeck. 'That would place her in your vicinity.'

'Then why didn't I see her?' asked Ewart with surprise.

'That's a conundrum we may never solve, sir.'

'What about the explosion itself?'

'Oh, we'll certainly find the man behind that.'

'Was it this Tranter fellow?'

'No,' said Colbeck with a confident smile. 'I'm not even sure that he was anywhere near the station at the time. It's someone else, sir – and we're getting closer to him all the time.'

'That's excellent news,' said Ewart. 'Are you sure that I can't press you to have some refreshment?'

'I'm afraid not, sir. But you could certainly press me to have a closer look at those items on your desk. Are they all Viking artefacts . . . ?'

Alice Kendrick had spent hours arranging items for sale at the market on the following day. She had been dreading the event because it would mean she would inevitably meet up with Owen Gale, the fishmonger. That, however, was no longer the case. Gale would see her as a friend rather than as an enemy. She could go to the market without any fears at all.

As she worked away, she heard a faint scratching sound, but she had no idea from where it came. Her first guess was that it was caused by a mouse and that troubled her. If a colony of mice moved in, she would have all manner of problems. Putting her scissors aside, she stood up and tried hard to concentrate on the noise. It was low, steady

337

and insistent. Alice could not decide whether it came from inside the house or outside it. When she went into the back kitchen, the scratching was marginally louder and accompanied by the faint cry of a cat.

'Patch!' she cried in delight.

Opening the back door, she bent down to scoop the animal up into her arms, holding him tight for a full minute. Patch was no longer crying. He gave a soft purr.

'Where have you been?' she asked. 'I've been so worried about you.'

The cat was unable to reply but his body provided some explanation. He was much thinner than he had been, and bits of his fur were missing. Alice pulled him even closer to her.

'Welcome home!' she said. 'I'll look after you, Patch. There won't be any mice here while you're around.' She moved to the pantry. 'Let's find you something to eat, shall we?'

When they got back to the hotel, Leeming and Hinton were still perplexed. Neither of them could understand how a woman could give evidence of having been close to a dramatic event when she had not actually been at the station.

'The stationmaster might be mistaken,' said Hinton.

'Not about something as important as this,' argued Leeming. 'He deals with passengers every day of the week and probably knows the names of half of them. If he swears that he didn't see Mrs Brightwell on the platform, then she was not there.'

'So why did she tell you that she was?'

'I have no idea.'

'I thought she was supposed to be very religious.'

'Even Christians can tell a lie when it's necessary,' said Leeming, 'though I haven't a clue what made Mrs Brightwell do it. Anyway,' he continued, 'let's turn to that fiddler. Did you get anything of use out of him?'

'Not really, Sergeant, but I did learn how he came to befriend Tranter. The man rescued him from a beating one night and Bray has been grateful ever since.'

'Did he know if Tranter had been here on the day of the explosion?'

'No, he didn't.'

'It was a waste of time talking to him, then.'

'No, it wasn't,' said Hinton. 'His life story was interesting. He and that violin of his have been everywhere. He even played at a friend's wedding once. There was only one problem with chatting to Bobby Bray.'

'What was it?'

'I had to pay him for the pleasure. He told me how much he'd have earned if I hadn't dragged him away, so I put my small change into his cap.'

Leeming laughed. 'You're too soft for this job, Alan,' he said. 'You have to be more careful with characters like Bray.'

They were seated in the lounge. Before they could continue the conversation, they saw Colbeck glide into the room. He sat beside them and asked for their respective reports. Hinton went first, describing his chat with Bray but omitting any mention of paying him.

'According to Mr Ewart,' said Colbeck, 'Mrs Brightwell was not in the station on the morning in question.'

'Yet she told me that she was,' said Leeming, taking out

his notebook and tapping it. 'I've got her statement in here. I refuse to believe that she was lying.'

'There are two possibilities,' decided Colbeck. 'First, she was not there but claimed that she had been. Mr Staines didn't see her and neither did Mr Ewart.'

'Then she was telling me a lie.'

'Not necessarily, Victor. Let me put another idea to you. Mrs Brightwell was there, after all, but she was dressed in such a way that she was not recognised.'

'What possible reason could she have to disguise herself?'

'I'm still trying to think of one.'

'Well, I fancy that your earlier suggestion was right, sir,' said Hinton. 'She was not in the station at the time of the explosion.'

'She was certainly not here as Mrs Brightwell,' insisted Colbeck, 'but she might have been posing as someone else. Yes, I know it sounds absurd,' he went on, raising both hands, 'but I can feel certain events fitting together at last. I'm also sure that there is a link between the two murders – Mrs Brightwell.'

Horace Nash was alone in his office when there was a tap on the door. A policeman entered and handed him a letter.

'I was told to give this to you by Inspector Keane,' he said. 'He's been talking to Ellie Duckett, the servant who discovered the body.'

'I know who she is,' snapped Nash, opening the letter. 'My God!' he said as he read the message. 'Why didn't the girl tell us this before?'

'She was too terrified to tell us anything, Superintendent. You know that. It's only since she calmed down a little that she thought the information might be useful.'

'It certainly is!'

Putting the letter aside, he reached for pen and paper before dashing off a short message. He handed it over.

'Take this to Inspector Colbeck as fast as you can,' he ordered. 'If he's not at Scawin's Hotel, someone there will know how to find him.'

After drinking a full saucer of milk and devouring the scraps of meat that Alice had found for him, Patch looked visibly better. When she tried to pick him up again, however, he eluded her grasp and went off into the other room, sniffing in every corner as if trying to find his way around again. At length, he came to his basket and, after sniffing it comprehensively, he hopped into it and curled up. Alice was delighted. It was just like old times. While she worked at the table, Patch was nestling in his bed. He had not been poisoned by Owen Gale, after all, and she felt guilty at having made that assumption. Where the animal had been, she could only guess but he had come home at last. That was all that mattered.

'The superintendent is not going to like this,' said Leeming. 'He wants us to bring this case to a swift conclusion, and not waste time helping the police with their investigation.'

'The inspector obviously doesn't see it as a waste of time,' said Hinton. 'When he read that message from Superintendent Nash, he simply told us that he had to go and ran out of here.'

They were still in the lounge of the hotel, mystified by the latest development. Hinton was wondering what had made Colbeck act so strangely. Leeming, however, was thinking about his son's birthday and accepting the fact that he would be unable to be there. It was galling.

Ellie Duckett was still dazed by the experience of finding her employer lying dead in her bedroom. She had only partially recovered from the shock but was desperate to help the police catch the killer. The information she had given to Inspector Keane had been harmless enough in her view, but it made him sit up with interest. He had sent a message to Superintendent Nash who, in turn, had summoned Colbeck. Along with Keane, both men were now sitting in the drawing room with Ellie.

Keane was a stringy man with a bushy moustache. He nudged the girl gently.

'Tell 'em what you told me, lass.'

'Can't you do that, Inspector?' she asked, nervously.

'They'd best hear it from your own lips.'

'Take your time, Ellie,' advised Colbeck. 'There's no hurry.'

'Thank you, sir,' she murmured.

It was minutes before she had composed herself. When she was ready, she looked around the faces of the three men before speaking.

'Mrs Brightwell treated me like a daughter,' she said. 'She made me feel special. I used to go for walks with her because she liked my company. It was a treat to get out of the house.'

'Did that make the other servants jealous?' asked Colbeck.

'No, not really. We're all good friends.'

'Tell 'em about the railway station, Ellie,' suggested Keane.

'Oh, yes,' she said. 'We were there. Me and Mrs Brightwell were there when that explosion went off. It frightened the life out of us.'

'Are you certain you were there?' asked Colbeck. 'Neither the stationmaster nor Mr Ewart saw you at the station. They know Mrs Brightwell by sight.'

Ellie lowered her head. 'It was a game she liked to play . . .'

When he was working at his desk, Nicholas Ewart was completely absorbed. He did not hear the doorbell being rung or the opening of the front door. There was also a brief conversation before his servant tapped on his study door and entered the room.

'You have a visitor, sir,' he explained.

Ewart was startled by the interruption. 'I told you that I wished to be alone.'

'Inspector Colbeck insists on seeing you.'

'Tell him that it's not a convenient time.'

'He won't leave until he's spoken to you, sir.'

'Oh, very well,' said Ewart, peevishly. 'Show him in.'

He got to his feet and manufactured a smile as Colbeck entered the study. Left alone with his guest, he indicated a chair. When Colbeck sat down, Ewart lowered himself into his own chair. Colbeck studied him for a few moments, then spoke with his usual politeness.

'I'm sorry to come at an awkward time, sir,' he said, 'but I wanted to know why you lied to me earlier.'

'I did no such thing,' protested Ewart.

'You told me that Mrs Brightwell was not at the station on the morning of the explosion there.'

'That was the truth, Inspector.'

'It was and it wasn't. The lady was not easily visible, perhaps, but she was certainly there. She was with Ellie Duckett, one of her servants. The reason that you didn't recognise her was that she was not dressed in her usual way. Mrs Brightwell was wearing far more subdued attire and had a wide-brimmed hat that covered most of her face. To complete her disguise,' said Colbeck, 'she pretended to hobble with the aid of a walking stick.'

'Why are you telling me this?' asked Ewart.

'Because you must have realised that it was not the only time that she wore that clothing so that she could watch you in secret, so to speak. In the early days of the excavation, Ellie told us, Mrs Brightwell went to see you at work two or three times. You were so busy in that trench that you didn't once look up.'

'If this is true,' said Ewart, smoothly, 'I must take your word for it. If Mrs Brightwell took pleasure from watching me at work, so be it. I'm surprised but not offended.'

'While I was at her house earlier on,' continued Colbeck, 'I took the opportunity to have a closer look at the window through which the burglar had gained access. It seemed to have been jemmied open. On closer inspection, I saw that it was the work of an amateur. No burglar would make such a mess.'

'I wish you would tell me why you're here, Inspector.'

'The man who came through that window didn't need to force it open, sir. It had been left unlocked for him. You see,' said Colbeck, 'he was not a burglar at all. He was

344

there by the invitation of Mrs Brightwell.'

'What – at that time of night?'

'Yes, sir. The lady was waiting for him in bed. But you knew that because you were the person she was expecting.'

Ewart remained calm. 'You have a vivid imagination, Inspector.'

'It all started at the railway station,' Colbeck went on. 'You took your sister there and installed her in a carriage, but you didn't linger anywhere near her because you had other business. Unknown to you, Mrs Brightwell and her servant had followed you there. At one point,' said Colbeck, 'they saw you step into the brake van for a few moments then step out again. They had no idea why you did that – until there was an explosion.'

'If you insist on making these ridiculous insinuations,' warned Ewart, 'I will demand to have my lawyer present.'

'You'll certainly need legal representation in court, sir, but you're intelligent enough to realise that. Let's go back to that explosion,' said Colbeck. 'You blamed the individual you described to us. Oddly enough, the description Mrs Brightwell provided us was remarkably similar. It's not surprising – you gave it to her.'

Ewart laughed. 'Why should I do that?'

'You would do anything to conceal your guilt.'

'I gave an honest account of why I was at the station, and I really believed at the time that Mrs Brightwell was not there.'

'But she was, Mr Ewart, and she was watching you carefully.'

'I was completely unaware of it.'

'You were soon made aware of it, sir, because you

had put a weapon in her hand. Mrs Brightwell was able to blackmail you. At least, that's my belief. You were the person who planted that bomb, and she knew it. The lady finally had the hold over you that she had dreamt about.'

'That's arrant nonsense.'

'I also believe that you had no intention of hurting anyone, especially not of causing a death. You're far too decent a man to consider that. You just wanted to cause minor damage and give everyone a fright. But your bomb ignited flammable items already inside the brake van. As a result, you burnt the guard to death and spread panic throughout the whole station.'

'That was not part of my plan,' said Ewart, losing any pretence of innocence. 'How was I to know those things were stored away in there?'

'What exactly was your plan, sir?'

'I wanted to exact revenge against the railway company. I only started a campaign of minor vandalism, but the NER was far more destructive than I could ever be. To build that station, they came inside the city walls themselves and constructed that excrescence on Toft Green, a site previously occupied by a Hospital for Poor Women. It was unforgivable!' howled Ewart. 'Part of our history was reduced to rubble because it was in the way of what they called progress. I love this city, Inspector,' he went on, tapping his chest, 'and I treasure its past. Our history is sacred. I couldn't stand by and watch it being swept away as if it were meaningless. Someone had to punish the railway company.'

'It's just a pity that Mrs Brightwell saw you doing it, sir.'

'Keep her out of this!'

'That's just not possible, sir,' said Colbeck, looking him

346

straight in the eye. 'The lady was desperately fond of you. She used the situation to her advantage. She made you come to her house at night – as her lover!'

'She was deranged!' yelled Ewart, jumping to his feet. 'Mrs Brightwell wanted more than a night in bed with me, Inspector. She tried to force me to marry her. Yes,' he went on, 'it's ludicrous, isn't it? She wanted to become Mrs Ewart and have an excuse to wear all that jewellery she adored so much. It was a ridiculous fantasy. How dare she think she could ever replace my dear Charlotte as a wife?'

'And yet you agreed to go to her room at night.'

'I had to take my opportunity while I could,' argued Ewart. 'I knew that she would be completely off guard. When I got there, she was wearing some of her most precious jewellery. All I had to do was to squeeze the life out of her and steal the contents of the safe. And if you hadn't turned up out of the blue,' he said, eyes ablaze, 'I'd have got away with it, wouldn't I?'

Slipping a hand inside his coat, Colbeck rose and took out a pair of handcuffs.

'I'm afraid that you'll have to come with me, sir,' he said.

'No, I won't.'

'You have to pay for your crimes.'

Ewart moved quickly, opening a drawer, and pulling out a dagger. He waved it menacingly at Colbeck. The inspector stood his ground.

'Superintendent Nash gave me four of his men in case I met with resistance. They're waiting outside the house,' said Colbeck.

'That doesn't frighten me, Inspector.'

'Do you really think you can kill five of us, Mr Ewart? We're trained for situations like this. None of us is a defenceless woman like Mrs Brightwell.' He took a step closer and held out a hand. 'Give me the weapon, please.'

'No,' cried the other, brandishing it.

'You already have too much blood on your hands.'

'The railway is the villain here. It showed no respect for the history of this wonderful city. It brought steam, stench, filth, ugliness and sheer pandemonium into our lives. It occupied us like an invading army.'

'You undervalue it, sir,' replied Colbeck. 'It rejuvenated this city and allowed it to reach its full potential. I'm told that sightseers pour into York in large numbers, and they don't come to look at the railway station. They enjoy visiting the historic buildings that you felt obliged to defend.'

'It was my duty!' yelled Ewart.

'I have duties as well, sir. Arresting you is one of them.'

'Goodbye, Inspector.'

And before Colbeck could stop him, Ewart took the dagger in both hands and plunged it into his own heart with as much force as he could muster. Face twisted in agony, he slumped to the floor and began to twitch and groan. Colbeck went quickly to his aid but there was nothing he could do to save the man. Nicholas Ewart had chosen his own way to die, among the beloved relics of the past that filled his study.

Edward Tallis was exercising his lungs by berating one of his detectives for the mistakes he had made. The man was squirming in embarrassment. However, the ordeal was soon cut short. A uniformed policeman arrived with a telegraph for the superintendent. The latter tore it open and read Colbeck's message. A smile spread across his face, and he felt a mood of benevolence coursing through him.

'Get out!' he told the detective.

Then he read the telegraph again.

Leeming and Hinton were seated in an otherwise empty compartment, waiting for Colbeck to finish his conversation on the platform with Gregory Maynard. The managing director of the North Eastern Railway was praising the inspector for solving the case that had brought him to York.

'I can't hear what he's saying to the inspector,' said Hinton, 'but Mr Maynard is obviously very pleased.'

'Then why doesn't he show it by giving us a reward?'

'You've already had a reward, Sergeant. You'll be home in time for Albert's birthday. What's more, you're taking the lad a tin of Rowntree's cocoa.'

'That's true,' said Leeming. 'I'll be very tempted to have it myself.'

The door opened and Colbeck stepped into the compartment. He sat opposite his colleagues and looked from one to the other.

'Mr Maynard was very pleased with our work,' he told them. 'He was amazed that the person who accidentally caused that explosion was so highly educated.'

'I was astonished as well,' admitted Hinton. 'Mr Ewart was such a pleasant man to talk to. I found it hard to believe that he'd commit murder.'

'He had many fine qualities, Alan. He loved this city so much that he became its self-appointed champion. When this railway station was built,' explained Colbeck, 'he was

349

horrified at the way it came right inside the city walls. That's why, in time, he began his campaign of vandalism here. Each time, the damage was more serious as he worked up to the culmination with that scare in the brake van.'

'It was much more than a scare,' said Leeming. 'It killed one person and injured a lot of others.'

'None of that was intentional, Victor. He just wanted to give people a fright.'

'Jack Follis certainly had one.'

'Mr Ewart planted that bomb when the brake van was empty. That shows his concern for people nearby. He gave thought to consequences. He didn't realise that the guard would come haring along so soon after he'd planted his device.'

'What about his friendship with Mrs Brightwell?' asked Hinton.

'Yes,' added Leeming, 'you still haven't told us the full story about how she came to be strangled.'

'And I'm not sure that I want to,' warned Colbeck.

'Why is that?'

'Some things are best left unsaid. Mr Ewart and Mrs Brightwell were essentially good people. They did a great deal for this city, and that's how they deserve to be remembered. Each of them was inspired by a passion that drove them on,' said Colbeck, sadly. 'It's unfortunate that their individual passions got wildly out of control.'

EDWARD MARSTON has written well over a hundred books. He is best known for his hugely successful Railway Detective series and he also writes the Bow Street Rivals series featuring twin detectives set during the Regency; the Home Front Detective novels set during the First World War; and the Ocean Liner mysteries.

edwardmarston.com